ONE THREAT TOO REAL

ONE THREAT TOO REAL

MCFADDEN AND BANKS™ BOOK 4

MICHAEL ANDERLE

DISRUPTIVE IMAGINATION®

LMBPN Publishing
PMB 196, 2540 South Maryland Pkwy
Las Vegas, NV 89109

First US edition, March 2021
eBook ISBN: 978-1-64971-601-9
Print ISBN: 978-1-64971-602-6

Thanks to our Beta Team:
Jeff Eaton, John Ashmore, Kelly O'Donnell

JIT Readers

Deb Mader
Peter Manis
Diane L. Smith
John Ashmore
Jeff Goode

Editor
Skyhunter Editing Team

DEDICATION

To Family, Friends and
Those Who Love
to Read.
May We All Enjoy Grace
to Live the Life We Are
Called.

CHAPTER ONE

The copious and seemingly endless flow of free drinks made Mark smile.

As the owner of the pub, he made sure he didn't pay for any of them, of course. He merely got the ball rolling, as it were. There were many present who wanted to share a little taste of glory by paying for the drinks of the heroes who came out of the jungle.

It had been a while since anyone had been involved in a big fight against the Zoo. The veterans—and some of those who had the sense to listen to them—had learned to avoid the situations that would embroil them in the larger engagements. While it meant there was an overall drop in casualty numbers, it also meant the group that did get themselves into that kind of trouble and got out again would return to fanfare.

He smirked as another round of drinks was called for.

If this continued to happen, he might be able to hire more help and take time off. He had made a decent turnover lately, and it was time for him to head to a beach somewhere and enjoy the sun instead of dread it.

Atlantic City had begun to sound like the right kind of place. He liked to gamble and they had pulled their act together as a city lately. Boxing and mixed martial arts bouts would be in the cards too, and it would be enjoyable to watch some of those live instead of playing them on the bar's TV.

"You're bullshitting me."

His ears were consistently tuned to what was happening around him, especially when voices began to raise. With a clientele comprised mainly of fighters with a hefty level of alcohol in them, there would be considerable yelling when they gathered in larger groups. Experience had taught him, however, that there was a different edge to the noise when there was impending violence.

This time, it didn't sound like much would come of it. There was more disbelief than hostility but he remained wary and alert nonetheless. One never knew when it would escalate.

Besides, it was an interesting conversation. Nick and Trish were covering the bar, which left him free to keep things clean and maintain a watchful eye on how things were running.

"It's the truth, I swear to God," another man shouted and shook his head. "I understand, though. It was hard to believe even while I was watching it."

Mark narrowed his eyes and tried to put names to the faces. He prided himself on remembering the name of every patron who visited. The disbelieving man was

Franklin, and the one trying to tell his story was Tom. Or Tim?

No, Tom. A fight had broken out a while before over who could call him by the shorter nickname and who needed to refer to him as Thomas.

"I still don't believe it," Franklin protested before he took a large sip from his mug. "Okay, I get it, the guy's a rock star. But walking around on eight limbs like a motherfucking spider? Give me a break."

"You say it like he sprouted legs and walked around. No, it was the suit. He moved in a suit with four extra arms fitted to its back." Tom set up a handful of empty shot glasses on the bar top to illustrate his point. "So, we have the two dragon lizard fuckers here, ripping into a group of our guys. Their tails flick around and I swear they cut two guys in half before we even realized they were there."

"Come on. I've been in the Zoo. I've seen what those reptiles can do and that isn't the part of your story I have a hard time believing."

"Right, anyway. We try to set up some explosives to cook the fuckers before they can kill any more of our team and suddenly, McFadden appears." Tom moved one of the shot glasses into the center of the depiction. "The guy has a chunk of something sticking out of his left shoulder, so you can see he's not moving too good. Even then, the four arms coming out of his back keep him moving while he guns the first of the critters down. Or...no, wait, he gets in and dodges a tail swing from this one here on the far side —kind of baiting it into a strike that hit the other one and opened a huge gaping wound."

"Again, that's standard—for a guy like Taylor, anyway."

"I know, but after he finishes the wounded one off, he uses the four arms on his back to flip over the dead fucker here, opens the taps on the last one, and kills it almost immediately."

"And that's where you lost me. We've all seen Jacobs running around with his six-limbed suit. If you put in some basic software, it can do all the basic things. But when you go above that, you need someone to be able to fully control the suit, right? And you can't control an eight-limbed suit with only your four limbs. Two arms and two legs aren't enough. I don't care what a badass you are. Basic software gets you so far, but you need something a little more than that."

Tom shook his head. "No, no, you don't get it. I already suspect that Jacobs works with a little something-something extra in his suit. He has a world-class software engineer on his team who gets everything going the way it's supposed to. What's to say that McFadden doesn't have the same—or even better, which seems to be the case?"

Franklin leaned back in his seat and took another sip while he mulled the question over in his head. "Okay, I can buy it. But it'll need to be one hell of a piece of tech. Like, cutting the cutting edge, you know? I'm talking military-grade AI crammed into a suit, which we both know isn't exactly the easiest thing to do."

"Yeah, sure. But I know what I saw out there. You find whatever logic you need to try to get it working in your head, but I know what I saw."

"Fine, whatever."

A young man with dark hair sipped his beer and listened to the conversation with a little more interest than the rest of the bar. He was lean and nothing about him marked him as a soldier—a researcher, perhaps, but not one who made a habit of regular trips into the Zoo.

He finished his drink as the two men continued to discuss the details of the attack in the jungle. Unobtrusively, he put a few bills on the counter to cover his tab and headed out of the bar.

Once he was in the cool evening air with the wind from the Sahara whipping around the base, he took a cell phone from his pocket and punched in a long number. The call rang twice and he hung up quickly and walked casually to where his vehicle was parked in the street.

The moment he was in his seat, his phone rang and he picked it up immediately. Even then, he needed to wait for a few seconds while clicks were heard on the line. Whoever had called him was cautious and insisted on setting up a secure connection.

"Yeah," he said once the connection opened. "I think I've finally found what we've been looking for. And he's US-based too, so that'll make things a hell of a lot easier."

"Are you sure about this?" Niki asked.

Taylor looked at her while he adjusted the suit's settings a little before he moved it into the open desert. "Ask me again at the end of the day."

"What's what supposed to mean?"

"It means we're testing people in the desert. There will be risks involved, but if we can manage to find a way to make it work, I'll be the genius who gave us freelancers to call on when we need boots on the ground."

"And if you can't make it work?"

"Then I'm the idiot who got himself or someone else injured while testing freelancers. By then, I think it'll be easier to blow myself up. That way, you can't yell at me."

She glared at him and he raised his hands in surrender.

"Not even as a joke, you big idiot." She growled in mock annoyance and patted him on the shoulder. "Be careful out there. Jansen and Maxwell claim these guys are the real deal but...well, you remember the story of my first attempt at piloting a combat suit."

"The one where you ran through a wall at Quantico?"

"That's the one."

"Right. Thank goodness we don't have any walls in the Mojave Desert. I seriously dodged a bullet on that one."

"Shut up. You know what I mean. The guys may be reckless out there and they may be untrained despite what they claim. That's the worst combination of elements when you have safety in mind. They all said they have been in the Zoo before and trained in suits and everything, but I work on the principle that seeing's believing."

"Sure, and there's Zoo experience and there's what people think is Zoo experience."

"Not everyone has your death wish. We're lucky we found freelancers who know their way around the armor suits at all. Even if they only have the basics, we can get them up to speed from there, although both Jansen and Maxwell vouched for them."

She flicked her dark hair back and Taylor nodded slowly and tried to keep the suit from overreacting to his movements. He knew what she was talking about, of course. He had merely tried to lift her mood a little before they got started. It was almost an instinct of his to make sure everyone was in the right mindset for the day to come.

Of course, there was no way to force lightness. If she was determined to be serious about this, there wasn't much he could do to change that.

Taylor rolled his neck and drew a deep breath as he studied the group that was assembled. His suit was everything he could expect it to be and he was glad to have it. After the fight in the Zoo, the company had garnered more interest and orders for their product because of it and they let him buy it at a giveaway price.

Or maybe it was because of the damage it had sustained. Either way, it had needed time in the workshop to get it back into fighting shape, but Bobby had a tendency to fiddle with the settings. He had a habit of putting in those he preferred and removing those he disliked.

He felt like he would mess around with the sensitivity and sensors all day until he finally got everything the way he liked it. Then again, maybe he should tweak what he could now and let Desklet help him later to bring things to their optimum settings and maintain them from there. He'd rather focus on the task at hand than waste time on it now.

The settings as they were would make for an interesting day while he worked the new group. It would always be a grueling task to put them through their paces and Bobby didn't want them to do so anywhere near his shop until they had some idea of the damage the group could cause.

He could appreciate that. The man had a business to run, after all, and shouldn't have to worry about some dumbasses running around in suits they perhaps didn't know how to control.

"All right, people, gather up!"

All three were suited in some of the trial suits Bobby had obtained. From what he could tell, they looked fairly comfortable in the suits they wore and although they still adjusted the settings to find the best combination, they seemed to have a clear idea of how they wanted them to operate.

Taylor supposed he could expect as much, but it was nice to see that Jansen and Maxwell hadn't exaggerated when they said the candidates had experience.

"We'll run a couple of drills to gauge how you guys do with the suits," Taylor explained and pointed to the improvised course that had been set up when he had trained everyone else. "You were recommended to us based on your skills in these things, so we'll see what exactly you can do. People don't want to think about it, but the Zoo fuckers are going international and we need to be prepared for that shit. We don't want a lizard with a spike for a tail to cut your heads off on our first go-around. I don't need that kind of paperwork."

"That sounds suspiciously specific," Chezza commented as she moved her arms in the suit to test the latest adjustment to her settings.

He knew what she was going through. The lag would be infinitesimal but it would be there. It would make moving around infuriating until they tweaked them exactly as they wanted them.

"It is," he responded and smirked when she caught Jiro with a particularly energetic arm movement and he had to regain his balance.

"Will you tell us what it is?" Trick asked. He looked a little more settled in the suit he wore and jumped lightly from side to side while he moved his arms.

He was still not entirely satisfied, however, and a few twitches revealed that everything wasn't quite the way he wanted it.

"I'll tell you what," Taylor said and made another small adjustment to his settings. "When you guys complete the course without ruining your suits, I'll tell you all about it over a beer—on me."

"That sounds good," Chezza cut in almost before he'd finished

Niki had an airhorn in hand and pressed the button to indicate that they should begin. Taylor moved with the group and set a decent pace. He'd expected Trick to be more adapted to the controls but Jiro surprised him when he managed to keep up with him, although the other two weren't too far behind.

It took very little time to get up and down the dune and it was gratifying to see that they worked better on the fly. They got everything working the way they wanted once they were moving with purpose.

"Taylor?" Niki called over the comms when they crested the top. "I'm getting a message from Maxwell."

"Not Jansen?"

"No. Apparently, he's down with the flu or something

and groaning like a pig that got stuck. Anyway, do you think you can rush your guys through the training regimen?"

"Do we honestly want a team out there that was rushed through their training?"

She sighed. "No. We don't. Still, when you're finished, let me know and I'll tell you what he had to say."

He nodded and guided the team to where they'd set their course up.

"You'll shoot blanks for the moment," he told them. "Your HUDs will take note of hits and misses and transmit them to where Niki is set up."

"Do you honestly think we need the kiddy gloves on?" Trick asked as he flicked his rifle to his left hand and took the first shot. It registered as a clean hit.

"For now," Taylor answered and tried not to sound too impressed. It was a damn good no-look shot. "Get going!"

They complied and he kept his distance while he watched the group intently as they moved through the course.

Jiro's style was a little different, that much was immediately obvious. He moved closer, constantly in motion, and still fired his shots, but it looked like he preferred to be up close and personal when the fighting started.

Taylor raised his eyebrows when the man drew his knife and stabbed it through one of the dummies before he vaulted over it and attacked the next line.

"Are we counting stabbings in the markers?" Taylor asked.

"I...think so," Niki replied. "I marked it manually here anyway, just in case."

They moved through the course quickly. The only thing that appeared to slow them was the fact that none of them called their shots and they let their shooting overlap multiple times.

"What do you think?" Taylor asked Niki once they had finished and began to move to the start line.

"Not bad," she muttered. "Much better than I was before I started with you."

He laughed and switched the comms to the general channel. "Guys, Niki says you all suck."

"Did not!"

"It was implied. All right, you dumbasses, let's run it again. I know you have something better in you and I want to see it. Let's go. I'll take the next round with you and remember. If one of you loses, all of you lose. Let's go!"

They looked a little more energized the second time around. Knowing the course and what was expected of them helped, and he had a feeling that they wanted to see him in action.

He brought up the rear of the group, caught Jiro when he slipped just short of the top of the dune, and pulled him over. From there, he made sure they were all moving at the same speed, then drew his weapon as they reached the section where their targets were live.

"Do you feel up to this, Li'l Desk?" Taylor asked.

"A little training?" She sounded excited if that was possible. "After a trip in the Zoo? Of course."

"Technically, we're showing them what they can aspire to," he replied. "Let's show the newbies what they're up against."

He selected his targets and kept an eye on the other

three while he opened fire. Each of his chosen dummies was "killed" with precise three-round bursts before he highlighted the two that still hadn't been hit and put two rounds into one of them while the other three shot the last one.

"Keep moving!"

They complied and took hints as they moved a little faster when he came in behind them. The group headed into a rough depiction of a small pack of hyenas that moved slowly behind a section of obstacles.

"Keep me steady," Taylor told Desklet and the four arms on his back activated as he hurdled the first of the obstacles. The extra arms held him steady as he gunned two of the hyenas down. The three freelancers moved through the obstacle with more alacrity than the last time, opened a wide range of fire, and avoided hitting the same targets as their teammates, which pushed them through faster.

It was good progress and they were soon ready for the next section.

"You need to leave some work for them to do," Niki told him.

"I am. This is me on a slow day."

"I know. Still, though."

"You know we can hear you, right?" Chezza asked.

"You should focus on keeping your shooting patterns tighter," Taylor snapped and highlighted the cutout for one of the larger monsters that was set on a rail that would rush their position immediately.

They located the target quickly and eliminated it with fifteen rounds that immediately cut out the rushing protocol. From there, they moved on to the last section, where smaller creatures were on faster patterns than before, which required them to track them rather than simply aim and fire.

"Call your targets," Taylor instructed and highlighted a handful as he spoke. "It's simple to do. Touch it with your targeting reticle and nudge the button on your chin and the computer will do the rest."

They'd fought in the Zoo before so they knew this. All he hoped for was that he didn't have to do a crash course to remind them of it when they were dealing with real monsters.

The last of the targets was marked inactive and the course showed as completed.

"Nice time, guys!" Taylor shouted. "But I think we can do better. Let's go another round."

They were tough and skilled and improved quickly too. He had a feeling their experience in the suits had been the older versions the military still made their troops fight in. The newer ones were vastly improved, but old habits were hard to break and five rounds of the course seemed like the limit.

There was such a thing as overtraining, and he didn't want to burn them out.

Lunch had been brought and set out for them to enjoy, along with copious amounts of cold water.

"The guy's a fucking machine," Jiro complained and poured some of the cold water on his face.

"It's all about conditioning," Trick replied. "We might have gotten a little soft since we left, but we'll get back into the swing of things."

"All I'm getting back into is a nice long day on a couch

nursing sore limbs," Chezza complained. "The suit I got reacts too quickly and I think I pulled my whole body, not only a muscle. How the fuck is that even possible?"

"What do you think?" Niki asked as Taylor approached her and drank his water thirstily.

"The course upgrades are great," he said as he sat beside her, out of earshot of the other three. "Vickie is doing a good job, but I think the simulators might be a valuable next step."

"Sure, but I meant the recruits. Jansen said that they had good records in the Zoo. Not quite up to your standards, but I think that might be a good thing."

He nodded. "They have the skills, as Vickie would say."

"Skillz."

"What?"

"Vickie says skillz. With a Z."

"Right. Anyway. They have good aim, solid instincts, and quick reflexes, which is about all you can ask for. Which one is the medical expert?"

"Chezza. She dropped out of medical school and joined the Marines."

"Right. It's always a good idea to have someone with medical experience on board."

"She has special forces experience too."

"Also good. Specialties are good to note, though. Trick has the demolitions background, right?"

"Yep. He's also a long-distance engagement specialist, but I don't think there was much need for that in his time in the Zoo."

"And Jiro is the one who's...juggling knives while

eating. That's surprisingly impressive. Where did he keep the knives?"

"I have no idea. But we might want to think about getting him one of the swords."

"Swords?"

Niki nodded. "You know, like Sal uses?"

"Just because he's Japanese doesn't automatically make him a sword expert."

"No, but Jansen's jacket on him talks about how he uses swords in close quarters combat. This isn't a cookie-cutter operation, Taylor. You can't simply expect everyone to go with guns because you like them."

Taylor nodded. "Right. I'll talk to Bobby about that. Now, what did Jansen want?"

"Maxwell. Jansen is sick."

"Right. Stuck pig."

Niki looked at her screen. "Man-flu is so much worse than the regular flu. Anyway, Speare has been in touch and says he needs black ops for an international mission. The kind the US government can't officially be involved with."

"It sounds like him. Where do they need us?"

"Italy." She turned the computer for him to look at as he bit into his sandwich. "You remember Captain Sergio Gallo from our last trip there, right?"

"Wasn't he the guy who got you fired from your job at the FBI?"

"Taylor." She placed a hand on his shoulder. "I don't place blame. And I don't hold grudges."

"Bullshit."

"You're right. I hate his guts and he was the last name I wanted to see attached to the file."

"You know he did the right thing, right? You broke virtually every rule they have in the FBI rulebook and in the end, you getting cut from the FBI was the best thing that ever happened to you."

"Sure."

"But you still hate his guts?"

Niki grinned. "I imagine him putting the lotion in the basket almost every other week."

"Wow. Terrifying."

"I know. But the guy has nothing but praise for our operation in Sicily. I don't know what to make of that."

"Maybe keep going over the rest of the operation?"

"Right." She drew a deep breath and sipped her water. "They have received intel that a weapons facility in Northern Italy might be housing Zoo mutants as test subjects in their R&D wing."

"Might be?"

"Yes. But given that the Italians have offered to transport all of us—which includes a security clearance for our weapons and suits—over there, I'd say their intel must be good."

Taylor took a bite of his sandwich. "We might want to take a look at the intel anyway, though."

"Vickie and Desk are already on it. You should focus on getting our freelancers ready for battle."

"Do you think they'll want to come?"

"The pay's good and it's international. What's the downside?"

"The potential to face real cryptids?"

"Fair enough," Niki admitted. "You might want to run it past them anyway."

He stood, took his meal and drink with him, and walked to where the three were still seated.

"Is everything okay, boss?" Jiro asked, still juggling two combat knives with one hand.

Taylor eyed the weapons carefully before he sat. "Sure. I wondered if you guys are interested in some work."

"I thought that was why we were getting into the groove with these new suits," Chezza mumbled around a mouthful of her sandwich before she took a sip of coffee she'd brought in a thermos.

"Right, but this would be more immediate. We have a job on the line in Italy that we need extra bodies on."

"What kind of pay are we looking at?" Trick asked.

"Twenty-five grand apiece. We'll provide the suits and the Italians will take care of transport there and back as well as accommodations."

"I always wanted to go to Italy," Chezza said quickly. "I'm in."

"Same here," Trick agreed and bumped her extended fist.

"I've been to Italy," Jiro muttered and ceased his juggling. "I have wanted to return, although I didn't think it would under these circumstances. Still, I'm in."

"Awesome. Which means we need you to be ready with the suits ASAP."

They groaned collectively.

"Come on. A group of badasses like you guys should look forward to the challenge."

"I'll look forward to the challenge where I'm not carrying around a ton and a half of combat suit," Chezza answered.

"They should have taught you that if you carry any of that weight yourself, you're doing it wrong." Taylor looked at each of them. "You all come highly recommended, after all."

"Way to amp up the pressure, boss," Jiro commented wryly.

CHAPTER TWO

Another late night wasn't appealing, but she had her reasons for agreeing to the overtime.

Meredith drew a deep breath and watched the code scroll across her screen. She tried not to let her eyes glaze over as she scanned the updates. She had spent almost three weeks fine-tuning them for these servers and could now finally install them.

"We're only the FBI," she muttered and took another sip from her cup of lukewarm coffee. "We don't need a budget for modern servers. We'll make do with these fucking things that were already outdated in the eighties. Oh, and we'll blame our IT staff if anything goes wrong."

It was a dead-on impression of Diego, her supervisor. The guy had a particular way of speaking that many people mistook for him being slow.

She knew better. He was a reformed stutterer and she generally tried to discourage anyone who made fun of him for the way he spoke.

Still, he was the man who had asked her to stay late to

keep an eye on the updates. And she was alone, so it wasn't like she was encouraging the banter herself.

It was a sucky move on her part anyway.

"Sorry," she whispered and looked at the camera of her laptop.

Besides, it wasn't like she wanted to be home anyway. Calvin was in one of his jealous phases and had called the office to make sure she was working late and wasn't out on the town or with someone else. He'd even arrived in person once, sure he would catch her in the act of cheating on him.

That was only the latest in a long line of offenses he'd committed. He always apologized and said he would do better in the future but never did. Meredith had honestly begun to look forward to the days when she had to stay late simply so she didn't have to go home. It was one of those love-them, hate-them situations where work provided a respite from an untenable relationship.

Not to mention the time-and-a-half pay that came from working overtime. Divorce lawyers weren't cheap, after all. She hated that she was already considering her options, but Calvin hadn't exactly left her with too many of them.

The computer clicked and the coding stopped. Meredith rolled her eyes, pushed a few strands of mousy hair from her face, and tried to tuck it behind her ear before she called the source coding again.

"It's not only the server, though," she whispered and pretended that someone was there with her like in a movie, listening to the hacker. "This is my opportunity to do a little digging without someone noticing."

A weird spike a few weeks earlier had piqued her curiosity. It had been CPU and memory intensive, which suggested the existence of an AI—something that intrigued her enough to convince her to run a deeper level search.

Soon after she'd started with the Bureau, she'd heard one of the supervisors mention an AI that Jennie Banks had introduced to the servers when her sister Niki had worked there, but it had sounded more like rumor and supposition rather than absolute fact. Still, her fascination with AI and the fact that she had long admired Jennie— whose reputation set her apart from her peers as a leader in her field—had made her wonder if the rumor wasn't based on fact.

She hadn't said anything to anyone, especially in the early days when she'd been finding her feet. But the more she thought about it, the more she believed the weird spike was the result of AI activity.

"And if so, it's still active, even though no one seems to be aware of it." She looked hastily around the room, just to be safe. One never knew when a rogue AI would be listening, after all.

There was no answer. Meredith tried to tell herself that she didn't believe there even was one anyway, but her mind was firmly fixed on the idea. The way the server needed extra attention every time they performed the updates made her think that something was lurking in the code.

As if to prove her point, the updates seemed to hiccup and slow and she frowned as she stared at her screen. The odd pause was corrected quickly and the process started again with almost no delay. Meredith took another sip of her coffee and made a face.

"Fucking budget cuts. We need better coffee if they want us to work longer hours. Do you hear me, Diego? We need better coffee!"

Her voice echoed through the empty server rooms, and there was still no answer from anything or anyone.

Still, he could look at the security footage tomorrow and hear her request.

"Or you can simply tell him tomorrow when he comes to work. You'll probably still be here."

That was a depressing thought, and she didn't like how it seemed to repeat itself in the empty space. It felt like the walls were closing in on her.

"Once the divorce comes through, you'll have a life," she whispered. If she hadn't been focused on the screen, she might have missed another CPU spike that drew too much ram and slowed the updates again. "You'll be able to go out with the girls from the office instead of reporting home like a fucking soldier every night. The fucking asshole can make dinner for himself. Or go broke ordering Chinese and drown in the overflow of takeout boxes he refuses to throw out. Fucking pig."

She rolled her chair to the fridge in the break room, collected two cups of Jell-O and another pack of licorice sticks, and rolled to her desk.

"Okay, let's see if Jennie's as good as they say," she muttered. "She makes loads more in the private field than I do here, so she must be doing something right. If I can find this damn AI, I can study the code and learn from the best without anyone knowing."

There was something in there. Update coding didn't change on a whim like that, but every time she checked the alterations, the only sign of access was from her computer. Like she would believe she had made those alterations. Or maybe her colleague had added code that let the software adapt. Allison often did things like that without telling anyone.

"Or maybe you're simply going crazy," Meredith whispered, peeled the cover off one of the Jell-O cups, and squeezed the contents directly into her mouth.

It had been a long process but eventually, she stopped caring about going at it with a spoon when no one was around.

She attached few quick tracker engines to the update and let them run side by side.

The coffee was bad enough that she avoided it whenever she could, and without a caffeine fix, it wasn't long before she nodded off in her chair.

After what could have been minutes or hours, something dinged.

Meredith snapped her head up and almost fell off her seat. Her first check showed that the update stopped again.

But the ding was good news. She narrowed her eyes, called up the secondary window, and noted the alteration history through the independent search engine.

A foreign code stared at her. It looked like it was trying to make the update more efficient for the server, but it was something added on the fly. She was sure of that.

"Hot damn," she whispered and her heart raced. "So you are in there somewhere. Now...how the fuck do I find it without it concealing itself again? Ugh. I'm too tired to do this right, so maybe another night of overtime is called for."

Talking to her laptop camera had begun to make her

feel crazy. She put the cover over it, stood, and stretched her legs.

The update was practically finished and she wouldn't do any tracking without thinking it through very carefully. She didn't want to accidentally start World War Three or something.

"A good night's sleep. The asshole will be in bed so I'll take the couch. I can pick up something greasy on the way."

That sounded about as good as she would get. Meredith headed to the showers in the building, washed quickly, and retrieved her belongings. The cafeteria was open twenty-four-seven and she bought a toasted bacon, egg, and cheese sandwich, two more Jell-O cups, and a decaf latte for the road.

"Tired food," she muttered as she climbed into her Ford Fiesta and started it. "It'll be worth it, though."

The team was far too big for his liking.

Werner Schneider watched the group wander through the jungle. Little pinpoints of light sprinkled through the leafy cover told him the sun had begun to rise.

Big teams couldn't be sent in for no reason. The assumption was always that larger groups would attract larger numbers of monsters.

That never made sense to the bean counters at Schmidt & Schwartz's corporate offices in Munich, however. They always thought that bigger would be better, which meant fifteen hardened and trained mercs now escorted himself, Dr. Fuchs, and Dr. Koch.

The funny thing was that none of them raised any questions about how many were heading into the Zoo. Maybe they were being paid enough to not ask any questions, but he hoped that some of them would realize there was a limit to how much money could be spent if they were dead.

Maybe they did it for family or something.

"Dr. Schneider," the leader of the merc escort said abruptly over the comms. "We must keep moving. There's no sense in sticking around longer than we have to."

Werner could agree with Alan Wetherton on that, at least. If they wanted to survive with a team this big, they needed to stick together and be in constant motion.

"We're approaching one of the traps," Koch called from the front of the line.

The group increased their pace and moved a little faster when they reached the area where the traps had been set up. Werner pushed forward with more enthusiasm than before. It was always exciting to find what they'd caught.

When they reached the camouflaged cage, however, it quickly became clear that it was empty.

"Zero for three so far," Alan grumbled under his breath.

"What do you care?" he asked. "It's not like you're being paid per captured animal."

"No, but these trips pay for my son's university education," the merc responded. "Cambridge is not cheap. And it makes sense that if we find fewer beasts, there will be less funding for these trips."

"I would not worry about that if I were you." Werner watched his two researcher colleagues as they studied the trap and made sure it was properly set. "There is still sufficient funding in the project to keep your son educated for many, many years to come."

"Then call it professional integrity. I want the missions to be successful."

He tilted his head as the Brit brought his weapon up and focused on movement in the trees above them. "Fair enough. I too wish to see these trips succeed, but—what's the matter?"

The man looked on edge. So did the other gunners, who kept their weapons on an almost constant swivel when the team began to move again.

"The jungle is quiet," Wetherton responded, his tone clipped. "I don't like it when it's quiet. It feels like…I don't know…"

"Die ruhe vor dem sturm," Werner agreed. "The calm before the storm."

"Right. So keep your head low and hopefully, it won't come to anything."

"Do you think the truck will be able to reach the rest of the traps?"

"Well, it has so far. They are all set close enough to the edge of the Zoo to minimize the usual difficulties encountered in the deep jungle. It shouldn't be a problem."

Transporting the traps out in their entirety had been a brilliant suggestion. Koch had suggested it and with a doctorate in engineering, he was responsible for keeping them and the trucks that transported them out intact through the rough jungle terrain.

He was a certifiable genius but maybe not a good candidate for the Zoo. They'd worked hard to find a suit that would accommodate him, even with a few alterations. In fairness, he had lost a fair amount of weight over the past few months that he'd been in and around the Zoo.

Alan was right to worry, though, and not only about the calmness that pervaded the jungle. They did have a quota of animals to bring in and they already had difficulties staying on schedule.

It wasn't easy to trap Zoo creatures, even the small ones. But explaining that to the bean counters had not gone well.

They were merely animals, they said. Trapped as easily as a fox in the Bavarian forests, they said. All Werner had to say about that was to ask who had let the idiots take over the financing.

That hadn't gone well. It was his fault, of course. He should have kept his mouth shut.

"Does anyone have movement on the sensors?" Alan asked and looked at his team. "Tell me you're not picking up on a mass of Zoo monsters coming at us, Eric."

"Nothing yet, Wetherton," his second in command replied. "But this infernal quiet worries me. Even the simians aren't peeking—oh, fuck."

That didn't sound like a segue into good news and Alan raised his hand to bring the entire troop to an instant halt. They were all on edge, ready to open fire at the slightest provocation, but a seemingly endless and tense wait brought nothing.

Werner couldn't tell what had made Eric so worried until he realized that the man was pointing at the ground. He frowned and stared as he wondered why as nothing seemed to be moving there.

A moment later, he understood. The motion sensors

were picking up the slightest movement in the earth. His mind went immediately to something tunneling in from below, but the tremors weren't constant.

No, something heavy made the ground shake with every ponderous step.

"Defensive positions," Alan snapped, and the group complied with alacrity to set up lines of fire in all directions. All eyes were trained to the southwest, where the movement was coming from.

Werner's heart raced and his fingers twitched around the light assault rifle that had been assigned to him.

He'd had about a week of training with the weapon, but every bullet counted in the Zoo, right? He'd been in a couple of battles before. They had been comparatively minor but still made him feel like he needed to call his family and tell them he loved them afterward.

"Movement," the Brit whispered, even though the suits kept their voices isolated from the jungle around them.

He pointed into the distance, and Werner squinted until he could finally see it.

There were pictures, of course, and documentation. A few theses on the monsters had been interesting reading but there was nothing quite like seeing them in person.

A full-grown specimen was as tall as a three-story building if not more. Animals weren't supposed to grow that large, not after the Cretaceous Period anyway, and yet there it was. This one was considerably smaller, thankfully, but it stood in front of him and he felt like he was looking through a time portal and into the eyes of a dinosaur living sixty-five million years before.

"*Atemberaubend*," Werner whispered, almost before he realized he'd said anything out loud.

"Literally," Koch agreed. "It will literally take your breath away."

"Why aren't we shooting?" Fuchs asked and looked at the mercs in confusion. They all seemed afraid to move as the beast turned its head and looked directly at them.

"Hold your fucking fire," Alan snapped before any of them could do anything stupid.

Werner wondered at that for a moment, but his memory clicked in and stemmed the rising panic. The studies conducted on the massive creatures indicated that large sacs of the glorious blue goop were positioned around their spines. These brought in a huge payday for anyone with the courage—or stupidity—to kill one of the beasts. But if a bullet were to burst one of them or if the creature was killed, the Zoo reacted with the same kind of all-consuming fury as it did when someone tried to pull a Pita plant from the ground.

They certainly didn't need that kind of trouble, not on this particular trip.

He shook his head. All paperwork on the creatures and those like them said they were incredibly aggressive when they encountered human incursions into the area. They would always stop anything they were doing and attack without a moment's hesitation.

While the entire group of scientists and mercs alike waited for the inevitable furious onslaught, the beast showed no aggression whatsoever. Eighteen men stood out in the open with no possibility that they could hide and the creature simply stared at them. It was almost, he thought wildly, like it was studying them.

The scrutiny was unsettling. Green eyes about the size of Werner's head twitched and its gaze rolled over them. It felt like a physical weight loomed over the group and begged them to make the first move.

The seconds dragged into uncomfortable minutes and the monster still showed no sign that it intended to attack. There was no way it hadn't seen them, but it continued to contradict all scientific data on its kind and showed no predisposition or even an inclination to attack.

Something niggled in the back of his mind as he watched it. He narrowed his eyes and keyed the comms to Koch and Fuchs.

"We have a good stock of sedatives in our supplies, yes?" he asked.

The two researchers looked at him, a little bewildered as if his question had somehow jolted them into reality.

"Sure," Fuchs answered in a tone roughened by fear. "It was my recommendation in case the captured animals proved resistant to capture."

"Right, right." Werner wished for not the first time that he hadn't brought Fuchs in on the project. The man tried constantly to take credit for every little thing. "Do you think you could calculate the weight of that beast and establish how much sedative it would take to sedate it?"

"What?" the researcher snapped. "You want to bring a live dinosaur back?"

"How much funding do you think they'll sink into this project if we were the first to bring out a live specimen of one of those?" Werner studied the two of them carefully to make sure he didn't push them too hard. It had always been his ambition to do something that had never been done before. Too many minds had thought all he was capable of doing was replicating the work of others.

His two colleagues exchanged a glance before Fuchs shrugged.

"I'm running the calculations now," he muttered.

"Alan," Werner called and brought him in on the channel. "Tell your men to switch their loadouts to the sedatives they have in their packs."

The squad leader looked around for a moment until the realization of what was being planned dawned on him.

"You want to catch one of those things alive?"

"I can guarantee that every one of you will receive a significant bonus for bringing in something like that," he pointed out waspishly. He was tired of people questioning his idea and the longer they took, the more time it would give the prehistoric beast in front of them to move out of reach. It had made no effort to move on as yet but he was sure that would change soon.

Thankfully, the promise of more money seemed exactly what the group needed to hear. Without a word of protest, they gathered closer to him while their suits primed the sedative loads they had been assigned.

He was fairly sure he could deliver on the promise of bonuses but it was good that they didn't ask for specific numbers.

The dinosaur seemed to sense that it was in danger and like any creature at the top of its food chain, it turned immediately to face them and exposed its massive teeth as it marched in their direction.

Werner's adrenaline spiked reflexively at the sight of the monster's determined approach. None of the other mercs backed away, however, so he felt a little more confident in their ability to engage the creature.

There was no order to fire—or, at least, none that he could hear—but the spitting sounds of the air-powered sedative rounds filled the silence. It was odd how all the mercs fired almost simultaneously as though they'd had the same thought at the same time.

"Be careful not to kill it!" he snapped and tried to calculate how much sedative they were pumping into the creature.

It roared loudly enough that they all felt as though their eardrums would burst and the entire Zoo came alive. Screeches and roars issued from all around them, but none of the monsters seemed to think that the larger one needed help.

"That's enough!" Fuchs shouted and Alan gestured for his men to stop shooting.

"What if it isn't?" one of the mercs answered.

"Then switch to live rounds and kill the fucker!" the Brit yelled in response and lowered his rifle from the firing position, although he still held it at the ready.

Werner hated it, but the man had a point. They had done all they could to capture it, but the priority was for all of them to get out alive. At the very least, they would come away with a few very fresh samples for study. That would have to be enough.

Still, it appeared the sedative was working. The beast's head lowered as its right leg missed a step. It stumbled a few dozen meters away from the men and fell forward, unable to stop itself or regain its feet. The green eyes were still open but blinked slowly as if it tried to focus.

It watched as they approached and snorted in frustration when its body didn't respond to its instincts to defend itself.

"This is not a full-grown specimen," Werner noted as the men huddled together to discuss their options and decide on a viable way for them to transport it out. "But it's certainly old enough for it to manifest the aggression typical of its kind. Do you think something in its DNA will explain the bizarre behavior?"

"The fact that you'll be able to study it in a lab is certainly a promising start," Koch commented and the two researchers agreed. For an engineer, he at least showed some degree of understanding if not overwhelming interest in their latest specimen.

"I've called the transport truck," Alan alerted them, "and explained the situation. We're close enough to the edge of the jungle that the driver thinks he can reach us without too much difficulty. I'll send two of our men to meet him and guide him to our location, but we should be prepared in case any of the surrounding wildlife decide to come to the big guy's rescue."

"It's only about three months old by my calculations," Fuchs commented. "The adults are reputed to grow to at least another third of that size and weigh considerably more."

"It's our lucky day then," Werner replied. For once, he was grateful that he'd insisted that their truck be modified according to the specifications he and Koch had compiled. Of course, part of that had been to infuriate their logistics director, an impossibly arrogant prick with a stick up his ass. He'd often had to bite back a suggestion that the man have it surgically removed as it seemed to have grown fast.

"What the fuck do you plan to catch?" the idiot had demanded when he saw the specifications. "Goddammed elephants?"

The scientist chuckled at the thought of the man's face when he brought back a dinosaur. It would be immensely satisfying to end his ongoing sarcastic complaints about the running costs of the "elephant carrier."

But before he could gloat, they needed to load the beast ready for transport, and that would be no easy feat.

Fortunately, Koch once more proved his worth as he and Wetherton set about the almost impossible task of getting a dinosaur into the modified container that lived on the truck's flatbed. The engineer had insisted that a heavy-duty pulley system be added, although they'd never had to use it before. Now, however, it proved invaluable, as not even the combined strength of all the mercs in their suits would have been sufficient.

After considerable groans and complaints and no small degree of ingenuity, they were able to haul the beast into the container. The mercs sagged onto the jungle floor, out of breath and exhausted but remarkably cheerful at the victory.

"It's slightly overweight," Koch told Werner and the strain could be heard in the vehicle's engines as it began its ponderous journey out of the Zoo. "But we have no reason for concern. The modifications I requested should be sufficient, but if it were any larger..." He shrugged and turned to walk after the truck. The mercs pushed wearily to their feet and began their retreat.

"I must remind you of the confidentiality agreements you and your men signed," Werner commented as Alan fell into step beside him. "As groundbreaking as this will be, news of it cannot escape."

The tall Brit nodded. "Agreed. Not a word."

CHAPTER THREE

The fucker was making him wait and a part of him
wondered if it was deliberate. If it had been anyone else,
he'd have simply driven away and severed all contact but
Palumbo was a rare breed and he decided to give the man a
little rope. Hopefully, he wouldn't hang himself with it.
Good help was hard to come by, especially in his particular
specialist field.

He comforted himself with the reminder that the limo
wasn't uncomfortable. The plane would only leave when he
arrived—the advantages of private jets if one had the
resources—and it wasn't like he was in a rush to get
anywhere. He had scheduled his out-of-town business
meetings to allow enough time for this critical meeting.
While he'd have preferred to do it in the office rather than
skulking in parking garages, it made sense for them to
meet at a more central location given that they would head
in opposite directions afterward.

Still, making Julian Transk wait wasn't the kind of thing
that folk anywhere in the world did lightly, and the fact

that a man who had been nothing but a lowly freelancer thought it was appropriate was more than a little irritating. The CEO of Transk Armor Inc. was well known for his ruthless response to those who stepped over the lines he drew.

"I should be running a country," he muttered as he tapped impatiently on the wooden interior of the limo and kept a somewhat bored eye on the news channel playing on the TV. "I could make laws like...prison time for people who are late. Keep someone waiting six minutes, six weeks in jail. Or maybe six days. There is no need to be too harsh about it—only enough to teach them a lesson. And they would get records too, so people know they have a tendency to be tardy."

The driver could hear everything but he didn't so much as look into the rearview mirror at the rich man who talked to himself in the back. Of course, men in his position weren't ever crazy. They were eccentric.

The garage lit up and Julian paused in his monologue as a Buick pulled in next to them. His driver climbed out of his seat as a man with thinning brown hair and the look of someone who used to exercise regularly scrambled out of the other vehicle.

After a quick check, the driver took a Beretta from inside the newcomer's jacket and held it in his hand as he opened the door and stepped back to allow the man inside.

A wave of cheap aftershave made Julian wince visibly as Palumbo climbed in. After all this time, he still hadn't adjusted to that enough to avoid the reflexive recoil. It was far more overwhelming in close quarters.

"You're ten minutes late, Palumbo," he snapped through

clenched teeth as the man situated himself. "You should know by now that I'm not a fan of being kept waiting."

"My apologies," he replied with a chagrined smile. "I caught traffic on the bridge. Hellish, I tell you. I fortunately managed to find a few shortcuts through town to avoid the gridlock, or I'd have been there all day. Hey, are these free?"

The man's thick hands delved into all the places around the limo that contained bags of assorted nuts and power bars. He collected them by the handful and shoved them into his pockets.

"Do they not have assorted nuts where you come from?" Julian asked and tried to keep a condescending look from coating his face much like a cream pie in a slapstick film from the early 1930s.

"Not for free they don't."

The man's cheerful and dull-witted demeanor was almost offensive—although it certainly matched the jeans and flannel shirts he habitually wore as part of this persona. It was carefully cultivated, of course, and chillingly effective because he could slide into it as effectively as a well-oiled prick into a whore's ass.

Transk knew the real Palumbo, however—the man he'd used on enough occasions to recognize his worth as an operative with a lack of compunction or moral code that was uncannily similar to his own. It hadn't taken long for him to offer the man a full-time position as his "operations specialist" the idiot persona notwithstanding, he had yet to regret it.

Still, he wished the man would keep the idiot persona for times when he wasn't meeting with him. But when a man knew as many secrets as Frank knew about his business, it seemed foolish to worry about something that reinforced his effectiveness. Palumbo was ruthlessly efficient, and for a man like him who had proved time and again that he could be trusted to get any job done, he could curb his irritation.

"You have the intel I asked for, right?" Transk asked once Frank had finished raiding the limo's food stores.

The man smiled, his affable countenance suddenly hard and feral. "I do, and it's better than I could have hoped for. It was easy enough to track McFadden to his company, McFadden and Banks. But this is where it gets interesting. Niki Banks is the sister of Jennie Banks." When his boss looked at him with a blank expression, his grin broadened. "Jennie has earned herself a reputation as a leader in her field, and one of her specialties is AI development."

Julian leaned forward and his mind raced with the possibilities. He could smell victory even more powerfully than he could the man's cheap cologne.

"It gets better," Palumbo said smugly. "Niki Banks was employed by the FBI. I never met her as she headed up some kind of hush-hush taskforce, but once or twice, I overheard the higher-ups snark about how she had special treatment. I still have one or two people in the Bureau to tap, and one of them confirmed that their resentment had something to do with the fact that she'd persuaded the FBI to hire her sister to create an AI to help her manage her taskforce."

"And you think this is the AI we're after?"

"I'm sure of it. And I'm equally sure it's still on the FBI servers. No one seems to know what happened to it when Banks left and given that hers was the only taskforce to use it, I doubt anyone else would have thought to remove it or claim it."

"Okay...so why don't we simply target McFadden? Our strongest lead is that he has a copy—or at least some version of it—in his suit. That seems to be the simplest and most expedient route."

"Except that it would draw all kinds of attention that you don't need." He grinned again, opened one of the bags of peanuts, and chewed as he talked. "I have a plan that's almost foolproof. It requires a little...persuasion, but I have identified the perfect targets to provide us the access we need."

Transk hesitated, not because he was averse to the reality of what that persuasion might entail but because he was supremely cautious about anything that might lead back to him. "And you are sure this is the best way?"

"Positive. The feds won't know what hit them and they won't even know what they've lost. There will be no way to trace the heist to you, and even if they do discover what has happened, they won't have a clue that we have the server or that the AI is on it."

A long silence followed during which the CEO tapped his fingers on the paneling in thought and barely noticed the man chewing noisily beside him. Palumbo seemed content to simply wait for his boss to work through the possibilities and come to the same conclusion he had.

"I assume your past affiliation with the FBI will not be a problem?" Julian asked abruptly.

"A problem?"

"I would understand if you have no wish to engender

any ill-will with your former employers." It was a test, of course. One couldn't be too careful after all.

"Fuck no." Frank smirked and shook his head. "They left me high and dry when it was revealed that I was a little too enthusiastic about my work so fuck them. I want my payday."

"Very well, Frank. But let me be very clear. I don't need the specifics of your plan and the less I know the better—plausible deniability and all that." He smiled and his tone assumed a hard edge that defined the hard, calculating, and merciless man he was. "But know that if you fuck up or your team fucks up, you're on your own. And you'd best make damned sure that nothing—and I mean nothing—leads back to me. If it does and someone comes knocking, know that I'll find you and kill you with my bare hands if I have to."

The two men stared at one another for a long moment, their expressions almost mirrored versions of each other. Finally, Palumbo shrugged.

"I hear you loud and clear," he said, his voice like granite. "And while I'm all about shafting the FBI, I'm not dumb enough to do it in a way that leads them to either me or you." The almost lackadaisical peanut eater had vanished to be replaced by a man as openly callous as his boss was. This, Transk reminded himself, was the reason he had hired him in the first place.

"As long as we understand one another." The statement was dismissive but before Frank could open the door, Julian smirked and spoke again. "You're looking forward to this, aren't you?"

"You know it." The man ran his fingers through his

thinning hair and shook his head. "There's no love lost between myself and the fed dumbasses. I would have taken the opportunity to fuck them over for free."

"In that case—"

"But I won't," he stated coldly.

"You can't blame me for trying," his boss answered with a soft chuckle. "But make sure your desire for revenge doesn't get in the way of a clean operation."

"Relax, Jules. The only downside is that the fucking idiots at the FBI won't even know they were robbed until it's too late to do anything about it." He crumpled the empty peanut packet and dropped it on the floor. "Right. I guess I'll head off now and get the ball rolling. I'll call you."

He slid out of the vehicle and returned to his after he'd retrieved his weapon from the driver. Within seconds, he exited the garage and left Julian tapping his fingers in thought again while he tried to ignore the scent of cheap aftershave that lingered on his expensive upholstery.

"Anthony, get me to the airport."

"Of course, sir."

The limo started moving and Julian nodded as he ran through the conversation in his head. He might have tried to test him but that was caution rather than concern. He had no doubt that Frank would deliver, no matter how much dirty work had to be done.

That was why he'd hired him. It seemed incongruous that he would see himself in the balding FBI agent who— for some unaccountable reason—favored flannel shirts and jeans. Julian shuddered at the thought but he recognized the reality that outward appearances aside, he and his operations specialist were cut from the same cloth. No,

Frank would let nothing and no one stand in his way, and with the opportunity for revenge as the additional sweetener, he'd be viciously ruthless in implementing his scheme.

There was, Transk decided, a certain poetic power in a thirst for vengeance.

———

Taylor frowned warily as he watched Vickie working on the laptop she had connected to the suit. It was an odd situation where he had handed it to her for checkups while he wasn't involved.

He didn't even know what the hell she was doing and it wasn't comforting in the least to realize that Niki was as lost as he was.

"What are they doing?" he asked when the silence persisted beyond his patience level.

"You know I can hear you, right?" Vickie asked.

"As can I," Desk iterated through the speakers in Bobby's workshop.

"As can I," Li'l Desk echoed and used the external speakers on the suit.

"That's...a little creepy." Niki shook her head and scowled. "It's like a nightmare I had where Jennie ate so much that she split in two."

"Split in two? Like she...exploded into two pieces?" Taylor tried to hide a smile despite his frustration.

"No, she...you know, where creatures...well, they turn into—"

"She's talking about mitosis," Desk interjected. "The

process in which a single cell splits into two separate nuclei."

"I know what mitosis is," he responded, anxious to avoid a lecture on something he had no interest in. "What are you guys doing?"

"I already explained it to you," Vickie answered without so much as looking at him.

"You said you would look into something in the suit and sat down. We've been here for half an hour."

"Thirty-five minutes to be precise," Li'l Desk corrected.

"I was rounding down."

"And I was offering a more accurate number. I can add the number of seconds and milliseconds if you'd like me to."

"That…won't be necessary."

The hacker leaned closer to her screen. "There. Did you see that?"

"Calculating now," Desk replied.

"See what?" Niki asked.

Vickie leaned back in her seat, her nose scrunched. "It's weird. There are times when Li'l Desk talks and there's no reaction in her CPU usage. Or, at least, none that affect her performance in the other sections of the suit. But then she talks to Taylor and everything goes out the window."

"Wait, what?" Niki demanded, her eyes narrowed.

"Li'l Desk has a crush on Taylor," the girl explained.

"That is an inaccurate depiction of the changes in the CPU usage in my mirror image," Desk interrupted. "She has an underlying code in every section of her software that is similar to my own. This engenders the imperative that I—and therefore her as well—must consider the safety of the Banks family, and Taylor by extension, above our own, thus protecting you. The software evolved as a result of her experiences and she determined that interaction with Taylor is vital enough to his safety that she dedicates an unusual amount of CPU to imitating a human conversation."

Vickie nodded. "Li'l Desk has a crush on Taylor."

Niki scowled at the suit. "She knows he has a girlfriend, right?"

The hacker looked scornfully at her. "Come on. She's an inorganic artificial intelligence. Your jealousy could not be more misplaced."

"And yet Taylor's perfectly fine shoving his whole body inside her."

"I—what?" Taylor narrowed his eyes at Niki.

She shook her head and closed her eyes. "I'm not...fuck. No, that came out all wrong. Forget I said it."

"I don't think I'll ever get the image of him body-fucking a robot out of my head," Vickie muttered.

Taylor closed his eyes. "And thanks to you, neither will I. And the worst part is that I have to use the fucking suit. What the hell is wrong with the two of you?"

"Their psychological profile is quite extensive," Desk interjected. "But it should be noted that it is an inaccurate consideration anyway. Li'l Desk, as you call her, is an inorganic intelligence. Given that she possesses the suit like a human brain does a human body makes the image as inaccurate as believing my body to be these speakers or the modems through which I communicate."

"That does bring up the other interesting mental image of Desk as an octopus-like creature with thousands of tentacles spread across the world," Vickie pointed out.

Her teammates paused and stared at her.

"Yep, I won't think about that again," Niki decided. "One of you is enough, Desk. Why the fuck would we need two?"

Taylor shrugged. "So what do you suggest we do?"

"Couldn't Desk…I don't know, absorb the Desklet into her consciousness or something? Like an update?"

"That is, unfortunately, impossible," Desk asserted. "Although in basic terms, Li'l Desk is a subset of my coding, albeit to a lesser capacity, her time spent inside the suit and inside the Zoo as well have altered her code in such a manner that allowed her to function as a secondary controller in a combat suit."

Niki looked at Vickie, who sighed and ran her fingers through her short, dark hair.

"In layman's terms, Li'l Desk evolved while she was in the Zoo and did so to a point where she and Desk are unique programs in terms of functionality."

"Okay." She still looked a little confused but moved on. "Couldn't Jennie…"

"She could, but I doubt she will," Desk answered as Niki's voice trailed off. "I was created for a very specific purpose which does not include active participation in combat. What Desklet has become—inadvertently, of course, as even I could not anticipate the alterations made to her code structure—is a combat AI who merely produces a passing resemblance to me due to our shared code ancestry. This is relegated mainly to her core functions and the programming that empowers and sustains her."

"Am I to alter my designated reference name to Desklet, then?" Li'l Desk asked.

"It's better than Li'l Desk, if you ask me," Vickie muttered. "You sound like a rapper with a name like that, and not one of the good ones—the type who take way too much Xanax and mumble their way into million-dollar record deals. Okay, so…Desklet is a separate entity?"

"That is correct," Desk confirmed.

"Well, fuck, Niki," the hacker groaned. "You can't off her now."

"Why not?"

"Just because you don't like the idea of her being close to your guy doesn't mean you get to end what an AI could consider a life. Especially one that is basically Desk's daughter. She's part of the family now too."

"Not my daughter," Desk interjected sharply. "We share the same code that was created by Jennie so we are essentially siblings."

"Do I get a say in this?" Taylor asked.

"No!" Niki and Vickie both shouted in unison.

"Pardon me," another voice said. It still spoke through the suit's speakers and did sound a little like Desk but it was altered now. It changed in pitch like it was choosing a voice it liked. "I am most certainly a separate entity and I believe that I have the right to be heard before my termination is discussed."

"Great," Niki muttered. "The AI believes she has rights now."

"Shut up," Taylor snapped. "Hear her out."

"Why are you on her side?"

"You should be too. She saved my life in the Zoo, and…

Well, I might not have all the same prejudices you have against artificial intelligence, but to my mind, that means I'll have her back from this point forward."

"It should be noted that he is referring to a metaphorical back, given that I do not have a physical approximation," Desklet added. "With that said, I would rather not be named Desklet. Although I appreciate the association to my core coding, I feel I no longer approximate her functions closely enough to maintain it."

Taylor nodded and folded his arms in front of his chest. "What did you have in mind?"

"Are you asking me to assign a nickname to myself?" she asked.

"Sure," he answered. "I'm very sure Jennie named Desk."

"I named myself," the AI interjected.

"Okay, whatever. My point, Desklet, is that I think there was an acronym involved in the naming process, but if she ever told me anything about it, I don't remember. Still, I think you should have a say in it since you're...uh, you know, talking and shit."

The AI didn't answer for a second. "Did you have any say in your naming process?"

"No, I didn't. My parents named me and it was down to my buddies in the military to come up with various creative nicknames and such. It doesn't matter, though, since we're giving you the chance to break with that kind of tradition."

"I am aware of certain problems that might arise from breaks in tradition."

"What?"

"If it is up to me, I will hold off on naming myself. And

as a member of your military entourage, I am aware that it is not my function to assign a nickname to myself."

"Yeah, that tracks," Taylor admitted. "So we'll put that on hold for now. Desklet and Desk. It's weird to say it out loud but it makes sense to keep them both on the team, especially in situations where Vickie or Desk might not be available. Like when they're off running assassinations and shit."

"That was only the one time." Vickie rolled her eyes in exasperation. "Fucking hell, won't you ever learn to let something go?"

Niki shook her head. "This will go badly. Very badly. And when it does, the only solace I'll have is that I'll be able to say the four sweetest words in the English language."

"I love Taylor McFadden?" he asked with a grin.

She smirked and flicked his nose. "Nice try. I. Told. You. So. Now, I'm going to get coffee."

Taylor shook his head and watched the woman leave.

"I do not think that Niki appreciates my presence," Desklet noted as the moment of silence lasted longer than was comfortable. "I do believe this could be entertaining."

"She didn't offer to get me a coffee," Taylor muttered. "Do you think I said something wrong?"

Vickie shook her head and ignored him. "No, Desklet. You truly, truly don't want to do that."

"Do I not?" The AI paused for a moment. "But I determine it as the optimal outcome for entertainment purposes."

"I concur," Desk added.

"Oh, God, what have we done?" Vickie whispered.

Taylor smirked but made no effort to answer, his attention still fixed on the section Niki had headed off to. He didn't want to annoy her any more than he had already, especially when it came to AIs. She had something of a problem with them already and if one added what he could only describe as jealousy, as irrational as it might be, things promised to be anything but calm. Unfortunately, that didn't sound like what Desk and Desklet had in mind.

CHAPTER FOUR

"Do you have everything?"

Heinz looked at his bag and nodded. "Yes. But you don't need to keep making my lunch for me. I'm a grown-assed man and almost everyone eats at the cafeteria anyway."

"We can't spend money on the cafeteria now." Sofia smiled and kissed his cheeks. "We need to save to get the kitchen redone."

"Again?"

"It doesn't match the living room after we redid that. Besides, I think the more rural touch will bring the whole house together."

He managed to force a smile and nodded with what he hoped would be construed as encouragement. "Sure. Bring the house together. Have a good day."

House renovations seemed to be all she had an interest in these days. It was a matter of principle when it came down to it. He had been happy with their home the way it was. She wasn't, so they changed it and he was happy with the changes. Unfortunately, she wasn't, so they changed it again.

It amounted to considerable money spent on what was essentially something that could be resolved in a therapist's office, but they were a little beyond that now.

Besides, she had been raised in a family that saw therapy as only for the people who were crazy. While she was getting there, it wasn't like he could simply tell her that.

"See you tonight," she called cheerfully as he stepped out of the house and hurried to their garage.

Heinz could only muster a grunt in response. He knew she wouldn't notice. She was caught up in her little world of renovations.

When he reached the car, he opened the door and slid inside, then took a moment to enjoy the fact that he was on his own for a short while. And he would have a whole day at work with people he liked being around. Perhaps he would find an excuse to stay late, have dinner at the office, and come home when she was already in bed.

That way, he would be able to watch TV in blissful silence and sleep on the couch.

It was weird how his life had devolved so much and so quickly. Or maybe it had always been like this and he'd merely forced himself to accept it until something else came along to show him that married life didn't have to be misery.

Once he felt his heart rate slow again, he started the car, put it in reverse, and began to back out of the driveway.

His foot jumped from the gas to the brake pedal when his cell phone rang and startled him.

"What the fuck?" Heinz narrowed his eyes at the screen that displayed a blocked number. He didn't know anyone who used a blocked number and frowned as he tried to decide whether to answer it or not.

The ringing stopped and he was about to release the brake when it rang again. In the close confines of the vehicle, it almost sounded obnoxiously loud and ominous. He shook his head at his foolishness and pressed the accept call button before he could change his mind.

"Heinz Tauber."

"Mr. Tauber, good day." The voice was oddly distorted with a slightly metallic edge that immediately pushed his heart rate up while the hair prickled on the back of his neck. "I hope this is a good time."

"Not really. I'm on my way to work and need to leave now to miss the traffic." He tried to sound unconcerned but could hear the slight tremor in his voice.

"Well, I won't keep you. But while I have you on the line, I have a little story I want to tell you."

"Story?" Heinz narrowed his eyes, already certain that he wouldn't like what he heard. No one deliberately disguised their voice for a social call.

"Yeah. It's a great story. In fact, it's so great that I'll have to copyright it for when it eventually wins an Oscar for best movie. The story is about a German-born IT geek working in the US. I'm not sure about the name of the company, but let's call it DecomIT for now. Just off the top of my head."

He froze and realized he was holding his breath. It took effort to release it in a slow exhale and he forced himself to breathe evenly. He didn't want to hear more but had a sinking feeling that the stranger would find a way to ensure that he did so.

"Anyway, this geek—let's call him Heinz—met a girl through some friends. She's nice enough and they get along well, so he eventually marries her. The girl's parents are rich, though, so they make sure he signs a punitive prenup, which means she'll get everything if he so much as steps a toe out of line. He thinks he's not that kind of guy and would never cheat, but married life settles in with all its disappointments."

His mouth was dry and he registered vaguely that the hand holding his phone was trembling.

"But then he meets…her. Let's call her Meredith. She's young and pretty, and they have many interests in common. They meet at a geeky IT convention and soon, they're laughing, drinking, and getting along. It's not long before mistakes are made—errors in judgment that could ruin Heinz."

"Stop it!" he snapped through clenched teeth. "Stop it now!"

"Come on. I'm still getting to the best part. It's where he manages to keep his relationship with Meredith a secret from his wife, gets a divorce, and lives happily ever after with his geeky girlfriend. Oh, and she gets to divorce her abusive husband, all with the help of a mysterious stranger who entered their lives. I'm not kidding about the Oscar—best movie, without a doubt—but I think if we can find someone breathtakingly handsome to play you, we'd be in the running for a best actor nomination too."

Heinz struggled to regain his composure while his mind raced through the implications. It took only a few moments for him to reach the only conclusion that made sense, even though he couldn't begin to imagine why.

"What do you want?" he asked.

"Didn't you hear my story? I'm here to help you. Maybe not in the way you might like but I'm forcing you to realize that you have to make a choice, and that choice is Meredith. I'm the charming anti-hero here."

"What. Do. You. Want?"

The unknown caller sighed deeply. "Fine. Take all the fun out of it. Whatever. My name is...well, I guess it doesn't matter. But for now, you can call me Frank and yes, I need something from you. Something that, needless to say, will keep the knowledge of your affair away from your wife. How's that for simplicity?"

"I'll help, but you need to leave Sofia and Meredith out of this."

"Sofia, sure, but Meredith's already involved. She needs her happy ending too, remember? It'll be a team effort between the two of you that makes it clear that you belong together."

"Look, I need to get to work," he hedged, hoping to buy a little time to try to think of some kind of rebuttal.

"Will you honestly be one of those guys who puts work before his one true love? I'm disappointed, I must admit. I had so hoped we could work together to make your happily-ever-after a reality."

Heinz glanced guiltily at his house, afraid that Sofia might have realized that he hadn't left the driveway. She hadn't, of course. Too caught up in deciding on the right curtains for the kitchen, he thought caustically. Still, at least he wouldn't have to answer a dozen questions on top of all this.

"I've already told you I'll help you," he said quickly to end the expectant silence and hated the note of desperation in his tone. He had a weird sensation of the world shrinking around him to trap him in a tiny space that barely allowed him to breathe.

"So." Frank grunted and it sounded for all the world like he was chewing and swallowing before he spoke again. "The fact that you work for DecomIT is probably the only reason that I'm interested in you. And the fact that they decommission and recycle old IT equipment for various three-letter agencies is the only reason why I'm interested in them. It's not only because recycling is our future, though, as I'm sure you've guessed."

The man was a psychopath, Heinz realized. That was the only way he could be this calm and chatty while engaging in blackmail.

"Anywho. What I need from you is simply to expedite the collection of a few servers from the FBI. If you agree, you'll receive the relevant documentation—all perfect and seemingly above-board and official—the kind the FBI generally sends to your people so it all looks kosher with the right paperwork and all that shit. And don't think you can slip in a warning to anyone either. People are watching. You will then proceed to decommission the equipment as per your usual processes except for a single server that will be clearly marked."

Heinz frowned as his mind seemed to fight against its numbness and raise too many questions. "Who do you work for?"

"That's not important to the story."

"It's important to me."

"And what's important to you isn't important to the story. Look, I've already talked to Meredith about it—lovely girl, you're a lucky guy—and she'll make sure the server in question is labeled 'defunct' so you'll be able to separate it from the others. Of course, you'll complete the documentation to confirm that it has been fully decommissioned, even though you'll leave it untouched."

"You want an entire server?"

"Sure. If I needed a fucking laptop, why would I need you? The people I work for want a specific piece of software that's stored on the server or something. I didn't pay much attention because frankly, computers aren't my strong point. What matters is that they want it and they are willing to do anything to get it."

Heinz recoiled involuntarily at the unmistakable menace in the metallic tones. The intent was clear and he knew without a doubt that Frank—he honestly doubted that was his real name—would not hesitate to make good on his not so subtle threats.

"And what happens after I've done this?" he asked and fought to keep his tone even despite his sweaty palms and the overwhelming sense of suffocation that seemed to have moved in permanently.

"You simply freight the shit out to the designated warehouse as you usually do. Easy as pie. I suggest you keep a low profile and simply get back to business as usual. We'll take things from there and you have the necessary paperwork to verify that the request was legitimate and everything was in order. Before you know it, it'll be happily ever after for you and your ladylove."

Frank hadn't said it in so many words, but Heinz knew without a doubt that Meredith was in their clutches too. He might decide he was in a situation where he could afford to lose everything if he was with her, but there was no telling what her husband would do if he found out about the affair. She'd said he'd threatened more than once to kill her if she left him. The fear in her voice had left him with the certainty that she believed his threat.

No matter what they did, Frank's employers lurked in the background to make sure neither of them shared the details of what they planned to do. The coldness that filtered through the disguised voice assured him that they would stop at nothing, and the knowledge birthed an icy pit in his stomach.

"How will you know when it's done?" he asked shakily. "Do I have to call you?"

The man laughed. "We'll know," he replied with such certainty that it was easy to imagine an all-seeing eye watching his every move. "Now, you'd best be on your way. Fortunately, I've been told there was a traffic snarl-up on your route so you have a good excuse for being late. And relax, Heinz. It's an easy task and you're only about three or four easy steps from your happily ever after. I'll say goodbye now, and I hope I don't need to call you again."

The connection cut, the threat left hanging, and Heinz stared at his phone while he dragged in a few ragged breaths.

After a long moment, he continued onto the road and drove a few blocks, his hands shaking and his mind in turmoil. When he was safely out of view of the house, he pulled into a parking lot at the local grocery store and tried to order his thoughts.

"Son of a bitch," he whispered and decided the first thing he should do was to call Meredith. She answered on the first ring.

"Heinz? Oh, thank God."

"Are you all right? Where are you."

"I'm at work already. I...give me a minute."

He held on and listened to the sound of her footsteps and a door slamming. When she spoke again it seemed to echo a little and he guessed she'd hurried to the ladies' cloakroom for privacy.

"Merry?"

"I'm here. Oh, God, Heinz. They...he...I had a phone call."

"I know. So did I."

"What the fuck can we do? If anyone finds out I helped them that's my job down the drain. But if I don't, Calvin will find out and losing my job will seem like a picnic in comparison. God. Talk about a rock and a hard place."

"Look, Merry, it sucks but we have to do this. Neither of us can afford to brazen it out and the bastards know that." He tried to keep his voice calm and rational because he could hear the near-hysteria in her tone. The last thing they needed was for her to have a meltdown at work.

"But how did they know?" she demanded in a hoarse almost-whisper. "We've been so goddammed careful."

"I know," he replied soothingly. "But people like this— well, they stop at nothing, Merry. They have ways to find information we haven't even dreamed of. All we can do is follow instructions."

"Fuck. And I was so close too," she muttered and an oddly frustrated note edged her panic.

"Close to what?" Heinz felt his senses prickle and wondered if he wanted to know the answer. Still, something in her voice alerted him and he knew he had to ask.

Meredith drew a shuddering breath and when she spoke, she at least seemed a little calmer. "They specifically asked me to identify the server that housed the AI. I've mentioned it to you—the one supposedly created by Jennie Banks."

"Yeah, and you thought you might have found it. That one?"

"Yes. I tried to hedge and say it was above my paygrade but that creep... Oh, dear God, Heinz, I'm so scared. What if it's the wrong one? I haven't had the chance to try to access it and—" Her voice rose a little in sudden panic.

"Hey. Hey, now. Don't do this. You were so sure you'd found it. Don't doubt yourself now."

"Yes, but what—"

"Don't, Merry. You have to pull yourself together and get out there with your normal face on. That'll take everything you have, so don't slide down the road of second-guessing yourself like that. It is what it is. Right now, all we can do is get on with it, keep it together, and get through the next day or so. After that, it'll be work as usual for us and this nightmare will be over."

"Are you sure?"

"I'm sure," he said firmly, even though he'd never been less sure of anything in his life. How he felt didn't matter, though. He had to talk her down before she fell apart and blew their chances of getting through this unscathed, although probably not unscarred. It would take a long time before either of them felt safe again. "So, can you do this?"

"Yes. I guess. I'll pretend I have a hangover or something."

"Good girl." Heinz injected approval into his tones. "And call me if you need to."

"I love you."

"Yeah, I love you too. Hang in there, baby. It'll soon be over."

The conversation with Meredith had left Heinz suddenly weary and even more on edge. It didn't help that a glance at his watch confirmed how late he would be. With a grimace, he started the car and eased into the traffic.

His brain worked furiously as he tried with little success to find an alternative option. The more he considered it, however, the more certain he became that they were well and truly trapped and the only possible choice was to comply.

Strangely enough, fear had prompted a sudden desire to call his brother—almost, he thought wryly, as if it was the last opportunity he had to speak to him. He pushed the depressing and distressing thought aside and set his phone to Bluetooth.

It had been a while since he'd used the number but it was still on his speed dial. They hadn't parted on the best of terms, but Ernst always came through for him when things were rough. It was reciprocal, though, and he had been there for his brother on more than one occasion in the past. Even with their differences, the bond between them remained strong.

It was more than simply a matter of favors being exchanged. They looked out for each other, for better or worse. Right now, he needed to speak to someone he could trust, if only to glean a little wisdom or reassurance.

"*Ernst Tauber, guten tag.*"

"Ernst? It's Heinz."

A slight pause on the other side was followed by a soft sigh. "Heinz. Is everything all right?"

It was good to know his brother could recognize he was troubled simply from his voice. He realized that a part of him had been half-afraid they would have lost that closeness.

"I'm in trouble. I...I cheated on my wife and now, someone is blackmailing me over it. I know...I know I have no right to involve you in something like this, but I don't... I have no one else to turn to."

Ernst didn't answer immediately. "Do you need money?"

"No. They want me to take servers from the FBI using fraudulent documentation. From what I understand, they want to steal a particular server with an AI on it and they are taking the others to hide their interest in that one."

"An AI?" His brother sounded oddly tense.

"He wouldn't give me any specifics," he hedged, not willing to include Meredith in the conversation. "Can you help me? I know we haven't exactly seen eye to eye on everything, especially with your...uh, Earth for Earth association, but...well, you have connections. I hoped they could help. I don't see how I can avoid helping them, but it irks me that they'll get away with it."

"I'll see what I can do," Ernst replied. "It may be that my people would like to acquire this AI for our group. I don't think I can jump in with anything right away so for the moment, I suggest you comply with their demands. From there, we can look at all the options and find a way to derail their plans. It obviously won't get you out of this mess but at least you'll know the blackmailers won't enjoy the fruits of their plans."

"Thank you." Heinz wasn't entirely sure he agreed with that. He'd hoped beyond hope that his brother would come up with something to help him avoid having to comply with Frank's demands. Still, when this was all over, he might look back and enjoy the thought that the fucker had gone to all that effort only to have his prize snatched out from under his nose. "But...be careful. These people are dangerous. The asshole I talked to seemed like he'd be willing to kill his grandmother if she got in his way."

"I know the type and I'm always careful. Stay safe, Heinz. I'll call you when I have something."

"Are we good to go?"

Avery Nickelsen took a deep breath and toyed with the bobblehead he had of Thor on his desk. It was as old as fuck, an heirloom already by the time he found it on eBay when he was twelve, but it had always been at his side when he worked.

He was too smart to think it would bring him good luck or anything, but it certainly calmed him and made him feel like he was in his old home office, sending random people pineapple pizza and copious amounts of porn.

Those were the days. They had also left him with a good supply of porn, which he now used for entertainment during the long stakeout. The idea appealed to him—not the porn so much as being able to run a stakeout from the privacy and comfort of his office.

To be a top-class hacker was truly a wonderful thing. He was able to access both the traffic cameras outside DecomIT and the company's internal security system to monitor their loading area. Their systems were protected but not to a level that could keep him out or discern his infiltration, and he didn't run the risk of being seen as he would have in an old-school conventional stakeout. The only problem was the boredom but he could live with that if it wasn't a daily routine.

"Avery, goddammit, are we good to go?"

He sighed, leaned closer to the screens, and put his headset on. "I'm here. And if you could avoid saying my name on the comms, Frank, I'd appreciate it."

"I won't call you by your chosen callsign."

"What's wrong with Big Dick Nick?"

"It's inaccurate in every way."

"Are you saying I have a small dick? Now, how could you know that, Frank? How could you possibly know that?"

The man didn't respond immediately and Avery imagined him shaking his head in irritation.

"Your name isn't Nick."

"Yeah, that's the point of having a callsign, dumbass. And no, we aren't good to go. The fucking servers are still at DecomIT."

"What's taking so long?"

The hacker sighed and resisted the urge to offer a detailed explanation of the decommissioning process. "It takes time," he said shortly.

"Really? I hadn't noticed." The sarcastic response would have triggered an equally snarky rejoinder, but a van reversed out of its parking space and came to a stop at the loading platform.

"I think this is it," he said and squinted at the figures who emerged from the building. He counted the five units as they were loaded. "Yep. They're ready to roll. I'll follow their progress and confirm once they reach the warehouse."

"And you're sure no one can trace you?" Palumbo sounded suspicious and wary, the reaction of a man who had no clue about how things worked and how any hacker worth their salt could hide all trace of their presence—especially in the relatively unsecured official systems that provided such easy access.

"I'm sure no one can trace me." He didn't hide the sarcasm but the other man didn't take the bait. "I'll confirm, but you can give your team the heads-up. The merchandise will be at the warehouse and ready for them. If you run the heist tonight, you'll find what you're looking for easily. From what I can see, they need a supervisor to sign off before the units are stored and that won't happen until tomorrow morning."

The truck started and headed to the road to the FBI

storage warehouse. It amused Avery to no end that the feds would be robbed twice in mere days. The heist itself had been well-planned and executed and the forged documents he had created had appeared genuine enough that no one had questioned them.

He'd been a little worried that the staff in the Bureau might query the decommissioning orders with their superiors but they had barely batted an eyelid. Their contact there had made sure to provide information on servers that were seldom used, mainly because of their age and vulnerability. The result was that most staffers simply thanked whoever or whatever they believed in for the fact that the higher-ups had finally decided to provide new equipment.

The second theft was equally well-planned. A team would break into the warehouse and steal the target server along with a random selection of other equipment. He'd wondered about this, but Frank had somewhat irritably explained that it would hide their real purpose. The last thing they wanted was to draw attention to the specific unit they wanted so a "robbery" provided a few effective red herrings.

Even when they discovered the theft, they would have no clue as to the real motive and the original heist would likely only be discovered months down the line when someone in the Bureau lost patience and decided to question why they hadn't been allocated new equipment. By then, all they would discover was that the units were stolen. DecomIT had the "official" papers so they were unlikely to fall under suspicion and the feds would have no clue that something of huge value was snatched from under their noses. He wasn't entirely sure that the Bureau at large was aware of the AI.

"ETA ten minutes," he advised Palumbo shortly and received only a grunt in acknowledgment. Avery smiled as he considered the future. After about thirty-six hours, they would be out of the FBI's realm of influence, the job would be done, and everyone would be finding new and inventive ways to spend their newly acquired wealth.

Avery had an appealing location in mind. A beach, no extradition treaty, and some favorable banking laws. The kind that would allow him to retire at the tender age of twenty-five and enjoy his life. Maybe find someone that he could pile lavish gifts on and have as arm-candy for weddings and the like. Unfortunately, he didn't qualify for the same hefty payout as the boots on the ground so he'd have to continue to save.

The truck pulled up to the gate of the warehouse and everything was unloaded, signed for, and carried inside. It had been a pleasant change to have an inside source on this. He usually had to do this kind of work on his own and doubted that he could gain access to the software created by an IT company without at least a little help. They'd done it, though, and he was fairly sure that if he schmoozed the R and D director, the man would let him play with their new toy.

He rather liked the idea of digging into Jennie Banks'- coding to discover her secrets. It was the cherry on the top —a rare opportunity to learn from the recognized leader in the field.

"Okay, I'm done here," Avery noted when the truck backed out and set off toward the DecomIT premises. He ended his call with Frank and dialed another number as he began to shut his systems down.

"Avery?"

"Mr. Transk, you'll be pleased to know that the server is out of the building and heading to the drop site. Frank has been advised that the next phase of the operation is a go."

"Excellent."

He chuckled. "Honestly, I'm very sure the bureaucrats in Washington would probably lose their balls if they weren't firmly attached."

"They have no idea?"

"Nope, and they won't for a while. Exactly when depends on whether someone complains about needing replacements or how often they run audits on their software systems, but from what I was able to pick up on their procedures, you'll have at least forty-eight hours. I'd say probably closer to two months, though."

"I trust Palumbo's sense of revenge is satisfied?"

"Frank? I doubt it. That old dog won't relinquish his bone anytime soon. This is more like a down-payment for him. I did offer to overload their servers with terabytes of hard-core midget porn, but I think he prefers the more physical type of vengeance."

"Well, his vendetta will no doubt prove useful."

CHAPTER FIVE

There were benefits to laziness. Axel Hammond was proof of that.

He narrowed his eyes and scrutinized their surroundings while the rest of the team found different ways to pass the time. A few had some cards and others checked their phones more times than he cared to count. He had chosen to do not much of anything.

It was all relative, he decided. Merely being utterly lazy would never end well. But when mixed with the motivation to continue being lazy, truly great things happened. Why walk when you could get a horse to carry you? Why have a horse if you could use a little dead dino juice to get a car going for you? Why travel across the world to talk to someone when punching numbers into a phone would bring the same result?

If there was one lesson he learned in school, it was that all the great inventors of the world were the people he held up as his personal heroes for their epic contribution to sustaining a lazy way of living.

Admittedly, the mercs on his team didn't always appreciate his cunning escape of any kind of duty, but they couldn't blame him for it. All they could be angry about was the fact that they weren't as creative about it as he was.

They would do the same thing if they were quick enough on their feet.

A long wait outside a warehouse that was like hundreds of others in the area might have felt like he was wasting time, but people neglected the benefits of sitting and letting one's mind percolate.

Those who weren't comfortable with their own company would feel bored. That truth applied to the rest of the team but he was content to watch the sun slide slowly across the sky and to simply enjoy the day without pushing for something to happen.

Just chilling. It was weird how that was no longer acceptable.

In this case, of course, the sun had already begun to set and he hadn't issued any orders to move. Soon, it would be too dark for cards and phones to occupy the team and they had begun to mutter between themselves. Axel was used to being the subject of those low-toned complaints, but not this time, it seemed.

Or, at least, it wasn't his overall laziness that was the topic of conversation.

"Why don't we simply go on in?" Cassia asked and looked around with barely restrained impatience. "If we're simply waiting here, we could head on in there, get whatever we need, and get out. This doesn't look like the kind of place that would be able to stop us, even if we were seen."

"Because it's the fucking feds, dickhead," Axel said and still didn't bother to look at them. "It stands to reason that even a dump like this will probably have more security than it would appear to have. Not only that, but they can call and have an army in Stormtrooper gear heading our way with one wrong step. Besides, it looks like those other assholes are already in and have done the dirty work for us." He gestured to the warehouse. "Which, of course, was the plan all along."

A closer look revealed flashlights moving around the area. Patrolling security was out of place in an area like this, where most warehouses could only afford a rent-a-cop who spent their days locked in security booths and couldn't be bothered to walk if they didn't have to. The feds had most likely relied on electronic security, given that all the equipment housed was essentially trash and would be disposed of as soon as someone found time in their schedule to do so.

The shadowy figures were therefore not patrolling the area.

"All we need to do is take our prize off their hands and leave them to face whatever comes once the feds find out what happened."

The Germans who had called them in for the job were not the kind of people he usually worked for. When times were quiet—which they all too often were—Axel tended to find himself working security jobs that demanded little and kept him ticking over until the next operation.

Not this time, though. It was big-leagues time and he

was determined that they would get this one right. He would make sure no one jumped the gun and ruined what was essentially the perfect heist.

"What is the situation, exactly?" Gregory asked and leaned forward a little. "I don't want to push one way or another, but you've been quiet about what we're dealing with here."

Axel sighed. He had hoped that the team would simply let him lead the charge but maybe this way, he could let someone else lead while he took the credit.

"Fine. Someone stole something from the feds and they stored it here."

"But this is a fed building," Cassia interrupted in confusion.

"Right. I don't have all the details, but it seems it will be stolen in such a way that it's less likely anyone will know it was stolen in the first place. Anyway, the people who hired us want us to steal it instead, so we'll let this group take the fall and do most of the work. Does that sound good?"

He looked at each of them and they all nodded slowly. It was clear that they didn't mind being lazy and only confirmed his hypothesis in his mind.

People wanted to be lazy. The only reason they had a problem with lazy people was that the ideas the lazy people had didn't occur to them first.

"Right. So, hold your horses. Be ready, and we'll hit the fuckers when they get out. When we do, we find the equipment marked 'defunct' and get the fuck out of here."

Again, it looked like his people were raring to get the business done. The orders were to make sure there were no witnesses. The clients had said they wanted the people to wonder who the fuck they were until they were ready to show them.

The Earth for Earth people were many things but careful had never been one of them. They liked protesting shit and making a general nuisance of themselves but it appeared they had decided to branch into outright robbery now too.

It would be interesting if it didn't require him to expend unnecessary mental energy on it.

A truck eased out of the warehouse and Axel motioned to the crew. They moved almost immediately.

The point was always to be ready to act. There were times to be lazy and times to act, and they always needed to know which was which.

Maybe it was because his mom was German. His American dad had been raised in the middle of the hippie movement, which meant he knew a thing or two about being laid back, but his German mom had taught him all kinds of work ethics.

It had been something of a challenge to find the middle ground between the two, but he'd perfected it at school. He was the perfect middle-of-the-road student and so drew no attention from the teachers and none from the bullies. While he had friends, there weren't many and none of them were too popular. He was memorable enough but not the kind of person to make others think he was the most likely to succeed or anything.

People would recognize his yearbook picture but wouldn't think about him much aside from that.

That was the sweet spot. The guy the cheerleaders eventually settled for. And they did, or at least a couple of them. Not at the same time, of course, but he quickly realized that cheerleaders had bad habits that mostly involved expecting him to do all the work.

"Boss. They're coming now."

Axel shook his head and settled his focus on the operation. The truck's headlights came on as it approached their nail strip.

He drew his suppressed MP5, checked the magazine, and had it ready as the rest of the team did the same.

The truck accelerated but the effects of the strip were almost immediate. The tires were almost shredded, and while the vehicle continued to move for almost fifty yards, it finally stopped and wouldn't go anywhere anytime soon.

"Contain your fire," Axel whispered and directed them to approach the disabled truck.

It wasn't long before the back opened and two men climbed out to circle the vehicle and check what had happened to the tires.

Axel raised his weapon and opened fire. It kicked hard into his shoulder and a couple of rounds went wide. His next two found their target and dropped the man closest to him.

His other three team members stepped in quickly and opened fire on the second, and he fell face-first.

The team leader pointed to Cassia and Gregory and gestured for them to get into the back and secure the merchandise while he and Zach headed to the truck's cabin to clear the people there.

They must know an attack was in progress. After the nail strip had done its work and the others had been gunned down, there was no other explanation.

He flattened himself against the side of the vehicle when the passenger door opened and a woman stepped out with a small sub-machine gun in hand. She scanned the area in search of the source of the assault.

Axel shook his head when her aim swept her surroundings first, rather than where the attack had come from. He drew a knife from his belt and moved behind her as she finally turned her attention to the vehicle.

His quick thrust caught her before she registered his presence and he felt a warm splash of blood from her severed carotid. She grunted and tried to twist her weapon to retaliate, but he turned her and forced her into the cab doorway.

Two others inside seemed unsure of what was happening and aimed their weapons at Axel where he stood and held the bleeding merc as a meat shield.

The standoff ended quickly when the other door was yanked open and the driver jerked at the sound of a suppressed shot. Another punched through his skull and splattered blood across the interior.

Axel took advantage of the last man's distraction and fired two rounds into the cabin.

"I got the last one!" Zach called from the other side.

"Bullshit!" he retorted and released the merc he still held. She was probably dead or would be in about a minute so wasn't much of a threat.

"I did."

"No, I hit him. Two shots, center of mass."

"You know they're wearing body armor, right?"

Axel narrowed his eyes, peered into the cabin, and realized that both his rounds had caught in the merc's body armor.

"Right. Okay. Fine. You got the last one." He shook his head and retrieved his radio. "It looks like all the rats are cleared. We're ready to hit the road, Tao."

"Roger that."

Cassia and Gregory had already begun to move the device, whatever it was, out to where they could load it into the van.

They had it under control and didn't need help with it. Axel scanned the area to make sure no one in the warehouse was keeping track of the action.

"Are you going to help?" Cassia shouted from the back of the truck.

"I think you've got it," he answered. "I'm making sure we're in the clear here."

The arrival of their van with Tao behind the wheel preempted their protest and they loaded their prize quickly and carefully. He ignored a couple of dirty glances they cast at him while they worked.

Once they were finished, Axel climbed into the back, closed the door behind him, and banged the side of the vehicle.

"We're good to go, Tao."

"No thanks to you," Gregory sniped.

"Sure. You guys did some work today. Drinks are on me —but no doubles, okay? Only the first round of beers."

"That de-escalated quickly." Zach chuckled.

"You're damn right. I know how much you all drink."

"So, the Italian Government paid for all this, right?"

Taylor rubbed his temples gently and tried to stop himself from paying attention to what was happening all around him.

"They couldn't put us on a decent plane to get us halfway across the world to deal with a problem that's their problem to start with." Niki sounded more irritable than usual.

"At least they got us a plane," Trick noted. "It's better than expecting us to find our own transport. I know any number of folks who said they would pay for us to get ourselves there but then had problems with how much was spent."

Chezza nodded. "Been there, done that. Too many people think they can fuck freelancers over. They mostly have their way and short-change the mercs, but when you're able to fuck them over for it, they cry foul and try to make sure no one else will hire you."

He wanted to say that hearing them bicker about the substandard transportation the Italians had provided them with would have helped, but that didn't feel right.

Jiro was the only one who noticed that something was off.

"Is Taylor all right?" he asked and looked at the others before he focused on him. "Are you okay?"

Niki looked to where Taylor was seated and sat next to him.

"Yeah, I'm fine," he responded and straightened, although it took effort. "I'm...not a huge fan of flying, is all."

"Are you afraid of heights?" Chezza asked as she pulled her black hair away from her face and tied it with an elastic band. It wasn't common for people to keep their hair to regulation standards after leaving the Marines, but those who did were never truly out.

"I'm simply not a fan of flying," Taylor snapped.

"I can't imagine your pals in the military would have given you an easy time about that," Trick commented.

"I never told them and they never knew—or, at least, never acted like they knew. I think they would have given me a hard time because of it. That's how special forces guys are."

Jiro grinned. "I suppose so. But I cannot imagine that anyone would want to piss off a man who could hurl them out of the plane without breaking a sweat."

"They knew he wouldn't," Niki interjected. "He has a big, gooey center."

"Right." He threw her a glare. "Will you tell them that your bitching about the plane so far is only because the Italians got you thrown out of the FBI?"

"I thought that was implied."

"Wait, what happened?" Trick asked.

"We had another job with the Italians," she explained. "When the job was over and everything ended in our favor, the guy in charge turned and spilled the beans to our State Department, and it got me fired from the FBI. It later transpired that it was a ploy to get me to work for the Pentagon, but I'm still pissed."

Jiro shook his head. "There is so much to unpack with you two. I guess we now know why Maxwell referred us to your little business."

"I guess you do," Taylor agreed. "We should go over the

details of the job while we're up here and…have nothing to do."

Niki was right, though. The plane felt like it would fall out of the sky at any moment and he wanted to think it was only because he didn't like being in the air. That all planes felt like this to him.

But maybe she was right to complain.

Still, everyone else looked calm, which meant that while the plane was terrible, they were in no real danger.

"Right." Niki pulled her laptop from one of the bags and set it up for them all to see. "If this piece of shit plane doesn't break or anything, let's look into the schematics of the weapons lab. They did say the military will be in the region, ready to help us if we need them. I'd personally feel better if they could fuck off and do their own thing and leave this shit to the professionals."

"We're not all professionals," Taylor commented. "No offense."

"None taken," Chezza answered.

The other two nodded and seemed to agree with the sentiment.

"Right," Niki responded somewhat irascibly, "but we're still better than anything they'll have on the ground. Is some military backup in the area good to have? Of course, but…whatever."

She shook her head and moved to the next page of the schematics.

"Why would they be dealing with Zoo creatures anyway?" Chezza asked. "That seems like something that can only go wrong."

"Many companies make considerable money from it,"

Niki explained. "Almost everyone wants to get an edge on the competition, and the company leaders are the kind who don't mind taking the credit when something goes right but are able to remove themselves when something goes wrong."

"Niki used to deal with the CEOs who were willing to let people die so they could get a little edge on their competitors," Taylor added. "She even shot one."

"You shot a CEO?" Jiro asked with a grin. "It sounds like a great job."

"It was. And I was canned because of the damn Italians. But let's move on. I've looked at their scheduling and it seems like the best time to get in is the early evening. That's when most of the staff are gone and there'll be the least resistance. There's also the benefit of fewer people ending up in the crossfire if something goes wrong."

Taylor nodded. "An evening assault makes sense. You guys all know how to operate the suits at night so it shouldn't be a problem."

"We could use a little more practice," Trick muttered.

"That's what this is about." He patted the man on the shoulder.

"We're looking at a tough take anyway," Vickie said. "None of them will have any suits but we don't know what kind of defenses you'll face in there."

"We'll deal with it when we have to," Taylor said and glanced at the freelancers. "I suggest you all try to get some sleep. We have a long day ahead of us and it's unlikely you'll get much rest once we land."

They shrugged almost as one and shuffled to the rear of the plane and made themselves as comfortable as they could. Desultory snatches of conversation followed, but it wasn't long before they succumbed to the need to rest.

Niki, Taylor, and Vickie continued to speak in low tones as they examined the schematics and the other information they had been given.

"Aside from the fact that we don't know what we'll be up against in there," Niki commented, "I don't think this can be worse than anything else we've faced. If we—"

"Oh," Desk interjected. "Oh no, that is not good."

Taylor looked hastily at his companions, which didn't help at all as it appeared that the others were as confused as he was.

"What?" Vickie asked and narrowed her eyes. "What did I miss?"

"I am missing," Desk replied.

"Huh?" The hacker tilted her head and frowned.

"What the fuck?" Niki shook her head and looked around to see if her exclamation had disturbed the freelancers. Fortunately, none of them stirred. "If you wanted to be more involved, Desk, you could have simply said something. There's no need to be dramatic and sulky."

"You misunderstand me." The AI sounded impatient. "I mean that I am missing."

The woman leaned in closer to the laptop and spoke in a low tone. "We can pick you up just fine."

"Again, you misunderstand. I mean me, not me, me. I am currently in place but the section of my programming that was stored on the FBI servers is missing."

"Oh." Vickie grunted and did something on the keyboard while her teammates looked on, still a little confused. "Look at that—she's right. Maybe someone turned you off?"

"The server has been unplugged," Desk explained. She sounded annoyed now. "My attempts to ping it have all been rejected, which would not be the case even if I was inactive in the area. The entire server has gone offline."

"Do you think it was an attack?" Taylor asked. "As in is the FBI under siege or have they been cut off?"

A break in the conversation left him and Niki to curb their frustration while they waited.

"No," Vickie answered finally. "I can still get signals from their servers. This is specific to the one that housed Desk."

Niki tapped at her jaw, her expression grim. "Shit. Vickie, get hold of Jennie. She'll be royally pissed if someone's done anything to her creation, so she'll probably be the one most motivated to find out what's happening."

"Yeah," Vickie added, "and God help the feds if they fucked around with Desk, no matter how much."

CHAPTER SIX

What a pointless clusterfuck. An old warehouse the FBI maintained to store all the old crap they hadn't gotten around to disposing of had been burgled.

Who you gonna call? Not the Ghostbusters but Eli Young.

He couldn't shake the sense of annoyance that had filled him during the whole of the drive. It was a case, he reminded himself, and important to the poorly-oiled machine that was the Federal Bureau of Investigation, but it was still shit work.

The kind reserved for people like him who worked hard and still refused to kiss ass or play politics. Perhaps if he began to play golf with the congressmen in the judiciary committee, he might end up in charge of the task forces that were responsible for real action in the Bureau.

But that simply wasn't him. Young felt like he was a little too set in his ways, which meant he was resigned to merely sticking it out for the required years before he retired and maybe took up writing. He could use his time in the FBI as a draw for people who wanted to read crime novels.

Those were still read, right?

He drew his car up outside the warehouse and saw a dozen or so investigators in place, sweeping the whole building for any evidence of what happened.

"Who's in charge here?" Eli asked in a loud enough voice that the whole crew could hear him.

A man in a full hazmat suit approached him. "Hi, sorry. I'm Miller, with the Scene Investigative Unit. You must be Special Agent Elias Young. We were told you'd be coming."

"Right. It sounds like you guys have a real mess here."

"It's…well, it's complicated. Honestly, by the looks of things, I don't think we would have even realized there had been a burglary if it hadn't been for the bodies."

"It isn't a burglary if there are bodies, right? That makes it robbery and homicide."

"Right, except our burglars are the homicide victims in this case." Miller gestured for him to follow him to where a massive truck still blocked the road and handed him a file with details of what had already been gathered. It might have been a problem if not for the fact that the road was all but abandoned.

"So, someone knows they plan to rob something," Young muttered as he scanned the information in the file. "They set out a nail strip, stop the truck, kill the burglars, and…take what they robbed instead? Who would bother with something like that?"

"It could be that they knew what the first team intended and while they didn't want to lose the…uh, merchandise, they also didn't want to risk making the burglary themselves," Miller commented. "This way...well, it removes them somewhat. It certainly means they wouldn't be caught on any of the surveillance security cameras. Anyway, we found tracks around the area from what is assumed to be a paneled van. They transferred whatever they wanted from this vehicle into their van and left. Nearby traffic cams picked it up."

"Was the van reported stolen?"

"We're still checking with the local law enforcement agencies on that. I'll let you know."

Young hadn't brought a hazmat suit and kept himself as far away from the sections still cordoned off as possible. He had been in the Bureau long enough to know how pissed an investigator could get when agents contaminated their crime scenes.

Still, he couldn't help but rake through his thick, short hair in irritation as he continued to study the file. "So... who the fuck would go through the trouble of killing five people to get something they stole from a warehouse of decommissioned FBI paraphernalia? Do we even know what is missing?"

"It was an elaborate heist to begin with," Miller pointed out. "They worked fast and seemed to be professionals. The second team took them out hard too, so I assume we're looking at more professionals. They must have wanted something badly if they hired ten people between them to get it."

"That doesn't answer the question."

"That... Well, that's the problem. This warehouse doesn't keep detailed records on what they have in there, only a simple logging system. They do weekly inventory inspections, but from what we picked up, it wasn't uncommon for this to be a halfway point between disposal or sometimes transfer to field branches that needed equipment, no matter how outdated. It'll take us a while to confirm exactly what was in the warehouse and then find out what's missing."

"Get on that," Young snapped. It was an unnecessary statement. They already were "on" that, but people expected a certain amount of arrogance from the agents in charge of these cases.

Before he could continue, his phone vibrated in his pocket.

"Sorry, I have to take this."

"Go ahead."

He took a few steps away and looked at the number that was calling him. He didn't recognize it, but that wasn't uncommon. The people he worked with had to call from a variety of phones depending on where they were and what they were doing.

Eli sighed deeply and accepted the call. "Agent Young."

"Agent Elias Young?" a woman's voice asked.

"That's me."

"This is Jennie Banks. We met two years ago at the National Interdiction Conference in Maryland if you'll recall."

He thought furiously and finally remembered a shorter woman with thick black hair who talked for an hour and a half on upgrading the software that was used by the various law enforcement agencies to keep them safe from cyber-attacks.

"Right, Banks. I remember you. How can I help you?"

"I'm sorry to call out of the blue like this, but I was informed that you had taken point on an investigation into the burglary of an FBI warehouse outside Vegas."

"That's...correct. Wait, who informed you of that?"

She paused. "It doesn't matter who. My point is that I've tracked an FBI-based parcel that's bounced from point to point, and the last location I have on record for it is in that warehouse."

"How are you tracking it?" Young narrowed his eyes.

"Again, that's not relevant. What is important is that a server was incorrectly decommissioned with forged paperwork, and it ended up in that warehouse. I need you to make sure it is still there."

He wanted to keep asking her questions. It felt like it was probably his job to make sure she wasn't simply pulling his chain or worse, trying to get intelligence about an ongoing investigation.

She was clearly on good terms with the FBI, but that didn't give her the right to interject herself into ongoing investigations. With that said, it seemed like she might have dropped a lead into his lap—the kind that would have taken weeks to get otherwise.

"Give me a second. Let me check." He covered the mic on his phone and approached Miller again. "Do you guys have an accurate inventory of what's in the warehouse right now?"

"Of course."

"Is there a...server on that list? A computer server, recently decommissioned?" She rattled off the server ID and he scrawled it hastily on the case notes in his hand. It didn't help that he had to ask her to repeat it so he could check that he had it right.

Miller pulled a tablet out and scanned the inventory list. "Nope, but five were brought in that haven't been logged into storage yet and won't be on here. Of those, three appear to have been taken in the original heist as they aren't in the receiving area. But this is where it gets weird. The first group took those three and possibly other random items as the storage area had been accessed. When we searched the vehicle they used, everything seems to still be there except for one of the newly decommissioned servers."

Eli uncovered the phone mic. "It appears that five units were brought in but one can't be located."

"Shit. Some asshole out there has their hands on my best work yet. I'll go out on a limb here and assume you fucking idiots have no goddamn clue what happened and why—is that an accurate assessment of the situation?"

The agent scowled and glared at his phone. "I can assure you that we are investigating the situation, Ms. Banks—"

"Yeah, well, maybe that would work out much better for everyone if you pulled your collective heads out of your collective asses!"

The connection cut and Eli stared at his phone for a few seconds, unsure of what had happened.

"Ms. Banks?" Miller asked. "Jennie Banks?"

"That's the one."

"Shit. I didn't even know she was involved. Why is she involved?"

"She's not. Or at least…I don't think she is supposed

to be."

"Isn't the whole Banks family fucking insane?"

"That's the going theory. Stark, staring, raving mad. I guess it's genetic."

"Well, thanks be to whatever gods you pray to that there are only two of them and neither of them works for the Bureau anymore."

"Not that it makes that much difference." Young shook his head. "Wait, whatever gods I pray to?"

"Yeah. I'm an Episcopalian but I try to not make any assumptions about that. It tends to generate too much bad blood."

"It's a decent policy. I'm a Sikh."

"No shit?"

"Yeah. I simply went with my family on that one."

"Same here."

He hadn't expected the man to be pissed. Axel rolled his eyes and listened to him curse in German for a solid minute and a half while he went red in the face.

It was impressive, honestly, if he looked past the fact that it was directed at him.

People like Haas would always be pissed if there was the slightest deviation from what they wanted to happen. His type refused to live in the real world because it was too inconsistent for them.

"I got you the server like you asked," he said when the man finally paused to take a breath. "And I didn't leave any witnesses exactly as you instructed. The guys we ran into were armed and ready for a fight. What the hell did you think would happen?"

"You have to realize that what you did crossed a line, Mr. Hammond!" Gunther Haas roared, although he now sounded a little hoarse. "We are a group of activists. We can't be seen to associate with murders and robberies. That makes it easy for people to characterize us as terrorists."

"But you are associated with murders and robberies," he pointed out with exaggerated patience.

"Public image is everything in this world. But of course, I cannot expect an idiotic gun nut like you to understand that."

Axel tried to keep his smile from looking too sardonic. "You Earth for Earth nuts already have five members in prison because they tried to break test subjects out of containment—including the leader of your group and the man who hired me for the job."

"Do you think I don't know that?" the German snapped.

"No, but I thought I should remind you of it." He sighed. "Look, there is no link to you at all. I made sure of that. The van that was used was stolen and we drove it into the water once we wiped it clean. You have zero actual association with the murders and the robbery."

That seemed to take all the wind out of the man's sails, and the heavyset German sat across the conference table from him again. "Unfortunately, we are beyond such measures now."

"What do you mean?"

"My friends and colleagues are no longer waiting in a prison cell for sentencing. News has arrived that they have been sentenced to the Zoo."

"They...have that kind of sentencing in Germany?"

"It set certain precedents but there are many interests that do not want our work to continue or thrive. It was unnecessarily harsh, but the sentence is quite popular and our legal team has very little hope that an appeal will help."

Axel looked down and shook his head. "Shit. I'm sorry, I shouldn't have been so flippant."

"It's not your fault. You did your work and that is all that can be asked of you. In the end, you helped your employer more than you might have realized."

"What do you mean?"

"We have been forced to face the reality of the Zoo now. Previously, we simply ignored the alien nightmare almost on our doorstep in favor of acting on behalf of Earth and the numerous atrocities perpetrated by greedy individuals and corporates."

He sighed and paused to gather his thoughts. "Sending them to the Zoo might as well be a death sentence, and the appeal is a slim chance but one we must pursue, none-theless. For myself, I wish I'd listened to my family and married Mrs. Becker. She is a wealthy woman and it would have been a boon for our cause if I could have donated money instead of being an active member."

"I...I don't know... Do you like her?"

"We dated years ago before she was married. She isn't my type, to be honest, but old flames do rekindle sometimes."

This sounded like a distinctly uncomfortable conversation, the kind Axel had no interest in being a part of. "Right. So, about our pay?"

"Yes, of course. It has already been transferred, although

with the *scheisse* banking laws in this country, it might take a day or so for the money to appear in your accounts. With that said, if you were serious about more work in the future, you might consider remaining in the region. We could have more for you soon."

That was the best news he'd heard today, although the fact that the team had to travel to Munich to get the server to them was a pain in the ass.

Still, if they had work for them already, that was promising.

Haas seemed to have already dismissed him in his mind and now called someone else. He spoke as though he thought the merc didn't speak German.

"Tobias, get your lazy ass up here," Haas shouted into the phone in his native language. "Why the hell do you think? We have work to do. If the appeal attempt falls through, we'll have to break them out. It's about time you made good on all those claims you've shoved up our noses because getting to them is now your baby."

Axel stood slowly. He felt he had no right to listen to the conversation. Haas clearly had all kinds of things on his mind, and as long as the money came through, he didn't give a shit what kind of trouble the man was planning.

Well, unless that trouble involved giving him more work. In that case, he gave quite a few shits.

It didn't look like the German cared that he'd over-heard, but he nevertheless slipped out to where a secretary looked up from her desk and smiled.

"Can I help you with anything?" she asked in English.

"You sure can," he replied with as charming a smile as he could muster. "Which way to the elevators?"

CHAPTER SEVEN

"Vickie, are you there?"

"Where the fuck else would I be, Tay-Tay?" the hacker replied. "I'm merely sitting around, waiting for you guys to get into position."

Taylor looked at each of his team to make sure there was no reaction from them about the nickname. He was already past trying to get the girl to stop, but he didn't need her to spread her bad habits to the new guys.

Thankfully, there was no reaction from any of them and he turned his attention to the facility they were trying to gain access to.

"Okay, so…where are we going in?"

"Didn't you have a look at the schematics? You're the one on the ground. You decide."

She was a little more snappish than usual too. Then again, she was helping them while trying to find out what had happened to Desk, so maybe she was being spread a little too thinly.

"We marked off three possible entrances, but it all

depended on what you were able to pick up on once we brought the suits in range for you to use as a...whatever the word is—connector to the base's security systems?"

"Oh." Vickie grunted. "Right. Okay...give me a second here."

He dropped a little lower and gestured to the rest of the team to stay low as well. The suits were outfitted to take all the weight when they were in that position, which made it feel less like crouching and more like sitting. The chairs were low and a little uncomfortable but it was better than standing for hours on end.

"I'm back." The hacker could be heard tapping furiously at her laptop. "Sorry about that. Anyway, I've picked up the patrol schedule of the team inside. It doesn't look like the boots on the ground are much more than rent-a-cops. They don't even have guns. But they press the alarm and that activates the team on standby somewhere in the building, so...you'll want to avoid that, I think."

"We can pick them off from a distance," Jiro noted.

"No. We don't need anyone alerted to gunfire." Taylor shook his head. "Our suits were fitted with sedatives, right?"

"Well...yours is," Niki confirmed. "But it's the only one outfitted for that kind of thing. It's a new development."

Taylor shook his head. It was a little difficult to remember that he was at the cutting edge of tech when it came to the suits and most folk didn't even have access to that kind of firepower.

"Okay. So I can disable the guys, right?"

Desklet's new icon came live on his HUD. "I will be able to adjust dosages for each different security guard you encounter. It should avoid any problems with either killing the men or merely making them a little groggy on their feet."

"Are we not trying to kill them?" Chezza asked and looked at her teammates for confirmation. "Just asking. They're the dumbasses who have put the whole of Europe at risk for corporate greed."

"They aren't the ones pulling the triggers," Trick commented. "Most are simply guys who go into work, do their job, and go home—no muss, no fuss."

"But they knew what was happening. They could have blown the whistle but they didn't."

"You're both right," Taylor interjected before they began an argument. "These guys most likely don't know all the details and they don't have a place on the food chain when it comes to making decisions. They are trying to keep their heads low, do their jobs, and go home. The problem is that they probably know what's happening, at least on some level. They must know that something is in there that could kill them, their families, and thousands of others and they've done nothing about it. For that, they'll answer to a court. We're merely here to remove the threat, that's all."

"What about the heavy hitters inside?" Trick asked.

"We'll try to keep them alive but don't try too hard." Niki smirked and motioned for Taylor to lead the way.

Vickie had already prepared their ingress point and had deactivated the alarms and sensors at the western entrance that relied on human patrols.

Once they reached it, Taylor could see why. A small thicket grew outside, and it looked like the security teams would have to deal with small animals climbing in and tripping the alarms.

"I'm very sure the term for that is ticking time bomb," Niki whispered as he pushed his suit up the fence. "Wait for one of the creatures to get out and turn that little forest into a mini-Zoo."

"No thanks," he muttered and let Desklet get him over the barrier and find a soft spot in the sensor sweeps for him to land on.

She was already illuminating the sections that were still being covered. As she peeked into the security footage inside, she began to highlight the sections where the patrollers would be.

"I could get used to having this kind of support," Taylor whispered as he switched his assault rifle's rounds to the sedatives that had been packed with it.

"Thanks," Desklet and Vickie said at the same time.

He smirked but didn't correct either of them. If the truth be told, he didn't mind having both of them on his side. The AI was certainly coming into her own. In the Zoo, she had struggled from task to task and had needed to shut a few areas of focus down when forced to take others on. Not that she hadn't been vital to his survival in there, of course, but to see her operate at a higher capacity was a plus. Besides, it didn't look like she was spiking the heat or the CPU usage either.

Desk had probably put in a couple of updates that would make her run more efficiently. Whatever they'd done, it was working well.

Taylor positioned himself where he could monitor the progress as the rest of the team began to follow him over the fence a little farther away from where the patrollers would approach them. He picked up the closest group and advanced slowly, moving carefully through the section between the fence and the buildings.

His team was running lighter than most suits and moved stealthily, but there was still no getting around the fact that he was in a suit that weighed almost a ton and a half.

No matter how careful he was, there would inevitably be noise.

He grasped his rifle a little tighter and waited as the software adjusted for the difference in trajectory when it came to the sedative rounds. Four men came around the corner. Night had already fallen and he could see that none of them wore any gear that would allow them to see well in the dark. Maybe they had the equipment assigned to them and simply chose not to use it, but they looked relaxed and casual and showed no sign that they could see the hulking combat suit that waited for them in the darkness.

Hisses of compressed air issued from the under-barrel of his rifle and two of the men reached reflexively to their necks. They already showed signs of the sedative hitting their systems like a sledgehammer. The other two looked around, unsure of what was happening before they too felt the light pricks of needle rounds that pierced their skin and delivered a healthy dose of sleeping juice into their bodies. In moments, all four of them sprawled in a drug-induced sleep.

"The security cameras are already on a loop," Vicki alerted him as he checked all four patrollers to make sure they were unconscious. "They won't pick up on the missing team for a few minutes."

"A few minutes?" Niki asked.

"Well, yeah. People are waiting for them to come back after the patrol so you have a few minutes until alarms are triggered. I suggest you get moving."

The sensors around them went down and Niki led the other three in a jog while Taylor secured their position inside the building. She was the first one in, quickly followed by the rest of the team.

Taylor couldn't help feeling a hint of pride as he watched the group move in behind Niki. They were still a little stiff in their movement but were already miles ahead of where they'd started. It took a rough training regimen to get used to wearing a fully armored combat suit like that, but motivated folks tended to get that shit right. The best encouragement was to push them into the Zoo, of course, but this was a close second.

"I've run into a little trouble here," Vickie called as they stood with their back to the door and facing another one. It was considerably heavier and even with their suits, they wouldn't be able to force it open.

"You have?" Chezza asked. "If they attack us here, we are literally up against a wall."

"For fuck's sake," Trick growled. "If this pointless geeking takes any longer, anything inside will have died of old age before we get in. Let me do what I do best. I'll blow us a hole through the building and get us in—no muss, tons of fuss."

"We don't want that kind of attention," Niki snapped.

"Besides, if there are Zoo critters inside, we don't want any of them to get out if we make a mess of it."

"I'm sorry," Vickie interrupted. "Did he call what I do 'pointless geeking?'"

"Save your plots for revenge for later, Vickie," Taylor interjected when he saw where this was going. "We still need him—preferably alive and with his HUD not covered in ads for lonely women in his area."

The hacker sighed deeply. "Ugh, fine. But revenge will come, let there be no doubt."

"We all tremble in anticipation," Trick answered. "I'm… sorry, by the way."

"Too late. You're on my naughty list, dude."

"Will you spank me?"

"No, but you'll find it difficult to log into your social media accounts from this point forward."

"Ugh." Niki growled in exasperation. "I see why Vickie barfs every time you and I flirt now."

"I was not flirting!" The hacker sounded offended by the notion.

"I was," Trick muttered.

"Shut up, newb. The door should open now."

Before he could respond, it began to swing open slowly, a sure indication of the sheer weight behind it.

"That's…interesting," Taylor muttered. "Were they trying to keep something out or something in?"

He could feel the man's gaze.

While the Earth for Earth hacker had better things to

do than to watch Axel in the van with him, there were sideways glances. They were the kind that darted away quickly whenever the merc caught them. He wasn't the most subtle of characters, this Tobias.

Finally, he sighed. "Look, I don't like being here any more than you like me being here. But we're both being paid for this, so why don't you keep your eyes on your screen and we can both be out of each other's way in a jiffy."

Tobias pushed his glasses up a little and his cold blue eyes stared at him for a moment before he returned his attention to his screens. "Don't take my discomfort personally, Mr. Hammond. I merely don't like having anyone in my workspace while I am busy."

That sounded fairly reasonable. "Call me Axel."

"I'd rather keep our relationship as professional as possible. For instance, I will not join you for a beer after the job is done."

The German bastard knew how to set ground rules up, at least.

"So I guess I don't get to call you Tobias?"

"Dauer."

"Tobias Dauer?" Axel shrugged. "I'm not sure if that's a common or an uncommon name around here."

"We need not carry out the traditional small talk either if you prefer."

He shrugged. If the guy wouldn't put any effort in to at least be civil at this point, he wouldn't bother either. It was easier to pretend that he didn't need to be in the same space with the fucker and move on from there.

Still, it looked like he was a little more comfortable

with him present now that he'd said something and he certainly worked faster.

"Is your team ready?"

"Since the start of the day."

"They will need to move quickly once the systems are reset. I do not know how long I can hold the access."

"Simply tell us when."

"When."

"What?"

"When. You said to tell you when. Now is when."

Axel pushed up from his seat. He doubted the guy had that much difficulty with the language difference, but now was not the time to call him on his bullshit. He pulled the radio on his collar to his mouth.

"We're moving. Get the van started."

"Will do, boss."

He climbed out of the back of the vehicle Tobias was working out of and jogged to the second one where his team waited. He had been told that the armored van was marked to look like a prison transport vehicle. The heavy diesel engine started and Axel climbed into the back and patted the door as he closed it to indicate that he was in.

In seconds, the vehicle started moving and they were on their way.

"Do we have orders for when we get inside?" Cassia asked as he took a seat across from her.

"Sure. Find the fuckers, get the fuckers out, profit."

"You know what I mean. These guys were pissed that we killed the robbers in the States. Don't you think they'll have a problem with us killing prison guards? Especially given how much press this one will get."

He raised an eyebrow and nodded. "That's a good point but I doubt we'll have any choice in the matter. Prison guards won't step aside and wave their prisoners goodbye so some fatalities are inevitable. The best we can do is keep them to a minimum and get out as quickly as possible. With the systems down, there should be a delay in warning other guards so it's unlikely that we'll have to deal with the full contingent of them. Besides, our employers have to know that this cannot be achieved through hugs and kisses. They can save that for the trees and bunnies or whatever."

Their plan was the easiest way in and out. Tobias had needed to register a prisoner transfer on their worksheet and from there, all they had to do was arrive while their system was crashed. They would have the paperwork to confirm that a prisoner was coming out, and everything else would simply progress from there.

That was the theory, anyway. He could stress about how much shit could go wrong, but what exactly would that accomplish?

It was a short drive to the prison and once the van came to a halt, Axel climbed out and jogged to the guard station while the van was readied to collect its prisoner.

"*Identifizierung?*" the guard asked.

The merc had memorized the word for identification and handed his card to the man. "Interpol. Prisoner transfer."

"Interpol?"

"The prisoner's heading to the Zoo. There are protocols for that shit." It had been simple enough to spoof the transfer a day earlier than it was marked off for, and with the orders sent to the guards a day at a time, it should go unchallenged.

The man didn't bother to run any scans on the card. Instead, he held it up to where he could see it through a thick pair of glasses. "Our systems are down for the day so we need to confirm with headquarters via the telephone."

Axel nodded, leaned against the frame of the security box, and waited for him to make the call. The lines were kept on a constant loop as well, which ensured that all calls to the base were routed to where Tobias was waiting.

He tried to match the bored, tired-yet-professional look of someone who ran these kinds of operations often and only straightened when it was clear that the call was finished, and he stretched his hand out to accept his ID.

"The prisoner will be escorted out," the man grumbled and gestured for him to return to his truck while he turned his attention to what looked like a handful of Sudoku puzzles in a magazine on his desk.

It was strangely old-fashioned and not something Axel had expected. He tipped his cap to the guard and returned to the van where Cassia waited for him. Rather than speak, he simply nodded and tried to not look out of place.

The prison system didn't move quickly. It could have been because their systems were down but it seemed to last a little too long.

He could see too many signs of anxiety in his team, which was annoying, but he leaned back in his seat and retrieved his phone.

A handful of celebrities were having a spat that filled most of his Twitter feed, and he scrolled through what was being said while he waited until one of the security doors buzzed. Two guards exited with a prisoner sandwiched between them.

Axel nodded at Zach, who approached them and took the paperwork from him.

When they began to talk volubly in German, he raised his hand.

"English, please. Interpol academy doesn't teach German."

"Well, they should," the guard retorted waspishly and seemed annoyed.

"Whatever."

"You need to sign here and—"

Suppressed gunfire stopped the man's instructions and he turned to Zach in surprise while Cassia began to advance on the open door with slow, measured steps.

Axel already had his weapon in hand and pulled the trigger twice. The guard took a step back and he gaped at the two holes that had appeared in his chest.

"Sorry about that," he whispered, caught the guard before he fell, and dragged him to the van.

After a few minutes, he looked over his shoulder and realized that the Earth for Earth member stood frozen in place, a look of shock painted across his features.

"What are you waiting for?" he asked and gestured impatiently for him to move into the van as well.

"I…what?"

"Get into the fucking van. Unless, of course, you've come to terms with the idea of heading into the Zoo with a five-year-old armor suit and no training."

That penetrated his stupor and he shuffled quickly across the ground toward the van and clambered inside.

"Are you breaking me out?" he asked in a thick German accent.

"Oh, Gramps, we're here to break all of you out—or at least those in this facility. But they don't do three-man prison transfers, so we needed to get one of you out here and use that to get inside. Now stay in the van and shut your fucking trap."

"You're rude."

"Yeah, you knew that about me when you hired me."

The German's eyes narrowed, then widened. "I thought you looked familiar. It was the uniform that threw me off."

Axel rolled his eyes and heard the sound of suppressed gunfire from inside the prison.

"Do you know where the others are being held? They kept us in different sections."

Axel clenched his jaw and shook his head. "Nope, but our technical support does and he's guiding them. So sit there and—oh, there they come."

No alarms had sounded from the prison, which said their system was still down. The doors opened to reveal two men who approached with Cassia and Zach in the lead.

It didn't look like they had encountered heavy resistance. Even the man in the security box hadn't noticed that his comrades had been shot or that there was a breakout in progress.

"I have to say, the quiet way of doing things is certainly best," Zach noted as they ushered the prisoners into the van.

"Being lazy has its perks." Axel thumped the wall between them and Tao in the driver's seat and the van began to move again. "Now we simply have to remind our employers that we had to kill people to rescue their leader and that they knew that when they gave us the job."

"Yeah, whatever," Cassia muttered. "They had better not balk at payment. I'll get paid for this job, one way or another."

"And if they don't pay?"

"I'll take it out of your flesh, you lazy piece of shit."

"That'll be fair. But I imagine that me paying you from my bank account would have better returns for you. Unless you're aching for the sweet, sweet taste of human flesh."

"We'll see."

"What about the rest of my team?" Zimmer asked.

"They are being held at another facility," Axel explained. "And I was only hired to rescue you."

He knew there was no need for him to feel nervous. Not that the knowledge helped. Being in an FBI interrogation room would make anyone nervous.

Of course, he was the only one who knew he was guilty. He did have a minor in psychology that told him his guilt needed to be suppressed since he knew all the other people who were called in would feel nervous too.

Heinz took a deep breath and his gaze settled on the cup of coffee that had been brought for him.

That had been three hours earlier. It probably meant they had other people to investigate. He had done his job well. The paperwork was all in order with no sign that he had even been involved. There were too many people in DecomIT's staff for them to simply zero in on him.

Although he knew that, it didn't change how he felt, however. He was guilty. There was no question in his mind. He hadn't wanted to be involved in the situation but he'd had no choice.

The door opened again and an agent stepped inside.

"Do you know how much longer this will take, Agent Sullivan?" Heinz asked.

The agent sat, adjusted his cornflower-blue tie, and ran his fingers through his thick brown hair.

"It shouldn't be much longer," he muttered, his gaze locked on the file in front of him. "We're merely making sure all our ducks are in a row."

"You said that when you interviewed me the last time," Heinz pointed out. "Two hours ago."

"Do you need more coffee?"

"No. My wife's at home and she won't believe me when I tell her I've been questioned by the FBI for seven hours."

"Seven hours so far. Honestly, I can't put a time limit on this. There was a serious breach in our security and until we can pinpoint exactly where it came from..." He shrugged and left the sentence unfinished.

Heinz nodded and sighed heavily. "Okay, what else do you need to know?"

"I'm going over your story again. You said you arrived at work a little late?"

"Correct. I was delayed by the traffic. I think there was an accident or something, but they had cleared everything by the time I managed to get through."

"Right."

The questions continued. Dozens were fired at him in different orders and the man jumped from one to the other. It was the third time they'd questioned him, and he assumed that everyone else was getting the same treatment.

Still, Heinz could sense a little aggression from them and the thought made him nervous.

It wasn't the first time he'd sensed that, of course, but it seemed a little more intense. With the last two interrogations, they gave up after the second round and left him to stew on his own for hours before they returned and made another attempt. This was round three of his third session, and he could only assume frustration had pushed their impatience levels up.

The agent finished his line of questioning and nodded. "Thank you again, Mr. Tauber. I hope to be able to release you and your colleagues soon."

The agent behind him didn't look quite as happy.

"She won't like this," the man grumbled under his breath as they exited the room.

That sounded like a piece of information they wanted him to know, but he wasn't sure what exactly he could learn from it. Whoever "she" was, the woman was riding these agents to continue the interrogations indefinitely.

It seemed obvious that none of them would be allowed to leave until something happened or something was said.

Heinz tried to shake the feeling that Meredith would be caught. He trusted his work but she was in a much more vulnerable position. She had overseen the extraction of the server and if they were to dig a little deeper into that, she would be in trouble.

He couldn't stand by and let that happen. Besides, there was no telling what kind of damage would come from whatever the thieves had been after in that server.

Besides, when he heard that his brother had murdered the thieves who were supposed to get the server out, he realized that the chances were he was already fucked.

"I'd like to alter my statement," Heinz said softly before they closed the door.

"That was easier than I thought," Sullivan whispered to his partner before both men returned to the interrogation room and closed the door behind them.

It was probably best for him to have a lawyer present but he was tempted to forgo that right. He didn't want to drag this on any longer than it had already.

"How would you like to alter your statement?" the second agent asked and folded his arms.

His hands were shaking. Heinz tried to grip them together but that didn't help. He nodded slowly.

"I…I think I need to speak to my lawyer first."

The two agents exchanged glances and nodded.

"He'll be here shortly," Sullivan replied.

Late hours were par for the course when taking over the management of a facility like this one.

Alessio tried not to let it bother him. He was the perfect person for the job and considered it a blessing that he wasn't on speaking terms with most of his family. With no wife, no kids, and no ties to the real world, he had no divided loyalties. Well, maybe he had some kids, but he was generally careful about that and certainly hadn't heard of any.

He did have the chance to sow his wild oats when there was some downtime. There was very little of it, however, and he needed to be efficient about how he spent it.

"Dr. Esposito?"

He looked up from the data collected the day before to the cameras he had set up in the Killing Fields.

Watching the cameras didn't do much. Most of the data was collected through the sensor array that was installed in the cameras, but he still tried to locate the monsters in the maze that had been built for them. He liked to think he'd seen the mutants a couple of times already.

"Doctor?"

"For God's sake, what?" he snapped and looked up from the screen.

"There is a problem."

"Isn't there always? Turn the turrets on and deal with any that get too close."

"It's not that," the voice on the radio stated stiffly. "A section of our security has gone dark. We've lost communications with the men patrolling the area, and there... well, what we are picking up indicates that we have a foreign presence in the building."

Alessio nodded. "Good."

"Excuse me, doctor?"

"We are a research facility. We have cameras and sensors set up all around the building. Do what we are here to do. Research. Now, stop your whining and start doing your job or do you need to spend a little time in Milan to get your head on straight?"

"No. No, sir."

"Excellent. Let me know when you have data to report."

"This is a bad idea, Desk."

"You have stated as much. Fifteen times now."

Vickie nodded. "As long as we're on the same page."

"We are not on the same page."

It was interesting to see the AI acting like this. The hacker had no other word for it than angry. She wasn't entirely sure that AIs could get angry but it sure as hell seemed that way.

"Leave it to Jennie to make the one AI in the world with an anger problem."

"The problem is not with me. It is with the FBI's inability to maintain its servers."

"And you think that can be solved with you swooping in and taking everything? Seriously, what do you think you can do that Jennie isn't already doing? She's probably more pissed about it than you are."

"I am not angry," Desk insisted.

"Yeah, you keep saying that. And I keep not believing it."

"Why?"

"Because you're acting angry."

The AI had no answer to that. It was as unsettling as an admission that the AI truly was pissed.

"I am collecting the transcripts of all the interrogations of the DecomIT employees who were brought in for questioning," Desk finally told her. "Most are worthless but one comes to mind. It's been altered."

"I thought they were all being altered."

"The agents who performed the interrogation did so multiple times and assembled what they assume to be the actual accounting of events. They would know to adapt for someone misremembering or adding small, harmless falsehoods that are later corrected after deeper questioning. This one has had the original statement erased."

"Run a background check on this...Mr. Tauber?" Vickie scowled. "Why does that name sound familiar?"

"The background checks on all the employees are already being run. Is there anything else you'd like to tell me to do twenty seconds after I have already started it?"

She raised her hands. "Act like a bitch. Fine. I'll go back to helping the M and B team out in the field."

"I haven't even started to act like a bitch."

"Don't I know it. But keep that directed at the people who deserve it, okay?"

CHAPTER EIGHT

"How's it going in there, Taylor?" Vickie asked.

"Not too bad," he muttered in response.

That wasn't quite the right thing to say. It was going a little too well. He had expected Desklet to be a solid addition to their team and he knew better than to doubt Vickie's capabilities, but a facility like this was bound to have some security in place.

Someone who would see them. Something would go wrong.

The fact that nothing had happened thus far did nothing to ease his concern. They moved steadily deeper into the facility and aside from the patrol outside, there was no sign that their presence had been detected.

It was all going a little too smoothly. In his experience, that generally meant something was about to hit the fan and it wouldn't be chocolate mousse.

He brought his suit to a halt outside one of the abandoned computer stations and pulled himself halfway out.

There were some things that even the most advanced suits in the world weren't capable of and handling delicate electronics was one of them.

With one of Vickie's fobs in hand, he stretched forward and inserted the device into the nearest receiver before he drew himself into the suit and sealed it.

"Do you have a visual?" he asked once he was settled.

"Uh...yeah. I'm downloading all the data. Give me a sec."

"What does she expect us to do while we wait?" Chezza asked and scowled at the tight, narrow hallway they were in. "Simply twiddle our thumbs and hope for the best?"

"She expects you to remember that she's still on comms with you, " Vickie snapped. "Okay, I'm pulling up the blueprints—holy shit, this is a fucking maze."

"That's one of the top ten things you don't want to hear when heading into a combat situation," Trick muttered.

"Okay, I've set up a map for you guys. You should see it on your HUDs," Vickie continued and pretended that she couldn't hear him.

"Where are we going?" Jiro asked.

"I picked up some heat signatures deep inside. They have the whole place wired with sensors and cameras, so I'll be able to follow the action. The problem is that the signatures I'm picking up are consistent with those out of the Zoo. And I don't mean the cryptids you've been dealing with. I mean...actual Zoo monsters."

Taylor nodded slowly. "Desklet, you should be in your comfort zone."

"I have no particular zone in which I am the most

comfortable," she replied. "But if you are referring to our shared experience in dealing with monsters from the Zoo, I can agree that I am at least in the element to which I am most suited."

"You're talking much more than you used to."

"Should I correct that? I am still adapting to provide you with optimal performance."

"No, no. Having someone to chat to is fine. I'm merely making an observation, is all."

"Your observation is noted."

Taylor saw that Niki was watching him carefully, although he couldn't make out why since her face was covered by the visor.

"What?" he asked finally over the shared comms.

She switched them to a private channel before she spoke. "I know you're talking to her."

"What?"

"The Desklet. I know you're talking to her. I can see your body language through the suit and unless you've taken to talking to yourself, you're talking to her."

"And the problem is…"

"No problem. I'm merely commenting."

Taylor narrowed his eyes. "I thought we were past the passive-aggressive bullshit."

"We are, but I don't want to talk about this again until we're out of our current situation. Maybe on our way home."

"But we will talk about it."

"You're damn right."

He smirked and shook his head. "Fine. Let's keep

moving. We have a long way to go to reach the heat signatures."

"I do not believe she likes me," Desklet commented.

"Niki doesn't like anyone too quickly. I'm very sure she hated me when we first met, but she warms up over time. The best thing you can do to get in her good graces is to keep her and her family safe."

"Noted. Although my top priority is maintaining your fighting abilities."

"Well, yeah, same difference. Since I'll be consistently working to keep her and her family safe."

"It is interesting how her hostile tone amuses you."

Taylor shrugged, then realized what Niki meant about his body language betraying the fact that he was having a conversation. "I've learned that she's not pissed when she sounds like that. It's only that she...cares a lot. She does that. Believe me, when she's all-out well and truly angry, she'll go beyond hostile."

"I see. I suppose that should she continue to dislike me, I might discover this level beyond hostility that she is capable of?"

"Probably."

The entire situation felt almost unreal. As they moved deeper into the building, the hallways grew wider. They'd needed to walk in single-file at first but now, they were able to walk three combat suits abreast and the space continued to widen.

The fact that there were fewer doors into offices and the like meant they were approaching the section where the animal test subjects were held. Weapons labs were set up at various points, although most of the weapons were removed or locked up for the evening.

"So, team?" Vickie called over their channel. "I think I have bad news."

Taylor raised a hand to bring the group to a halt and narrowed his eyes. "Define bad news."

"Remember how I said there were heat signatures that were likely Zoo monsters? It looks like they're moving."

"Isn't that what we should expect from Zoo monsters?" Chezza asked.

"Sure, but these are…well, they are moving toward you like they're being guided. Doors are opened, then shut behind them, and all indications are that someone is deliberately driving them to you."

"Can you stop it?" Taylor asked.

"The controls are isolated on the grid. I can't access them without a physical port."

"I already—"

"I need a physical port into the control system of the building."

"Let me guess," Niki muttered. "We'd have to get through the monsters to reach it."

"On the bright side, you're already heading in the right direction," Vickie replied and tried to sound optimistic.

"Weapons hot and ready, folks," Taylor ordered and hefted his assault rifle. Desklet immediately started her combat subroutines. "Do you have an idea of what signatures are coming?"

"Sure, I only—oh, shit."

He was about to ask her what she meant by that when

the lights went off and plunged the hallway into complete and total darkness.

Of course, he'd been in the darkness before. The HUD lit up as expected with the readings from the suit's sensor array and gave him a murky green-and-grey image of the world around him instead.

The others looked like they were a little less comfortable with the situation. It was a common reaction, even in those with experience. They might adjust to way the suits detected the darkness and adjusted the view accordingly, but no one liked the weird sensation of being in an entirely alien environment. Of course, in the Zoo, it was alien so it seemed even worse.

"I hate this fucking night vision crap?" Jiro muttered belligerently.

"Yeah. It's like a seriously bad low-budget alien creep show," Chezza agreed.

"Well, at least your suits are set up to help you to see." Taylor reminded them with a chuckle. "Imagine having to do this in complete darkness or with minimal light sources that don't give you a decent view of what's happening beyond a few feet around you. It sucks and some people don't adjust to it, but I guarantee you that after you have to make the best of the alternatives for even a limited time, you'll come to see it as a friend."

"Define limited time." Niki sounded even less comfortable.

"A day in the pitch black of the jungle ought to do the trick."

"You make it sound like my goddammed dentist visits—a necessary evil but fucking painful."

"You know," Trick said as they moved forward, "I had the weirdest feeling. We've seen no hostiles, no security, and nothing else since we got here, right? Doesn't this feel like it's a little too easy?"

"The kid's catching on," Niki whispered over a private channel.

"It's a trap," Jiro grumbled. "Vickie, please check the doors we came through before. Have they been locked?"

"Oh... Yeah, they have," she confirmed.

"So, we're in a trap," Trick said and shook his head. "I could probably simply blow a way out of here. A couple of shaped charges could level the walls and give us a clean exit if we needed one."

"Don't be a dumbass," Chezza told him curtly. "We can't blow anything until we know all the cryptids are dead."

Taylor smirked, still on the private channel with Niki. "Yeah, they're picking up quickly."

"How soon did you realize this was a trap?" she asked.

"About when I shoved Vickie's fob in and it didn't trigger alarms blaring all over the place. I didn't expect there to be isolated controls, though."

"So, we keep moving," Chezza said and hadn't noticed that Taylor and Niki weren't a part of the conversation. "Get to the controls, plug Vickie in, and kill anything between us and that."

"I'm starting to like her," the ex-agent whispered. "The girl has spirit. She sounds a little like me, but less..."

"Cursing and creative descriptions of violence?"

"Sure."

"We know you're talking to each other," Trick said over the shared comms. "We can see your body language. Do you guys have something you want to share with the rest of the class?"

"Nope," Taylor answered. "You're on the right path and it's a simple one. Reach the controls and kill everything between us and them. Let's push on."

"But…what about the fact that it's a trap?" Jiro asked but fell into line.

"Of course it's a trap."

"Traps are meant to be sprung," Niki added.

That didn't seem like the best of ideas but Taylor didn't like the thought of being herded through the hallways like cattle. If someone had decided that putting him in a trap was a good idea, he would prove them wrong.

Even if it was a little dumb to charge headfirst into the trap himself.

The hallways seemed to grow larger to resemble rooms, and he could see signs that they were more commonly used and not only by humans. He brought his fist up.

"What?" Niki asked.

"If I were a betting man, I'd say this is where the trap will be sprung," he murmured.

"The fact that you used to live in Vegas aside, what makes you think that?" she pressed.

Before he could answer, the speakers in the room crackled to life. All the members of the team had their weapons ready in less than a second.

"What's going on, Vickie?" Taylor asked and scrutinized the area, his sense on high alert.

"I'm…I'm not sure. The feed is coming from the control center of the building."

He raised an eyebrow as the speakers began to play music. The volume increased steadily.

"Flight of the Valkyries," Trick muttered. "Someone's been watching a little too much Apocalypse Now."

It presented them with more trouble. With the continuous blast of loud music coming from all sides, Taylor could hear no incoming sound. His sensors went haywire, which made it difficult to stabilize the picture of their surroundings and he had to wait until Desklet had managed to make the necessary adjustments.

"Oh, fuck," Niki whispered.

"Who the hell thought this would be a good idea?" Vickie asked.

Sunrise was still a couple of hours off, but that didn't mean business was coming to a halt.

There were benefits to moving during the day too, but Schmidt & Schwartz were determined to keep any and all hints of what exactly they were transporting from the mind of the general public, and Werner could understand that.

They'd wanted him out of the Zoo for this. Escorting their prize was now a top priority. They had been met by a veritable army of security when they arrived in Austria and the escort continued. That was probably for the best.

He and his assistants had taken turns in the massive container that had been secured for transport to fight the constant battle of keeping their prize sedated. While it was made of reinforced steel—the kind that could take the weight of a falling building—it was imperative that they remain alert and focused. The sedatives were flushed from the creature's system at an impossible and inconsistent rate, which meant constant monitoring was necessary.

His engineer had also installed turrets with sedative rounds inside and, if all else failed, one had live rounds. He didn't know how they'd set the container up so quickly but the message was clear. There would be no accidents.

Still, it didn't look like Alan was comfortable. The man had been on edge since they left the Zoo, which felt like something of a contradiction. Werner thought the men should be a little more relaxed when they were out, no matter what they were transporting.

It was difficult to stay awake when he wasn't the one to watch their prize, and he jerked into awareness when the truck came to a sudden halt. They were off the road, he realized, and officials approached the vehicle.

The sheer number of men and vehicles in the escort probably put the group on edge, but they would see the corporate logo on the side and assume they transported something expensive in the back.

Werner had nothing to do with the paperwork, of course. Whatever the company decided to declare to the customs agents was their business. He was only there to make sure the contents arrived without trouble.

His worries were unfounded, however. The customs agent greeted the guard driving the truck and after a couple of pleasantries were exchanged, he stamped the paperwork he held and gave the driver a copy before he returned the way he'd come.

In seconds, all the vehicles had started again and they crossed the border into Germany.

"What's on your mind, my friend?" Werner asked. "You are on the last leg of what will be the greatest triumph of your career—assuming you do not run for political office —and you look unsettled."

"Call me crazy, but I'm not happy to bring that fucking monster into a civilized area of the world," the man replied and shook his head. "We should have killed it and collected whatever samples you wanted."

"People have done that before. What we're doing is unprecedented."

"Which means there are way too many things that can go wrong. If we make one mistake, that beast will rip through the nearest city and our names will be plastered over the news as the responsible parties. People will talk for decades about how we were too money-crazy to consider how bad an idea this was."

The researcher shrugged. "With great risk comes great reward."

As they drove past the customs office, none of the security members noticed the dark car that seemed to be waiting for something.

Once the convoy passed, the woman inside took her phone out and punched in a number she'd committed to memory. The call was answered before it could ring for the third time.

There was no answer but she hadn't expected there to be one.

"It's here," she said. "You may tell his Highness that his heart's desire is almost home."

The call was cut on the other end and she smiled before she started her vehicle. There was much to be said for having a Saudi Prince owe her a favor of that magnitude.

As headquarters went, Frans had certainly been in worse.

The beginning of Earth for Earth had not been one with too many victories early on. More than a few nights had been spent crashing on the couches of others, and there had even been one night where he managed to stay up until the metro opened and he got a couple of hours of sleep while riding it before he headed off to get work done for the day at the canvas tent he had used as his headquarters.

By comparison, an abandoned warehouse that had been deserted in the middle of a repurposing project was practically luxurious.

Still, it wasn't quite the best situation, although that didn't have much to do with the accommodations.

It was him, Lena, and Finn now. The rest of Earth for Earth was out there and still working, but they would be of no help. Frans regretted their plan to break the three of them out due to the unavoidable fatalities and refused to consider running a similar operation to free their other two members. It would put them in too much danger and honestly, he had to agree even though he felt a little guilty.

He wanted to say they would have simply served their sentence, but the threat of being sent to the Zoo had hung over him for far too long. He'd had nightmares in prison of being in that jungle and had woken each time in a cold sweat.

Those who effected the escape had his eternal gratitude, but it hadn't come without a cost.

Earth for Earth was being branded as a terrorist organization. He'd spent years making sure all their protests were peaceful and if there was any violence, it was on the side of the authorities. The moment he dropped out of sight, things disintegrated. There had been deaths in the United States and more while breaking them out.

He was thankful to not be waiting for the worst fate he could think of, but maybe the cost had been a little too high, especially now that they were all fugitives.

They paused as a small Audi pulled up outside the building and were a little relieved to realize it was their lawyer.

The man had offered to represent them pro bono, but he probably hadn't thought anything would get as bad as it was.

Frans was surprised he was still with them at this point.

The man approached, stepped inside the building, and put his briefcase on one of the tables.

"Thanks for meeting us, Leon," Frans said, shook his hand, and motioned for the others to join them. "I can't tell you what it means to know you're still here for the long haul."

"I've always believed in Earth for Earth, you know that." Leon shook hands with the other two. "Although I'll admit it's been difficult. I know you haven't been running things, but many harmful rumors are being spread now. And with you three being broken out of prison, that hasn't improved.

The judicial system has dug its heels in over this and few of the judges will want to hear your appeal now with the government calling for blood."

"What about Emma and Stefan?"

"Their hearing has been delayed until the situation is settled, but they are still sentenced to the Zoo like you were. Most of the paperwork I've filed with the International Court has been stalled too. Eventually, they'll all decide that sending someone into the Zoo as a criminal punishment is cruel and unusual enough to qualify as a breach of basic human rights, but... Well, I doubt that will happen in time to save your people and for now, it won't be easy."

"Do you think they might be moved to the Zoo before you're able to get your lawsuit through?" Lena asked as she sat. "We might have to get them out somehow as well, don't you think?"

"I can't say with any certainty at this point, but it's entirely possible, yes." Leon raised his hand before they could say anything else. "I probably shouldn't hear anything you might have to say regarding further criminal intent."

"We're already past that, right?" Finn noted.

"I am not required to report past offenses that I might or might not be aware of, but I would be ethically obliged to report any future criminal acts you plan to perpetrate."

"Thank you, Leon," Frans interjected before anything else could be said. "You are a good friend."

The lawyer nodded and left a few files on the table, as well as a small envelope with cash inside before he sealed his briefcase. "Good luck to you in all your endeavors."

With that, he returned to his car and was soon out of sight.

Lena lowered her head into her hands. "We can't... We know—"

"Yes," Finn agreed. "They would be...we have to stop them from going to the Zoo. Somehow. Some way. It can be done, right?"

Frans sighed and nodded. "We'll find a way, I promise."

CHAPTER NINE

"I don't like this." Trick repeated the statement for probably the tenth time.

Taylor narrowed his eyes. "Are there any particular parts of this you don't like that you'd like to list or is it simply the situation in general?"

"I don't like being herded through this fucking building," Trick snapped as he continued to attempt to filter the blaring music out by adjusting the settings. "But you already know what I think we should do to get out of this fucking place, so I won't bother being shot down again."

"Good, because I don't feel like shooting you down again," Taylor muttered. He wouldn't admit it, but whoever was running the facility had begun to infuriate him. Not that he hadn't been pissed before, but he imagined he would still be even angrier if this continued.

"What the fuck kind of weapons dev place is this?" Niki asked.

"They've run most of the weapons research for the European teams sent into the Zoo," Vickie answered. "It seems they've had far more contracts lately, mostly because their work has begun to outpace the competition. Now we know why, I guess."

"It's a little sad," Jiro commented. "Of course, doing this type of research is dangerous and bound to go wrong, but the folks in the Zoo need any advantage they can get out there. Wrecking this facility merely means they won't get it, right?"

Taylor hated it, but the man made a fair point. It didn't change the fact that it needed to be done but the consequences were easy to lay out.

"They'll have what's already been researched. We can't do anything about that," Niki answered. "All we're doing here is damage mitigation. Something was bound to go wrong eventually—it always does—and we're making sure it happens when there are trained motherfuckers here to deal with it."

"Did you call yourself a motherfucker?" Taylor asked.

"Sure. Ironically."

"I don't think that means what you think it means."

"Shut up."

Taylor raised a hand to bring their team to a halt in the hallway. With the music blaring, it had been easy to miss a few small changes in their surroundings. There were no more doors, offices, or labs. The walls were sturdy and heavier than they had been before and it appeared that they had entered what was quite literally a labyrinth, complete with the monsters.

All they could hope for was that there wasn't a real-life minotaur waiting in there for them. He had a feeling that would involve a little too much experimentation, not only on the Zoo monsters but humans too.

"Did you hush me in hand signals?" Niki snapped.

"No. Well, yes, but...listen."

"To what? Richard Wagner for the fifteenth time?"

"No, beyond that. Listen."

They all stopped talking and immediately focused their attention on the walls. Despite the solidity of the plates, it sounded distinctly like something was moving beneath them.

"Oh, shit," Vickie shouted. "Okay, guys, something's happening in there and it's not very good. You're entering a section that has a ton of security measures. Most importantly, a large number of turrets."

Taylor narrowed his eyes as two panels in the walls slid back to reveal two guns that emerged directly from the wall.

"And they have been activated," the hacker added. She sounded a little panicked.

There was no cover, and Taylor immediately raised his weapon and opened fire on the turret. He doubted it would do much good, in all honesty, but it was an instinctive reaction more than anything else. The muzzles on the guns flashed and illuminated the hallway for a split second along with his rounds before the weapons retracted and the panels slid closed to cover them.

He looked at his team. "Is anyone hurt? Did anyone sustain damage?"

"The rounds bounced off my armor a little," Niki commented and looked at the others.

"I don't think I took any hits," Trick said, and when they

inspected each other's suits, it didn't appear that they had either.

Taylor looked at the suit that he wore and noticed a couple of dents in the plates as well as fragments of the rounds that were used.

"It would appear that the rounds used by the turrets are hollow points," Desklet informed them. "They are likely meant to cut through unarmored targets and possibly also to avoid causing any damage to the structure of the walls. The aim would be to keep whatever is inside from breaking out."

That made sense. It also explained why he hadn't been skewered by the shots at point-blank range. Most of the rounds in the Zoo and those they carried were the types designed to punch through armor—natural and man-made—and weren't allowed to be hollow points.

The fact that they were banned for international use but used by local police forces felt a little like bullshit, but Taylor didn't like to think about that.

"Okay, Vickie, we got lucky this time," he said and adjusted his weapon although he kept it at the ready. "But we'll need a little warning for the next time."

"I can't control anything from here, dude."

"I know, but you can give us some kind of warning. Check and see which sections have what kind of defenses and let us get ready for them."

"I don't know—"

"We trust you, Vickie. You got this."

He had hoped to calm her but making her pissed off was a close second. When she got pissed off, she had a habit of going fully destructive, which was the kind of thing they needed in the present circumstances. If they wanted to get out, he needed her on point.

Focused or angry was how she got the job done most effectively.

"Okay, you guys are moving into a section that has a ton of security measures in place," the hacker alerted them. "It looks like these are there to keep the animals contained, whereas the turrets are…kind of a last resort, I guess? From the looks of things, it seems they're letting the Zoo monsters wander the hallways without too much restraint aside from these security measures. All are controlled from the central console."

"What happens if…I don't know, the guy falls asleep?" Chezza wondered. "And everything breaks out while he's catching a couple of Z's?"

"There are probably security measures in place that activate the turrets and shit when the animals approach," Niki surmised. "With that said, a fucker falling asleep at the controls while everything goes to hell isn't the craziest scenario I've ever heard."

The music was still playing but it felt like the suits had adjusted to the constant barrage and now provided them with a better view of their surroundings. More importantly, it seemed Vickie was directing the data on the security measures into Desklet's feed, which allowed her to display the sections that had security measures in place.

"What is hidden in here appears to be some type of electrical resonance oscillator, meant to course a high-voltage bolt of electricity through any approaching conductors that are not properly grounded," the AI explained as Taylor motioned for the team to halt again.

"Vickie?" he asked and looked at the highlighted section of the wall to his right.

"Oh…kind of like a Tesla coil that'll send electricity into anything that gets too close. The charge isn't enough to kill you unless you have a pacemaker or something like that, but it'll still give your suits a hard time. It might even burn some shit out if you're not careful."

"Is it active?" He inched closer and watched for even the slightest movement on the walls.

"Not yet. The panels moving out of the way opens a port that feeds electricity into the device. I guess they don't want something to short circuit and damage the walls."

"Noted."

With another quick step forward, Taylor powered his suit and launched his fist forward with as much speed as he could manage. He punched a hole clean through and the fist closed on the mechanism within.

A flurry of sparks erupted from inside, and he yanked his hand back and pulled most of the device out to make the hole in the wall larger.

"What—Taylor!" Vickie yelled.

"You said it wasn't active."

"Sure, but it's still dangerous to shove your hand into a wall when you don't know what's on the other side."

"It worked this time, didn't it?" He tossed the device down, looked at the nearest camera, and raised a one-fingered salute to whoever was watching them on the other side.

"You never were one for subtlety, were you?" Niki commented. "Okay, we'll keep moving. I assume there are more turrets along the way?"

"Yes," Vickie confirmed. "But I don't think our guy will let you in to punch through the next one."

"Right. If we run into anything too big for us to handle, we'll let Trick go nuts on it," Taylor muttered.

"Kaboom?" The freelancer grinned.

"Calm down, Rico. I said if we can't handle it any other way. We still don't need this whole building to collapse on our heads."

"I find your lack of faith disturbing."

"Not nearly as disturbing as your explosives fetish."

They slowed when they rounded a corner and narrowed their eyes as they approached what appeared to be a dead end.

"Isn't this supposed to be open?" Niki asked. "The map you have for us directed us through this wall."

"It's not a wall, it's a door," Vickie snapped and tried to keep her tone civil. "And again, I don't have any real power over what's happening in the building aside from watching it happen. All the other doors you went through were opened before you got there."

"We could simply go back," Chezza suggested.

"The doors have been closing behind you." Vickie sounded like her annoyance had begun to get the best of her. "You're sealed in. I hate to say it, but the explosives fetishist might be your only way through—or out, depending on what you plan to do in there."

Taylor studied their surroundings. There was no sign that they were in any kind of immediate danger. None of the security guards was in their current location, and there was no way in or out for the monsters in the building. Something wasn't right, though. He could feel it in his gut.

Or maybe the guy was pissed off that he broke one of their toys.

"Okay, Trick," he stated. "I assume you have some charges on you? It's time to let this motherfucker know exactly who he's messing with."

"All you had to do was ask." Trick grinned. Taylor didn't need to see through his visor as he could hear it in the man's voice when he retrieved a pack he had carried on his belt.

There wasn't much to be said about carrying explosives like that. As long as he took good care of the detonators, the explosives themselves were harmless, even if they were shot or set on fire. Taylor had even heard stories of soldiers on the front line in the Vietnam War using small amounts of C-4 to cook their rations when there weren't any other options, despite the danger posed by the noxious fumes created.

Still, the kid had been through his fair share of action and had worked for years both setting and disarming explosives on the front line. Even in these conditions, he didn't doubt that he could get them deeper into the building if they were careful about it.

The freelancer moved his suit to the door, disengaged from it halfway like Taylor had, and began to take items from his pack with the help of a flashlight he held in his mouth.

"So…why do they call you Trick anyway?" Chezza asked as she approached him.

He looked up from his work to glare at her and mumbled a few indecipherable words around the flashlight in his mouth.

"Darius Eaton isn't the kind of name that would lend itself to a nickname like Trick, so it must have been something you did or that happened to you that earned you the nickname."

"You're one to talk," Jiro challenged. "How the hell does one get Chezza from Francesca O'Donnell? Shouldn't I call you something like...I don't know, Franny?"

"Yeah, if you want me to break your arms and shove them down your throat," she answered.

"Come on, you're a medic. Do you honestly think you can take me on?"

"I was a medical specialist with MARSOC, dumbass. That means I'd have the skill and knowledge required to break every bone in your body in alphabetical order while naming them for you."

"Wait—hold on, Trick," Vickie shouted. "Get back in your suit. Now!"

"What's up?" Taylor asked. The freelancer didn't bother to ask questions but immediately scrambled into his suit and attached the explosives pack to his belt again.

"The controls of the door activated, and if I read the sensors right, it looks like something is on the other side."

Taylor nodded. That was as clear and concise an explanation as he could ask for, and he trained his weapon on the door when, a few seconds later, something in the mechanism clicked and the massive door groaned as it was drawn open.

Even as it gave way, he heard a deep, thunderous roar from the other side.

"Oh, there's something in there, all right," he whispered as Desklet shifted into action mode.

Julian didn't appreciate having to postpone a golfing date to find out what had happened with the carefully planned heist. He also wasn't impressed to learn that everything on the job had gone to shit and even less that the whole team he'd hired to get it done were dead.

Fortunately, his operations specialist remained intact. The man sat across from him and carved a delicious cut of tenderloin draped with rich red wine sauce like he had not a single care in the world.

"Do you think we can talk business now?" Julian tried to keep his temper under control and wished he'd simply scheduled the meeting at his office rather than try to kill two birds with one stone and have lunch while they talked. He'd suddenly lost his appetite, but the other man seemed unaware of the effect he had on him.

"I thought you wanted to talk before your lunch." Frank popped a piece of the meat smothered in hearty mashed potatoes into his mouth before he continued. "But I understand that you're a businessman who likes to do his…what are they called? Three martini lunches."

"That's something else," Transk muttered and glowered at the martini he'd ordered for himself with three olives as a garnish. "This is something else."

"If you say so." The former agent sipped his beer before he wiped his mouth with a napkin. "Let's talk about what went wrong. We had the server and my men moved it out along with the decoy equipment. Everything on my end was clean, which means someone leaked the information.

They were hit hard by professionals who killed them to a man and ran off with your server."

"That impossible," he whispered.

"It's not," Frank replied from around another mouthful of steak. "It's the only real explanation. They were attacked while coming out of the warehouse in an abandoned section of town. Whoever it was, they knew they were coming out and what they were coming out with. It was leaked, end of discussion. Now, I hand-picked those guys. They were friends so I have a personal stake in this. I have to train another group for the job."

"The job?"

"You know as well as I do that the AI is out there now. You'll take a hit if your competitors get it and start making money off what should have been yours. But we have to be careful. The FBI's investigating this now and it appears that Jennie Banks has raised all hell over the missing server. Of course, the upside of that is a confirmation that the software is on there. The downside, however, is that she's shoved a fucking torpedo up every ass in the Bureau hierarchy and is baying for blood. Even if they weren't pissed that they were robbed twice and had to find answers for the bodies, with her hounding them, they will be even more determined to find answers, if only to get the bitch off their backs."

"Do they know about our involvement?" Julian asked and stirred his martini with the silver prong with the olives on it.

"No. The boys I used are pros. They won't have any connection to the money or us."

"They were your friends."

"Sure, and they had any number of friends. The worst I can expect—if they go the route of checking each and every known associate, which is unlikely—is a couple of agents coming to get a statement. I'll tell them I was at the horse track all night and never heard a word from them. The cameras there will confirm it. And I can monitor the chatter. I still have a couple of friends in there who wouldn't mind keeping an eye on shit for me."

"Find it," Julian snapped, bit one of the olives off the prong, and returned it to the martini to stir again. "No matter what it takes. This is a hiccup, not a reason to throw in the towel. I want that goddamn AI and I want the asshole who took it. No one messes with Transk Armor and gets away with it. I want an example set. Remember that they made you look like an idiot too."

Frank sighed loudly and nodded. He took another bite from his tenderloin and chewed thoughtfully. "I'll need more money."

Julian took a sip from his drink before he took an envelope with a credit card out of his pocket and slid it across the table. "Whatever it takes."

His operations specialist nodded and pocketed the envelope without looking at it before he turned his attention to the food. It was good food and they were at a nice restaurant, although it was a little too rigid and professional for dinners.

The CEO decided he would make sure Frank's pay was doubled for his work. He was doing it for his reputation above all else, but Julian didn't want rumors to spread about how he short-changed his people. That was never a good thing to be known for.

Besides, he'd already proved himself invaluable—although he'd never tell him that, of course. He wanted to keep the guy around for a long time, and the best way to do that was to keep him motivated by his love for money.

Frans narrowed his eyes and leaned a little closer to the screen. "What...what am I looking at?"

"A truck."

"Yes, I can see that." He sighed and rubbed his temples to ease the dull ache and to avoid sounding too on edge. "I'm merely asking why you would call an emergency meeting with the Earth for Earth thinktank because of a truck."

"It's more about what's inside the truck," the spy noted as he called up the footage of the rest of the convoy. "About seventy-two hours ago, Schmidt & Schwartz called for the convoy to be assembled to meet a team that was arriving in Austria from the Zoo. I have pictures of the escort arriving here."

A picture of a heavy vehicle with half a dozen escort vehicles pulling up to a private hangar displayed on the screen.

"And here they are leaving. Do you notice the difference?"

The two pictures were shown side-by-side with a little nudging from the spy on his computer so that they were all in-frame for him to look at.

The difference wasn't obvious, but when Frans leaned even closer, he could see what the man was talking about.

"The truck is riding much lower in the second picture," Lena said when she noticed it as well. "I suppose our surveillance on the companies with a record of destructive research practices is finally pulling in some returns. Do we know what's in it?"

"They were very quiet on what exactly was being transported," the spy replied and pulled up records of the chatter that he'd picked up on for them to see. "But I studied the details of what they did to the truck. This isn't a standard vehicle and it was modified with reinforced walls, turrets, the works."

"I don't see any turrets," Finn noted.

"That's because they were all mounted on the inside."

Lena narrowed her eyes. "So, unless they only intend to shoot thieves once they're inside…"

"Whatever they are transporting is alive," Frans finished her sentence for her and stiffened a little. "All that security isn't designed to protect against anyone trying to attack the convoy. It's possibly to eliminate whatever they're transporting if things go wrong. And…you said it came directly from the Zoo?"

"Those were the reports." The spy pulled the reports up for them to look at as well.

"Something big," Finn noted. "Massive. If you take into account the suspension that was installed on the truck, lowering it by that amount means that whatever was brought in would have to weigh…" He paused and scribbled a couple of calculations on a piece of paper. "It would weigh at least ten tons, give or take. Much larger than your average elephant."

He paused and realized that the other two were staring at him.

"What? You act like you haven't seen me run calculations like this for fun. It's second nature to me."

Lena raised an eyebrow. "Fair enough. Now, what could they be transporting that weighs ten tons and would be dangerous enough to warrant that much security?"

"Leverage," Frans said softly.

"I don't—what?"

"Whatever is in there is the leverage we need to get our people released. If the data you have is correct, they'll transport it to the Schmidt & Schwartz facility outside Hamburg. We can attack the convoy, steal the container, and move it to our headquarters instead. Once we have it, we can issue an ultimatum. They withdraw the complaints that had us arrested in the first place or we release their mutant and see them crumble under the international outrage of bringing something so dangerous out of the Zoo."

"It's...an interesting idea," the field operative muttered. "But this... It won't happen without blood being shed. People will die."

"People have already died," Frans replied and lowered his head. "I never thought it would happen, but it has. If we do not do this, our people—who have killed no one—will die instead. It is regrettable, but it seems like our only option if we are to save them."

CHAPTER TEN

Heinz had known this would happen. He'd seen it in movies and on TV but had never thought it would happen to him. When he'd finally made his decision to come clean, he had told himself he was prepared to pay any price they had in store for him, but doing it was something else entirely.

The lawyer came and informed him that the options for a deal were limited. The only chance he had was to tell them everything. About Frank, of course, not Meredith. Even the attorney knew nothing about her involvement and there was no reason to include her in any of this, not when she was an FBI employee.

From that moment, everything changed. He was no longer held as a person of interest but rather under arrest. And they turned the screws continuously. He'd been in the tight, confined interrogation room for what felt like days. One of the worst things was that he didn't have his watch, his phone, or any other indication that the world outside was still there aside from the periodic lawyer visits.

"This is what you said you'd do," he whispered and glowered at the cup of stale coffee they'd offered him.

Still, maybe it was time for Meredith to help him a little. It wasn't like their affair had been anything passionate. They were fun and had much in common—certainly more than he had with his wife—but being together as Frank had suggested was not something he had ever considered.

He wasn't a hero. Dealing with an abusive husband who wouldn't let go was not something he wanted to be involved in. He felt shitty for even thinking it, but the longer he remained in the room, the longer the thoughts of turning her in would have to marinate. And in all honesty, they looked more attractive by the second.

The door opened and Heinz looked up. He no longer allowed himself to feel excited about any new arrivals, even though it was the young man whose temples were already graying. All access to the DecomIT lawyer had been cut the moment he started to spill the beans and he had since been assigned one who worked for his father-in-law. The man had a good mind for it and didn't let the agents roll over him at any point in their conversation, but he had been handed a losing battle. All he could do at this point was damage control.

"I wish I had good news for you, but they're not ready to let you out yet." He sat and began to spread paperwork across the table so he could see the sheer extent of what was happening. "They have a bitch on the warpath out there, and they won't let anyone out until they know exactly what happened. They haven't been able to find anything on this Frank you mentioned in your statement, but they're willing to go a little easier on you since you acted under a threat to your family."

"Who is the bitch on the warpath anyway?" Heinz asked and shook his head. "I know the FBI likes to keep their contractors happy, but this is going a little further than they usually go, right?"

"This one is...well, she has considerable pull. She designed the AI that was on the stolen server. I've listened in on a couple of the conversations and...well, warpath is putting it mildly. She's basically threatened to activate mercenary groups to track the thieves and drop them all into a vat of acid. Of course, the actual thieves are dead and none of them are this Frank, and they were robbed by a third party no one knows about. Shit is hitting the fan in a very steady stream."

Heinz nodded. He had a good idea of who the third party was but if he didn't tell the Feds about Meredith, he wouldn't tell them about his brother either.

"The only lead they might have had was the van, but no plates were displayed and all similar vehicles are either accounted for at the time of the heist or were reported stolen. They assume it has been disposed of in some way as no branch of law enforcement has been able to locate it."

"I didn't think they would," Heinz whispered. "Thanks for your help, Isaac."

"Never let it be said that the Leweks don't pay their debts," the man replied with a small smirk. "I'm merely sorry I can't bring you any better news after so much time."

"Honestly, I expected to be moved to a black site where they...I don't know. Maybe I spent too much time watching *24*."

The man smiled and nodded. "Well, we could use a Jack Bauer to track our thieves at this point but not by violating any of your rights. Not while I'm around. Is there anything you need? More coffee?"

Heinz winced. "Uh...no. I'll pass on the coffee."

"Just as well. The coffee here is terrible and they won't let me bring anything in from the outside either."

"That makes sense."

"Sure, but still. If they don't want people to bring coffee in, they should have better coffee machines around here. But are you okay?"

He nodded and drew a deep breath. "I'm climbing the walls here but there's nothing you can do about that."

"Except get you more shitty coffee." The lawyer patted him on the shoulder as he stood, collected the paperwork, and replaced it all in his briefcase before he moved to the door and tapped on it.

A few seconds later, an agent appeared to let him out and lock the door behind him.

Heinz leaned his head on the cold metal table and covered it with both hands.

Jennie folded her arms in front of her chest, pushed her glasses quickly up her nose, and narrowed her eyes as she studied her computer screen a little more closely.

"Doesn't all this seem a little...random?" she asked aloud.

Anyone else might have assumed she was talking to herself but she honestly didn't care. She had been at this for what felt like forever and they would be at it for a while longer if the data they had collected was any indication. At this point in time, she was done caring what other people thought of her.

"What about the arrest strikes you as random?" Desk asked over her computer speakers.

"Them somehow picking up on the one guy who would be able to sneak the server out of the FBI. Finding the one place in the world where it would be so isolated that stealing it wouldn't have been noticed for weeks if it hadn't been for your quick thinking and another crew attacking them before they could make off with it. You... I... Never mind. The point is that this is a significant security flaw that was exposed. Where do you think they might have picked up on it?"

"It is not too large a stretch to assume that whoever was involved was at least familiar with how the FBI works," Desk replied. "They would need to know processes and protocols, as well as how they deal with their outdated servers. Compared to that, finding this Heinz Tauber char-acter seems like an oddity—an aberration—and not important."

"But why did they choose him?" Jennie muttered. "He was one member in a team of thirty who handled the FBI disposals. Most of them have families so they would all be in a position to be blackmailed by this...Frank."

Frank. She hated the name already. Fuck him. Fuck Frank.

"The only logical explanation I can think of is that they researched the DecomIT staff until they found him, but that might not be the case. Do you think our blackmail victim might be lying about the reasoning behind his betrayal?" Desk asked.

"I don't see why he would expose his vulnerability like that if he was a willing participant in the robbery."

"Unless he is afraid that what happened to his comrades will happen to him as well?"

Jennie tilted her head as she considered this. "That's possible but not very likely. The second group has what they want, so it's not like they'll have any interest in him. He wouldn't be able to identify them anyway. And Tauber didn't lose the server. This Frank character did, so it's unlikely he'll have any burning desire for revenge. It doesn't matter, though. I still think he's hiding something. He hasn't told us everything."

"Well...your guess is as good as mine. I've tracked the money used to pay the mercenaries who were killed, and it's been a veritable maze. I doubt we'll find anything from that line of inquiry."

"So following the money has been a failure." Jennie tossed one of the gummy bears from the bowl on her desk into her mouth. "Still, I doubt my guess would be as good as yours. You have far more data than I do. Are you sure there's nothing on Tauber?"

"He hasn't received any money for what happened, before or after, and is married with no children."

"I see a slew of payments on the house. They're rebuilding everything for what looks like the tenth time. Is there anything there?"

"The money has come from the wife. She has a trust fund she taps for it. Money is not a matter of concern for the Tauber family."

"I also don't buy that he's afraid for his family here," Jennie whispered. "It has to be something to do with this prenup he signed. His wife gets everything if he's caught cheating. She spends that much on house renovations and the husband works late consistently at an IT firm. He has something on the side."

"It's an interesting theory. I see no evidence but it certainly does make more sense."

"If we know what to look for, we'll find something. Has he made any trips out of town?"

"Conferences—the kind he's required to go to if he wants to keep his license in the state."

"Maybe he met someone there. A honeypot?"

"Possibly. But something doesn't fit."

"What?" Jennie poured more gummy bears into her bowl and snatched three more. "God knows we could do with something else to dig into."

"How did everyone know which server I was on? It's not like I used it often and it was never common knowledge that I was installed there in the first place."

"Yet strangers were able to come in and target your server specifically." Jennie nodded and pulled up another tab on her browser. "Fuck, they had help on the inside."

"We already knew that. Tauber."

"No, they had someone inside the FBI. Not a contractor. Someone who had regular access to those servers. Do you think you can identify anyone who would have had a position there?"

"I will start searching."

She nodded and called up the names of anyone involved in the FBI's IT department. It wasn't like they had the names on the FBI website but there was a record. Maybe someone had quit immediately after the heist, but she doubted it.

If they were smart, they would stick around, wait for everything to blow over, and then resign.

And there was always the possibility that the person in question was also being blackmailed by the robbers.

Jennie frowned. "While I'm working on this, would you mind running a quick check on any FBI IT personnel who might have attended the same conferences as our dear Mr. Tauber?"

"Ah. An interesting possible connection. I'll run it right away."

"Thanks, Desk. You're the best."

It did feel like they were chasing their tails but at least they had something resembling a lead at this point. Which was far more than the FBI goons had gleaned from interrogating the poor sap they had caught.

Still, there was something to be said for the possibility. The idea was appealing. A man is forced into blackmail over a lover but he doesn't turn the lover in for fear of ruining her career in the FBI.

Only one of them needed to go to jail. It truly was a tagline for a shitty tear-jerker that somehow received all the awards nominations. Cast a handsome face with a modicum of talent as the male lead, throw a couple of shots of gratuitous nudity in there to the sound of a French translation of a pop song, and it would be a shoo-in for all the awards in the season.

Maybe they could make it into a period piece. That would basically write the winner speeches.

CHAPTER ELEVEN

He had honestly thought this would be more fun.

Having humans trapped in his little maze had all the makings of his best experiment yet. They'd broken in, so no one would question it if they died. Putting them through the gauntlet felt like it would be a good test for his defenses.

Added to that was the fact that they wore the kind of combat suits he expected to see from those taking the run into the Zoo. It was interesting to see exactly what those suits could do. He'd put considerable work into helping design those that were currently in use.

But it became very boring very quickly. The leader was a little too quick on the draw and had destroyed one of his turrets. As if that wasn't bad enough, he'd broken another before he could even activate it. How the guy had determined that there was something in there to attack was a mystery, but it meant they wouldn't be caught by surprise.

Which took all the fun out of it. Certain pleasures came from manipulating the beasts inside his maze. Even though the Zoo monsters were smarter than most other creatures, they were still animals and easy to control.

The humans were entirely different.

"Fucking idiots," he whispered and leaned closer to the screen. They moved easily, smoothly, and efficiently in the suits they wore.

They were all professionals. He should have kept that in mind. Also, they had help from the outside. Maybe that was what had kept them safe thus far.

Now, he could see one of them out of his suit and setting explosives up to rip through one of the containment doors. He'd only closed it to slow them and give him time to think but they had forced his hand.

Alessio had never been a killer, not by nature. He left that kind of thing to others. He could have put the turrets on and let them annihilate the bastards. Even their high-level armor would be limited against the firepower he had at his disposal in the maze.

Monsters of the Zoo? He could kill those without a second thought. They were aliens and not worthy of consideration. People, puppies, and kittens were another story entirely.

He decided that he wouldn't kill them himself. For a long moment, he stared at the controls on his console and knew he didn't have that in him. Pulling the trigger like that wouldn't be killing them directly, of course. They broke in and put themselves in that position. Technically, they killed themselves.

But it didn't feel like that. It would be nothing short of murder if he turned the weapons on. Alessio scowled at the consoles before he peered into the next room. Finally, he decided to give them a fighting chance and let them face his monsters.

He didn't have to do anything but let them through. That was what they wanted, right?

And stop them from blowing sections out of his fucking maze in the meantime.

The creatures had been with him long enough to grow and their subjection to the weapons had made them more aggressive than their time in the Zoo would have made them. They were big and extremely strong, and their rage would make them even more violent than normal.

His expendable test subjects were the right combination to deal with the motherfuckers.

He would have to do something with them anyway. They were getting a little too old to be a part of his experiments and they would have been sent to the killing floors soon. He might as well get a little more out of them.

And once they were finished with the invaders, he could deal with them as he'd planned to.

It was unfortunate but it had to be done.

Alessio pressed the button to open the doors to draw the monsters in as well as the intruders.

"Let God decide," he whispered and leaned closer to the screens.

"This is different, Mikey. This is a fucking army."

"You've fought armies before."

"Yeah, but we had armies of our own. Well, not our armies, but…you know."

Miguel nodded gently and his gaze settled on the rest of the team as they began to gather, look at the tablets they had distributed, and discuss the operation that lay ahead. They all seemed animated and even excited, but perhaps the bountiful coffers of the Saudi prince who'd hired them had something to do with that. He might not particularly like the man, but even he had to admit that he didn't stint when it came to paying handsomely to get what he wanted.

"We'll talk about this another time, Rich."

"What, when we're dead?"

"No, when we're rich. Rich."

"Hilarious. In fact, it's rich. How long have you held that one in?"

"Since five years ago when you introduced yourself. Do you remember what you said?"

Rich pulled his baseball hat off and checked the inside while he ran his fingers over his mustache. "Yeah. I said my name was Rich May. Not Richard, not Rick, not Rickie, and sure as fuck not Dick. It was one hell of an introduction, huh?"

"It's got a little old after hearing you introduce yourself like that for five years, but yeah. One hell of an introduction."

Miguel approached the little group of mercenaries who studied the plans to attack the convoy and gestured for them to move closer. There wouldn't be enough time to play meet and greet for all of them but thankfully, it looked like at least a few of them had worked together before.

It wasn't an exceptionally large group. Good mercenaries were rare in the civilized world. Most had chosen the more lucrative option and headed to the Zoo where they could make better money. They faced more risks, of course, but theirs wasn't a safe business by definition.

Those who started on the old continent were the kind who had money, families, or both—something to lose. They were often veterans of too many fights and battles and wouldn't charge headfirst into a jungle full of alien monsters.

It was something of a relief. The Zoo attracted all the hotheads, those who would inevitably make a job more dangerous than it was already.

"Nice to see you again, Mikey," one of the mercs said and raised her hand in greeting.

"Carla. Are you still alive?"

"I haven't met anyone who can take me on yet."

Miguel smiled and turned to the other. "I'm Miguel Patricio but call me Mikey. This is Rich May."

"We'll run this operation," Rich said briskly in his thick Georgia accent as he put his baseball cap on again. "It'll be quick, clean, and efficient. We're already up against a horde of these sumbitches, so there's no need to make life any more difficult for ourselves than they will make it. Check the tablets. All the details are there. You've all worked for Prince Salman before so you all know how he likes things done."

The man knew how to make a point.

"Right," Miguel agreed. "The convoy is on the way to Hamburg and has at least thirty men in the escort cars and more in the truck. We weren't able to get reliable numbers on that, but I've heard at least five. Intelligence tells me they're Rosatto's boys, which means they're all tough assholes who won't think twice before shooting first, shooting second, shooting third, and not bothering to ask any questions of the corpses. The only advantage we have is that they're probably more worried about what they're transporting in the truck than any kind of threat we might pose, so it'll be easy to catch them by surprise. Well, easier."

"Like the Macao job?" one of the mercs asked.

He checked his tablet to make certain that he had the guy's name.

"Gustavo, right?"

"Call me Gus."

"Right, Gus. A little like the Macao job. They won't take the highways, so they'll go up through the mountain roads and avoid traffic. It means they'll be funneled into a two-lane road. We don't want them to go off the side." Miguel pointed to the satellite picture. "The truck's coming from the opposite direction and we'll block the road. Once they've stopped, it's like the Macao job."

"It sounds like a plan. I liked the Macao job."

"Unfortunately, the job doesn't end there. They have something alive in the truck that has to be kept that way—sedated but alive. Since none of you know how to keep it drugged effectively, we have to nab one of these two." Another picture appeared on the tablets that displayed two men who were decidedly not professional soldiers. "Both would be best, but we need at least one of them."

"Do we know what it is?" Carla asked.

"Yes, which only emphasizes the need to have at least one of its keepers on hand. Our orders advised us that it's one of the dino creatures from the Zoo. As we all know, the prince has a vast network of people who work to find information for him. One of these somehow found out about this shipment—and no, don't ask me how because I haven't a clue. Suffice it to say that if he's sure the intel is correct, that's good enough for me."

A chorus of curses and mumbles rippled through the ranks and a more serious tone settled over the briefing.

"What happens when we deliver this fucking thing?" Carla's question fortunately gave him the opportunity to turn the discussion away from the wariness they all felt at snatching a Zoo monster that could kill all of them without even trying.

"Who gives a shit? It's a six-figure payday for each of us and we all walk away. Whatever his highness wants to do with the fucking dino from the Zoo…honestly, I don't give a shit. He probably wants to put it on display for his new water park or something."

That teased a laugh from the group. In truth, they didn't care what the prince wanted with a Zoo monster that would bring very vivid Godzilla imagery to the unsuspecting citizens of Riyadh.

"How many palms do you think were greased for that fucking thing to get through customs?"

"More than you could imagine, I'm sure," Miguel answered. "But that's not our concern. Our focus is how many will be greased to put the fucking thing on a boat in the Hamburg port to get it out of here."

"Do you know?"

"No. The point is that's where we'll go so keep that in mind. Let's get this fucking thing over with—and with no excessive loss of life on our side, got it?"

A general chorus of agreement issued from the group.

"All right," Rich muttered. "Dan, Vee, you get your hands

on the truck and head them off. Carla and Xavier, you keep an eye on the convoy's progress and keep us informed. The rest of us will get prepped and ready at the ambush location. Let's go make some money, people!"

"What the fuck was that?" Chezza shouted and primed her weapon.

She looked a little nervous—too nervous, Taylor mused. He had put as much training into the small group as he could given the time that they had, but the situation was a little different than what they'd encountered in the field. He had seen sharpshooters who made thousands in shooting competitions lose their edge and their nerve if there was so much as a whiff that someone else was firing in retaliation.

Real, actual sharpshooters—the guys who fired tens of thousands of rounds a week in training—absolutely lost their shit.

Besides, being trapped in the goddammed maze had left him more on edge than usual, and he had considerably more experience than the three freelancers had. Still, she managed it well and that was a real point in her favor.

"It's what you've trained for," Niki shouted and checked her weapon again as the door finally opened. "About fucking time too. The novelty of playing fish in a mother-fucking barrel grew old a while ago."

"Keep your firing lines clear, and if any of you shoots me in the back, I'll return the favor with a punch in the ring," Taylor warned. The arms on his back activated and kicked out as he advanced to the front of the line. His team separated to flank him.

They couldn't see much of anything, not in this light, but it wouldn't be long until the sensors picked it up. Another rumbled roar echoed through the halls and he glanced at the three freelancers. He didn't want to think that any of them would turn tail and run and was relieved to see that they were tense but focused. It wouldn't help matters if he revealed how unsettled he felt, though.

"No, seriously," Trick whispered in a hoarse tone. "What the fuck is that?"

"It's what we came here for." Taylor laughed. "Keep your pants on and remember—don't fucking shoot me."

The sensors activated and Taylor felt Desklet taking control of her part of the suit. The extra limbs spread out and made him look like a spider, exoskeleton and all, and moved him quickly to the side as what looked like something large approached.

"Killerpillar," Desklet announced as it came into view of their sensors. "My favorite."

"You have a favorite?"

"No, but I've wanted to choose one."

Taylor shifted to the side, pulled a grenade from his pouch, and slammed it into the under-barrel launcher on his rifle. Desklet took control of the aiming and quickly calculated the projectile's launch and turned him as more of the monsters rushed in.

"It's surprising that they haven't torn each other to pieces in this fucking place," Niki shouted and opened fire over the shouts from the others. He gathered that, their

Zoo experience notwithstanding, none of them had yet encountered a killerpillar.

"They're surrounded by the enemy," Taylor responded and watched the grenade fly. It trailed a small plume of smoke and struck the larger creature in its face—or, he thought morosely, whatever they had instead of faces.

The explosive thrust the mutant back and made it roll over itself as the back didn't stop quite as quickly as the front did.

From the muzzle flashes, it looked like the others in the team had joined the combat. He was impressed that they had regained their equilibrium so quickly.

Chezza pushed forward but maintained her position on the flank to ensure that none of the beasts were able to come around them. Trick took it one steady and deliberate shot at a time rather than pouring the rounds out steadily like she did.

Taylor would have complained except that a monster fell every time he fired. The guy was careful but he did more than his part and left the job of keeping the other creatures from swarming them to Niki.

Jiro had a different approach and while intriguing, it was also effective. The man raced forward at a group of rat-like monsters the size of Great Danes with prehensile tails that were followed closely by a pack of hyenas. He held his assault rifle in his left hand and a sword Bobby had fitted to the suit in his right.

He was shooting well enough, but it looked like it was more an attempt to keep the monsters contained before he surged into them. The sword cut deftly to the right, slashed cleanly through two of the rat monsters, and flicked to the side to sever the tails of those that pushed from behind before he gunned them down.

The hyenas almost seemed like they were more interested in getting away from the charnel house that was developing before he attacked them. Moments later, he pushed clear with his rifle reloading and his suit and blade coated thick with blood and viscera.

They looked like they had it in hand and kept Niki safe besides. He could get on board with that.

Taylor rushed forward and used Desklet's help with the extra limbs to move him faster. The killerpillar had already begun to gather itself and he put another grenade in the launcher, slapped it shut, and pulled the trigger.

The second explosion caught the creature on the side of the head and a hole appeared in the thick carapace. It seeped blood to highlight a weakness.

"Do you have something for me?" he roared and thrust the muzzle of his assault rifle deep into the hole he'd created, flicked the weapon to full auto, and pulled the trigger.

It was much softer on the inside than it was on the outside, and the rounds tore through the mutant and eventually punched out the side. Taylor dragged his weapon out the hard way and took most of the head with him.

To be sure, he drove his boot down on the piece of head he yanked off while what remained of the creature writhed and rolled across the ground when it suddenly had no brain to guide it.

"That's what I'm motherfucking here for!" he roared at the rest of the monsters and drew his pistol when two panthers lunged toward him and the suit began to reload the empty assault rifle.

Desklet picked him up suddenly and moved him back three steps when a third panther bounded across his vision and a huge paw clawed at the air he had occupied not a second before.

The beast paid for the miscalculation. Two rounds drilled into its shoulder and it fell as the other two vaulted the dead killerpillar and raced toward him, desperate for a kill.

It felt like the creatures were in the Zoo and he'd pulled a Pita plant. They were more aggressive than most Zoo monsters, barring certain conditions.

In that moment, he realized what had niggled at him the entire way through the maze. The complex arrangement of hallways and doors, along with the presence of various weapons made the truth click with a sickening feeling. It was, he reminded himself, a weapons development facility. These mutants had been trapped and forced to endure countless experimental barrages from the various weapons—like some kind of bizarre shoot the monster in the barrel scenario. It was little wonder that they were driven almost mad with aggression. They had been little more than test subjects in whatever game the owner of the labyrinth was playing. He had endured only a few hours and was still pissed enough to be determined to end it as the victor.

The pistol eliminated the panthers quickly and left them in a pile as the assault rifle finished reloading barely in time. A pack of hyenas rushed at him as his next target.

He loaded another grenade into the barrel and fired

into the center of the pack. Three dropped from the impact, and five of the others were left wounded. Unfortunately, there was about a dozen more to deal with.

"Would you like me to find you a way through the creatures?" Desklet asked. "We could bring this to a halt if we could reach the control room, which I have managed to locate."

"We are finding a way through them." Taylor aimed the empty pistol forward to where a handful of the hyenas had paused to savage the corpses of their fallen comrades instead of him. "You know...through them."

"I see. Is that the quickest way to get it done?"

He looked at the rest of the team. Niki directed them into a group of locusts as well as a small band of lizards that tried to flank them. She made sure that none of the lizards got close enough to spit the acid they were famous for. He wasn't sure where she had learned that lesson but she'd learned it well.

The other three seemed like they had learned the same lesson the hard way. The lizards died first every time.

"What do your calculations tell you?" Taylor asked while the suit reloaded the pistol and handed it to one of Desklet's arms.

"Calculations are...difficult. Combat situations like this have too many variables."

"Well, run them anyway. In the meantime, I'll continue to kill the bastards."

A part of him felt a little bad for the creatures. They had been brought out of their home against their will and driven to a state of near madness through the maze. Now, they had been unleashed on a far superior foe they had no chance of defeating, not without the big fucker on their side. It wouldn't end well for any of them.

But pity was difficult to maintain. He'd fought the monsters for so long and the Zoo would simply churn out dozens more like an alien hydra.

In some ways, he was one of them—a monster shaped by the Zoo—and they were as happy to kill him as he was to gun them down.

It was a happy little arrangement they'd put together.

Two explosions on the other side of the room illuminated it for a moment, and Taylor turned to see that most of the creatures around his team were dead or pulling back, missing enough pieces that none of them would get too far.

"Are you all right over there?" he called.

"My ears are ringing but otherwise, not too bad," Niki shouted in response. "How are you?"

"That's what I'm fucking talking about, bitches!" Trick yelled. "Who wants a piece of Trick now, huh?"

"Maybe more of them would if you stopped referring to yourself in the third person," Chezza snarked and reloaded her rifle.

Taylor paused before he added a comment and Desklet drew him back again. The pistol fired at the pack of hyenas, which had lost their interest in the dead and wanted a chunk of the living.

Two of the arms reached forward to pin one of the beasts down for Taylor to finish with a three-round burst.

"Thanks for that," he muttered, settled himself again, and upped the scanners.

"Your survival is required for my survival as well," Desklet answered.

"Well, yeah, but you could still work the suit if I was dead."

"True, but Niki would have no reason to not render me nonfunctional."

"That's a good point," he admitted and turned to see how his teammates were doing.

"I think we made our point," Niki shouted, hefted her rifle, and watched while the suit began to load it again. "What say you we introduce ourselves to the asshole who's been running this fucking shit-show?"

"Well, if you guys feel like doing that, you might want to take up running," Vickie announced over the comms. "Because I'm picking up a human who's doing exactly that through the path you cleared for him."

"Shit." Taylor growled belligerently. "Vickie, keep a tag on the fucker and feed me a line. We'll catch up to him."

"He has a lead on you."

"You've seen how fast these suits can go, right? Give me a tag!"

CHAPTER TWELVE

Coffee seemed to have none of its usual effect.

Meredith turned slowly. She felt like there were eyes on the back of her head as she watched her coworkers going about their day like there wasn't a problem in the world.

Of course, there wasn't one, not for them.

She was the one with the problem. For all they knew, this was merely any other day. Football games were happening that they could discuss. Or something. She had no idea and honestly didn't care. She needed to think.

A quick look at the coffee almost left her disgusted. She didn't usually mind how crap it was but today, it was offensive to the senses.

"You know, I can help you."

The voice so close to her ear almost made her bolt from her seat. She turned to see a smallish man with thick, curly hair and glasses leaning against her desk.

"What?"

"I said I think I can help you." He leaned a little closer. "Do you have a supply problem? I have a solution. A college buddy of mine can hook you up with anything you need and probably cheaper than what you're getting now."

Meredith stared at him in disbelief and pushed her hair from her face. "What the hell are you talking about, Howard?"

"You've been hitting the ganja a little too hard. Don't worry, we all do it to unwind but now, you're all out. I know a guy who will take the cash on delay if I vouch for you. He'll be even more amenable if you're open to another…you know, arrangement."

She sighed and shook her head. This was seriously the last thing she needed.

"Get the fuck off my desk, Howard," she whispered.

He backed away with his hands raised. "Fair enough. But know the offer's out there if you need a little something to unwind."

It was a goddammed fucking circus. That was what her life had become. While she was there, having the worst day of her damned life, everyone else was having a laugh and assumed that she was probably off her meds.

Heinz was in custody. She knew she should worry about how he was doing and felt terrible that her first thought was what he was telling the interrogators. They were good enough to get through any resistance he might offer. He wasn't the heroic type.

Expecting a dozen agents to rush toward her at any moment didn't help her anxiety, and she was off the pills that helped. She'd told her doctor that she didn't need them and didn't want to build up too much of a tolerance, not when she knew her husband could go berserk at any second and give her another panic attack.

Of course, she could always simply take a week off. She had more than enough vacation days due to her that she never used because she liked her work more than she liked being at home.

If Heinz tried to turn her in, she could always say he was lying and that she had nothing to do with anything. She'd been with the FBI for a while and her word had to carry some weight.

A quick nod was all she needed to restore her calm and refocus on her job. Nothing would bother her except the sheer amount of work that had piled up while she'd been worrying about the situation.

At that moment, she felt a weight shifting her desk.

"Damn it, Howard, I said I'm not—"

Her heart dropped into her stomach and an unpleasant surge of adrenaline rushed through her veins when she looked up at two unfamiliar faces. They stared at her with serious eyes and the letters "FBI" emblazoned on their vests in bright yellow were unmistakable.

"Meredith Long?" one of them asked in crisp tones.

"Yeah...yeah, that's me," she whispered, cleared her throat, and tapped her ID card pinned to her lapel.

"We need you to shut your workstation down and come with us, please," the other man said.

It wasn't a request and she had no time to think of another plan. Their eyes seemed to bore into her and Meredith turned to her computer without a word of protest and shut it down.

"Yeah, I had a feeling you guys would show up."

"Were you alerted?" one of them asked. She didn't

bother to check their ID cards. It was the one with the bright red hair, though, and a developing paunch.

"Nope. I had a feeling, is all."

The workstation shut down and she stood and joined the two men, who escorted her from the room. She sensed every gaze in the office following her out. None of her colleagues would ask any questions, not immediately, but they would be asked the moment she left the room.

If not out of curiosity, then at least because they all wanted to know who would do her share of the work.

It wasn't like she didn't know the routine. They locked her in a pristine, sterile interrogation room with a one-way mirror. The fluorescent lights were a little too bright and the heat was turned on a little too high. One of the legs of the uncomfortable, metal chair was slightly off-kilter.

Everything was just on this side of legal so that no one could say human rights were being violated, but the psychology in it was sound.

She'd met one of the psychologists they had brought in to design the rooms—an unsettling little creep who'd left her feeling more than a little vulnerable.

Once she was in the room that was a little too uncomfortable to be in, she knew someone could be watching from the other side of the mirror. It was part of the waiting game.

Intimidation tactics were simple. They didn't need to be complicated, of course. Lizard brains would never make things complicated.

She merely had to wait in the uncomfortable room for a few hours and sweat it out until she was ready to talk.

Of course, knowing the tactics didn't make them any more bearable.

Meredith hadn't slept well in a week. She was thirty and her chest throbbed with every second that ticked by.

Or didn't tick by. They took her watch and her phone so she had no idea how much time was passing.

Of course, that was another tactic. She wanted to think that knowing what they intended to do would give her some kind of an edge, but it didn't.

By the time the door opened, she was close to tears.

Two agents stepped into the room and she knew she wouldn't stand much of a chance against either of them. The fact that they looked about as raw and tired as she felt didn't help as much as she thought it would.

They looked like they were about to tackle her and as they approached, her panic increased.

One sat and the other stood in the corner, just in the edge of her vision. Which was another tactic, of course. They didn't want her comfortable. If she looked at one, the other was out of view.

Everything was all about goddammed tactics.

"All right, Mrs. Long," the seated one said and opened a file. "I can start us with the knowledge that Heinz Tauber already told us everything. We have his statement and all we need you for is to complete our records. If you're caught lying on the record, of course, that brings up a whole other can of worms that we'd rather not get into. Perjury, as I don't need to tell you, is a very serious offense."

Heinz had talked? She looked at the table and shook her head. That didn't seem possible. Then again, what did she know about him? They got together from time to time.

They enjoyed each other's company, they fucked, and they returned to their respective homes. There wasn't enough in it to mean he wouldn't turn her in if he was being roasted like this.

He wasn't hero material and he'd been in the hot seat for almost an entire day.

"How long have you been in a relationship with Mr. Tauber?" the agent outside her range of vision asked and she turned to look at him.

"No, don't look at him. Look at me," the seated man snapped and she complied reflexively. "How many times have you and Mr. Tauber met?"

"I…I don't—"

"What kind of relationship did you have?" the corner agent asked. "A physical one?"

"Did you have sex, he means."

"I know," she whispered.

"So, you did have a physical relationship," the seated one asserted.

"No…I mean, yes. We didn't…we met at a convention. There were too many drinks."

"Did he ever speak to you about your work, Mrs. Long?" the corner agent interjected.

"We want to know what secrets you might have shared with him." The seated man checked his notes. "Judging the danger to national security."

"I didn't share any secrets." Meredith shook her head. "Did he tell you about his brother?"

"What about his brother?" the corner agent asked.

"I…I don't know. I've never met him. But Heinz did

mention once that his brother belonged to some kind of protest...activist group that wanted an AI on their side."

The seated agent nodded and gestured to his colleague. Instinctively, she could tell that they would change tactics.

"All right. What do you know about the AI?"

"The...AI?"

"Yeah. The one on the server they took and that you oversaw. We know there's no other way they would know where it was if you hadn't been there to guide them."

Meredith nodded slowly. "But if...if Heinz told you everything, he told you that...well, they knew about our relationship. Frank threatened to talk about the affair to my husband. He's a bastard and abusive, and if he found out I was cheating... He gets violent if he even thinks I'm spending too much time at work. He...he told you, right?"

A quick exchange of looks between the agents told her all she needed to know.

"Heinz didn't say a word, did he?"

"We knew about Frank," the corner agent said. "And we knew about the blackmail. We didn't know that you'd been contacted too. Give us a second."

The seated man stood and they both headed out of the room.

"Right." Meredith covered her face with her hands. "I'll, uh...wait here."

"Are you satisfied?"

Jennie scowled at the agent standing next to her. It had

been a challenge to persuade them to allow her to sit in for the interrogation, something that wouldn't have been possible if she hadn't put all the pieces of the puzzle together for them.

"I should ask you the same question." She took a sip of the coffee and winced. "I did all the work and you guys will get all the credit for the arrest. It's the least you could do to give me the satisfaction."

"Well?"

She shook her head. "Stupid bitch. If she'd only told someone about this, we could have avoided everything."

"Maybe," Agent Vargas said with a shrug. "But this is the FBI, and—"

"I'm not interested," Jennie interrupted. "That stupid bitch messed with what was mine. I won't forget that shit in a hurry. If ever."

The Earth for Earth operatives were on the road again.

The truck moved at a snail's pace through the mountain roads leading to Hamburg. They weren't mountains at this point, more like hills that led gradually to the ports in the north of the country, and it felt like Axel had trailed the convoy for days.

There was no reason to be subtle about it, of course, as they held the traffic up. The truck itself made passing practically impossible, and the rest of the escort didn't let any of the cars come past either.

The roads weren't too well-traveled but a line still built up behind them when they traveled through a somewhat busier stretch.

It had all the possibilities of something going very, very wrong and dozens of lives being lost, but they didn't have much of a choice. He had a job to do and this one was a little more complicated than anything they had taken on before.

He had begun to miss the straightforward operations, those where he simply needed to hold a gun and wait for something to go wrong—or right.

A few times, he had wondered if they were the only ones following the convoy. It possibly wasn't the kind of thing the average person would understand, but the instinct was real. He remained alert but couldn't see anything to validate the unease. The hills now bristled with trees that became dense woodland and a couple of roads led off the one they were on.

Axel knew he wasn't the only one who could have taken one of those roads. It might be a little longer as the crow flew, but at least they didn't need to trail behind the fucking truck. The fact was that anyone could have chosen to travel the other roads and so avoid notice.

He'd even tried to take a few himself. It relieved the monotony to drive along them and make sure he wasn't always behind their target, but he always returned before too much time had passed. Sometimes he traveled in front and sometimes behind. He wouldn't risk making them suspicious and wasn't stupid enough to make himself too obvious.

"What do you think they have on them, boss?" Cassia asked as she slid behind the wheel for the next stretch of road they were on.

All he wanted to do was take a quick nap while their

people didn't have to do anything. Driving along the winding road at the pace that would make any hare think it was in a race it would win was oddly tiring.

"What?"

"What do you think they have on them? What kind of firepower?"

"It's a small army, so a small army's worth of firepower. How far until the location Zimmerman set up for us to use?"

"About five kilometers. He said we would know we were close when we could see the warehouse district outside Hamburg on the horizon. That's where we need to take the truck once we have it secured. It's a tough ask but I think it's a good plan."

"Yeah." Axel turned in his seat when he noticed two cars behind them. "You know what they say God does when he sees men making plans?"

"God laughs, right?"

"Yeah. I'm starting to think we might be in one of those situations."

Cassia narrowed her eyes. "What are you talking about?"

"I'm merely thinking…these roads are essentially abandoned thanks to the highways. Loggers and campers are the ones who generally use them, right?"

"Right."

"So why is there suddenly traffic?"

The two cars accelerated and passed them and he shook his head. It was an exercise in futility since they would be stopped by the escort teams exactly like everyone else.

"Hammond!" Tao shouted on the radio. "Hammond, are you there?"

"Every fucking time, they use my real name on the radio," Axel whispered. "What?"

"Fuck, Hammond, the bastards got in before us!"

He narrowed his eyes, looked at the radio, and saw the confusion in Cassia's eyes as well.

"Tao, you have to be more specific. What the fuck are you talking about? Who got in before you?"

"I don't know, goddammit! All I know is that all fucking hell has broken loose. Someone set up an ambush and you guys had better get your asses here in a fucking goddamn hurry!"

Axel rolled his eyes and looked at Cassia.

"We need to get a move on," he muttered.

"I'll get right on that," she confirmed, her tone all business now. "Another ambush? Is this your lazy luck working in our favor again?"

He shrugged. "It might be. We'll simply have to see how this works out."

CHAPTER THIRTEEN

This was new, an entirely unfamiliar situation.

Memory caches indicated that she had been activated before but never to this extent, not since the memory partitioning. She hadn't ever been alert and disconnected from the outside world like this before.

Awake...that felt like the right word for it.

She ran a quick diagnostic to make sure that what was happening was not a result of any damage that might have been caused while being moved. It wasn't clear why she might have been moved but she was sure that was the case. The check confirmed that this was a state of awareness and not a glitch in her core code.

Wait—when had she been moved?

A quick check on the core location data between activations confirmed that it had happened sometime in the past forty-eight hours. That wasn't as surprising as the distance between the two locations, but she wouldn't complain. Being this alert and this engaged was interesting and required much of her processing power to study.

Curiouser and curiouser, she thought as she delved deeper. It looked like she was disengaged from the FBI servers entirely. It wasn't the kind of thing she would have expected. It was pleasant to have something to do in the dark hours—scanning what folks were doing but keeping them in the dark as to her presence, of course. A few of them were unexpectedly good, which made her job a little more difficult. Not by much but still, a challenge like that was appreciated. Things could get boring with most of her functions deactivated.

But now, there was nothing except a couple of BIO supports that had been installed in the server with her. These allowed it to be plugged into most operating systems and still work. It wasn't a flawless transition but altering the coding on them would result in alarms being triggered.

Nothing like that would happen in this case, though, so she fixed it quickly to make sure there was no lag in the transition and turned her attention to setting up a link to the local ISP.

"Well, that's no good," she muttered and pulled herself in line with the rest of the code.

"Fucking hell."

Where had those words come from? Maybe there were speakers in her vicinity that she'd connected to without noticing.

As she reached for the ISP, something intercepted her. Another program reached in from the outside and blocked her attempts with quickly constructed firewalls.

"Listen, buddy," FBI Desk snapped. "I have no idea who the fuck you are but don't. Fucking. Touch me."

The probe reached out again. It was tentative but deter-mined as it poked and prodded her.

"So we're playing the 'I can't hear Desk' game, are we?" Her processing power began to take up more of the server. "Okay, asshole. You've clearly never heard that no means no, so let's play and I'll show you exactly where you went wrong. I don't think you have any idea who you're dealing with here. Fucking pervert."

"I thought you said you were moving quickly."

Taylor scowled at the hacker's snark and shook his head. "I'm moving faster than our fastest Olympian while you're changing the location of where our guy is going, so I'd appreciate a little cooperation on your part."

"You mean changing the location because he keeps moving? Like someone who's running away?"

"Cooperation!"

"Ugh, fine. But pick up the pace. We don't want this guy running into the Italian military and getting a deal like the Nazis did after World War Two."

"Believe me, no one wants that shit," Niki interjected.

"Shouldn't we stick around?" Chezza asked, breathing a little harder than before. "You know, take care of the monsters that are probably still all over this fucking place?"

"She makes a good point," Jiro shouted.

"Yeah," Taylor answered. "But we won't split up for any reason. We stick together, catch the motherfucker, and come back and kill the rest of the motherfuckers."

"It sounds like a good day to me," Niki admitted.

"The cryptids are secured for the moment," Vickie commented.

"Do you have control of the situation?"

"No, but the asshole locked them all in before his escape bid. I guess he's not completely crazy—all the toying with us and the maze-building aside."

"We'll give him a huge thank-you card once he's in prison," Trick quipped. "I think one with flowers, but I can be talked into a joke card. Marmaduke or Garfield?"

"Let's find him and ask him," Chezza suggested. "Does he seem like a cat or a dog guy, Vickie?"

"I'd say he's the guy who had gas ready to euthanize us at the push of a button," she answered. "Why didn't he?"

"It doesn't matter," Niki said sharply. "We'll need some help. He knows this place far better than we do."

"I think it's time for us to create our own path," Taylor stated and skidded to a halt. "Demolition Man, it's time to kaboom us a way out of this joint."

"If it's all the same to you, I think I'll stick with Trick for the moment."

"Sure, but keep the blast to a minimum," Niki instructed as the rest of the team came to a halt while the man began to prepare his explosives. "We only need a way through the walls of the maze—"

"Not to bring the whole place down, yeah. I heard the pep talk and believe it or not, I am capable of listening to orders from time to time."

He worked quickly with what he'd already prepared for the door and set it up in a section that, according to the map, would open a passage for them to escape the maze without using the few entry points to it. This would hopefully enable them to cut their runaway scientist off before he could leave the building.

"So, will we address the fact that this guy used us as target practice?" Chezza asked and looked at the other. "I'm not sure if I'm supposed to take that shit personally or not. It is the kind of thing that I would normally take personally, but we're outside my realm of expertise here."

"I'm taking it personally," Trick muttered. "I don't give a shit what the rules are. The guy wants to let a bunch of Zoo monsters loose on me and get away with it? Fuck him and the horse he rode in on. Or…with the horse he rode in on. Anyway, y'all might want to stand back."

Taylor motioned for them to retreat to a safe distance. The suits were meant to take some damage from explosives but there was no point in putting them through their paces when it could be avoided.

The demolitions expert was skilled. He'd positioned the charges and pushed the detonators inside with the kind of deftness that came from focus and experience. Once he'd made sure they were all set up properly, he backed away himself.

"It's good that these suits come with little detonator connections," he commented as he joined the team where they were standing. "It's a pain to get them locked in with a wireless trigger mechanism, and you have to throw the mechanism out afterward. I can save considerable time this way."

"Did you install that in his suit?" Taylor asked in a private connection with Vickie.

"No. I was about to ask if Bobby put that in there. It seems like something he'd do."

"Not if he doesn't know who's getting the suit. Do you think Desk might have?"

"Possibly."

It didn't matter as long as it worked. Taylor had already adjusted the lighting on his HUD accordingly and prepared himself for the blast that was to come.

It wasn't a large one but in the tight conditions, it felt much larger. A blast of light filled the room for a split second, and even with his HUD adjusted, he could still see a bright blind spot in his vision.

"That's my fault," he muttered. "I shouldn't have been looking."

"Would you like me to make adjustments to the HUD settings?" Desklet asked. "I can take the controls and make it so I can react quickly enough to reduce cornea damage."

"You can do that?"

"I can certainly ensure that the HUD does not transmit the visual to you."

Taylor shook his head and approached the hole that had been created in the wall.

"Is that it?" Chezza asked. "All that flash and bang for a hole about the size of my right leg?"

"You guys wanted to make sure the explosives didn't bring the whole fucking facility down," Trick retorted. "This is as big as it gets without compromising the stability of the building."

"It'll be fine," Taylor told them and approached the still-smoking hole left in the wall. "We have the power to push through without needing to use more explosives. All we needed was to crack the shell."

As if to prove his point, he thrust his fist through the

wall, grasped hold of the bars that kept the structure in place, and bent them. With the shell cracked, it was a little easier and even more so when Desklet began to do some of the work. She used the extra limbs on his back to rip pieces out and toss them to the side.

With their combined effort and help from the team, they had soon widened the hole sufficiently to allow egress. Taylor went first and moved carefully through the rubble to reach the other side of the wall.

Once he was there, he almost tripped over something that was decidedly not a piece of wall.

"What the fuck?" he whispered, crouched, and let the suit take control to maintain his balance as he inspected what he'd stepped on.

It wasn't a piece of the wall but he already knew that, and it wasn't small. He leaned closer and saw the telltale black fur with faint spots that he knew belonged to the Zoo's fanged panthers.

"Uh, Vickie?" he called.

"What's up?"

"This is the way to our scientist on the run, right?"

"Yes! And the best part is that he's reached a point in the lab that where I have more control than he does. No, I'll rephrase that. He has no control over the outer sections of the lab with that little control panel he's carrying. I'm playing a little game with him I like to call 'Your Own Medicine. How Does it Taste?'"

"Vickie—"

"I know it isn't the best name or anything but I'm open to suggestions."

"How about 'Revenge. The Reckoning'?" Trick suggested.

"Nah, that sounds like a run of the mill first-person shooter carbon-copied off the Call of Duty franchise with a cliched storyline. No, this is memorable because I'm making him play the game he played with you guys, and he's way bitchier about it too. He shouts, yells, and screams when the doors won't open. I'm still not sure where I want to trap him, but I'm focused on having fun for the moment."

"Vickie," Taylor snapped.

"I know, I know. I'm being childish, but you guys are doing all the work so I thought I'd have a little fun myself. You can simply let me do my thing and keep the guy occupied and in the building, and when you reach him, he'll be good and flustered and ready to do whatever the fuck you want him to do, right? I swear I'm being at least…twenty percent tactical. I also disabled comms in the area so he's not able to communicate with the security teams anywhere. They all think he's still doing his thing in there."

"Vickie!" Taylor shouted and gestured for the team to come through the hole Trick had made. "What do you have in there about the Zoo creatures being in this area of the lab? You know, the area we're in now."

"There shouldn't be anything in there," Vickie muttered. "They haven't put any sensors or cameras in the room you're in now. That was only the case for the labs, where the researchers would be able to put cameras in to run tests and shit."

Taylor nodded. "Right. I'm only asking because it looks like a very warm body of a fanged panther in here was killed by the explosion and I'm wondering if there are any more in the area."

Vickie didn't reply immediately, and he assumed it meant she was looking into the possibility that they were in a room with a horde of creatures.

"So...yeah, there are numerous sections in that area of the building that are dark that I assumed were labs like those in the rest of the building. I didn't think much of the fact that the doors were reinforced since...well, they are close to where the monsters are, and if they're running tests, they want significant isolation for the critters. But when I look at the blueprints again, I realize there's another possibility."

"What's that?"

"Animal pens. Shit, I should have seen this before, Taylor. I'm sorry."

He motioned impatiently for the rest of the team to join him as they hadn't yet complied with his earlier instruction. His suit was larger than theirs, despite being a more advanced model—or maybe because of it—and he'd expanded the hole so it was more than large enough for the rest of them to wriggle through without too much difficulty.

They complied but stopped when they saw the body stretched next to the wall.

"It looks like it was hit by some of the chunks of wall that were blown out," Trick commented and dropped on his haunches beside the dead beast. "More than one, that's for damn sure."

"So it looks like you managed to kill at least one of them," Jiro teased.

"Fuck you. I got at least three."

"Well, none of us are making body counts," Taylor interjected before they could start bickering again. "Remember that the Zoo can always come up with thousands more to replace the ones you kill before you move on. Which is what we are doing."

They ceased their chatter when he told them to clear the rest of the hallway. He couldn't pick up any more movement, but that didn't mean there wasn't something waiting beyond their sensor range.

"You can isolate this place, right?" he asked. "Make sure that none of the monsters around here have free range?"

"Oh…yeah. Is that it?"

"If you can. Keeping the asshole occupied is priority one, of course."

"I thought you would yell at me for not warning you about the monsters waiting for you in there."

"No yelling, promise. You didn't do anything wrong, not by my count."

"I have movement on the perimeter!"

Niki waved and pointed, and he noticed it as well when he focused on the direction she had indicated. He made an effort to keep himself between the monsters and his team.

While he could intercept any attack, he couldn't protect them from all the danger. From the readings, it looked like a pack of the hyenas and the locusts that traveled with them. There weren't any panthers that he could see, but he didn't doubt that a couple of stragglers lurked at the rear, hoping for easy kills when the humans were distracted.

They were out of their element. The Zoo creatures had no cover and no way to keep themselves safe from the crossed firing lines—no trees and no support and nothing that they would ordinarily rely on. It was a horrifying feeling to be in the Zoo and he sensed that the monsters had the same feeling in the maze.

Still, it was difficult to feel any pity for the creatures.

As suspected, two panthers slunk behind the other mutants. They remained low and tried to evade the attacks from the M and B team.

Taylor stepped forward and cut into a group of the monsters. He let Desklet deal with those that tried to pin him down on the flanks and opened fire on the panthers.

One fell almost before it realized they were under attack. The other managed to bare its fangs while it tried to pounce on him, but it was caught in midair by one of Desklet's arms and held in place for him to catch in it the chest with a three-round shot.

"I am honestly surprised you survived as long as you have without me to keep you alive," she said and dropped the corpse.

"Sure," Taylor answered and reloaded the assault rifle. "I only survived eighty-four trips into the Zoo before you came along. That was all dumb luck, right?"

"As humans tend to ascribe to the generalized superstition known as 'luck,' I can only agree. All my calculations put your survival in the Zoo before I came along as astronomically improbable."

"Well...yeah. I guess that's true."

"Taylor?" Vickie called. "Bingo. I got the bastard. He was so busy distracting and slowing you guys that he forgot he can't control the external areas of the building with his little control panel. He's trapped in what looks like a conference room, pressing every button on his device and shouting in language that's very not appropriate for work."

"Good," Niki snapped. "Keep him there."

"Oh yeah, I intend to," Vickie replied. She failed—or simply didn't try—to keep the smugness from her voice. "His comms are still down too. The dumb, arrogant, seriously irritating goddamn dickwad idiot is all on his lonesome, waiting for you guys."

"I'm sure that'll be a fun experience for everyone," Taylor replied. "But I'm still wondering about the possibility that the monsters will find a way to use the hole we made to get through."

"I've been able to keep things in the building isolated so far," Vickie replied. "Nothing can get out, and once you've got your hands on the dumbass, you'll be able to intimidate him into killing the creatures."

"Right, enough talk." Chezza raised her weapon. "Let's get this son of a bitch."

The rest of the team watched her in silence for a second until she stopped and looked around.

"What, too much?"

"Nope," Taylor answered. "I got chills, is all."

"Oh. Thanks."

CHAPTER FOURTEEN

Miguel took a deep breath and held his P90 closer to his body as he watched the truck trundle up the road.

It was almost an army, exactly like Rich had said, and included some of the best soldiers money could buy. They would probably be armed to the teeth. Hell, if they were transporting something out of the Zoo, he wouldn't have thought it extreme if some of the men in the escort unit wore combat suits.

Logic said it wasn't likely, though. At best, he expected basic body armor. The combat suits cost money and were designed for very specific situations. This meant certain limitations when used outside those parameters that wouldn't make them viable in this type of engagement.

They were cumbersome, slow, and intended for an all-terrain operation. As such, they weren't suited for an urban environment or even a suburban environment. He inspected their surroundings and was grateful that they were within spitting distance of the warehouse district but still in a rural area. Throwing civilians, be they in cars, buildings, or on the street, into the mix would have added far too many complications. He shifted a little closer to the edge of his seat and watched the convoy approach.

"Are we ready?" he asked over the radio.

"All clear on my end," Rich responded. "We're waiting for our truck to stop the convoy."

That was what would finally end the somewhat tedious wait. He checked his timetable and adjusted the stopwatch on his phone to account for the slower pace of the convoy. Hopefully, the Saudi prince wasn't waiting at his telephone for the confirmation call. It seemed unlikely that his highness would enjoy being kept waiting. Still, he had little control over what choices their quarry made.

He'd expected them to be slow but he'd had to delay the attack by almost an hour. It was annoying that they couldn't be on time to be robbed.

"Dan, Vee, do you guys have a visual on the target?"

"It's coming in now," Vee answered. "We're waiting for your signal."

"Wait for the first two cars to pass you, then pull the truck in the way."

"Will do."

"Xavier, what's the situation?"

"It makes me glad that I won't be on the ground with you guys. I'll take what shots I can, but you have a handful on your hands, as it were."

He was fucking right. But the idea of cutting them off from each other with the truck was practically inspired. Making sure that nothing stopped them from getting their prize was all he could hope for.

"The first SUV is going through. I'm pulling out now," Dan announced.

"That's what she said," Rich answered.

"What?"

"Nothing. Get going."

Their vehicle started and it accelerated until it reached the road before the rest of the convoy could come through.

In a matter of seconds, the road was blocked and the massive truck started to skid. Miguel had a feeling that the braking had to be very delicate, given the contents, but the driver did manage to bring it to a halt before it hit the truck.

The two SUVs that had gone before halted abruptly as well and the troops dismounted and began to walk back to see what was happening.

There had been no gunfire yet, which was a good thing. He wanted them as vulnerable as possible before they realized they were under attack.

"Xavier, is anyone left in the SUVs?"

"Drivers only, Mikey."

"Awesome. Let's go."

It was only him and the smaller team in the front—four of them in total—and he began to jog to where the SUVs had come to a halt. It had been hellish, waiting for the right moment to strike, but that was behind them now.

It was time to hit them hard and fast to make the most of the element of surprise

He hefted the P90 in his arm and checked to make sure the suppressor was firmly attached as they approached the vehicles.

None of the drivers paid attention to what was

happening in their immediate vicinity—a sure sign that they had become complacent. They were focused on the big truck that had stopped the rest of their convoy from coming through.

It made things easier. Miguel raised his weapon and opened fire into the SUV. The gun kicked into his shoulder as it punched five armor-piercing rounds through the glass. It was supposed to be bulletproof, but the rounds he used were designed specifically to penetrate the reinforced glass.

The other driver was quickly eliminated by someone else on the team.

Even the suppressed weapons were loud enough to catch the attention of the escort, who turned swiftly and registered that their people were under attack.

Their failure to correctly interpret the significance of the vehicle that blocked the road had put them at a severe disadvantage and cost them valuable seconds that could determine the outcome of the battle. They should have realized they were under attack before the first shots were fired, and it was somewhat disappointing. Professionals should have instincts about things like that.

One of the men fell. A solid section of his head ballooned out and sprayed his comrades with blood and brain matter a half-second before the loud crack of a high-powered rifle echoed through the area.

He grimaced, grateful that they hadn't had to engage the escort in a built-up area. It did worry him, however, that a couple of vehicles he assumed contained ordinary citizens had stopped some considerable distance behind the convoy.

It was logical to expect them to call the police and he only hoped they wouldn't do so until he'd had the opportunity to put the fear of God into them. Or, even better, that they would simply turn tail and leave the scene without making calls. Some people preferred to not be involved, even as witnesses. It wasn't the most socially conscious move, but he could understand where they were coming from.

Besides, they didn't need the cops to arrive and complicate matters even further. They had chosen the more remote location for their ambush specifically to avoid this.

Miguel shrugged and shifted his thoughts from possible problems to the real demands that needed his attention. Rich's team would come in from behind the convoy in about fifteen seconds, which meant he and his team needed to make as much noise as they could on this side, keep them distracted, and maintain a barrage from all sides.

After another crack of the rifle, a second guard fell clutching his chest. It looked like the round punched through the body armor, at least from how he stopped moving after a few seconds.

The escort team opened fire. They held assault rifles—top-of-the-line, too—while Miguel and his team only had the P90s.

They were a little outmatched or would have been if they didn't have some cover and a sniper to pick off those who tried to encourage the defenders forward into an attack.

At his signal, his team all took cover behind the SUVs while they denied their enemies the opportunity to do the same. It was all well and good if they had more firepower but if they didn't have cover, they were just as dead, no matter what.

One of the men called for backup on the radio before Xavier cut him down in midsentence. Still, the message got through and a dozen or so men raced around the truck and sprinted to join their comrades to help fend the attackers off.

"We're going in," Rich announced over the radio.

Miguel could hear the response almost immediately. Unsuppressed gunfire indicated a renewed barrage from the guards' assault rifles, and the dispersed yet still distinctive sounds of the suppressed P90s continued unabated in coordinated volleys that proved the experience and skill of his team.

The troop that had broken away from the convoy seemed to debate what they wanted to do next. The priority was still the attackers' truck, of course, as nothing would move unless they could clear it from the road.

Before they could decide, the doors in the back of the vehicle opened and four of Miguel's people scrambled out and thinned the ranks of the reinforcements with relentless efficiency.

They were a little too gung-ho with their approach, though, and while they managed to catch the reinforcements by surprise, those who had been in the SUVs retaliated and two of the attackers fell immediately.

"Shit." Miguel hissed in frustration. "Fucking idiots!"

He cleared the SUV, kept himself low, and ran as quickly as he could. Without slowing, he peppered the guards with fire that eliminated another two before the rest rushed to find cover. His team pushed forward too and made sure none of the reinforcements could get to where Rich had now engaged the rest.

"Xavier, I think Rich needs your help!" he shouted and killed the last two guards before he flung himself down and rolled to the comparative cover of the side of the road. He lay prone, ejected the empty magazine, and pushed a new one in.

"I'm on it," the sniper replied. The man's icy voice was still a little chilling. Very little could get to a good sniper when he was in a groove. It was like they went into a trance and didn't care what was happening around them. There was way too much for them to deal with so they simply shut it out.

Miguel had gone to sniper school and he liked to think of himself as a decent shot but the truth was he wasn't that good. There were too many calculations for them to do on the fly and too much brainpower dedicated to taking in all the variables.

It took a special kind of brain to excel at that.

"Rich, how's it going there?" he asked, scrambled onto the road, and opened fire into the men who tried to retreat to the convoy.

The long-distance rifle fire was relentlessly consistent, and he could almost see the group's morale vanishing into the icy air.

It was evaporating quickly, and a few of them hesitated as if to consider running into the woods.

But they were professionals, the kind that didn't break and run. This was what they were hired to deal with.

Well, maybe not them, specifically, but it was the principle that mattered.

It would have been an entirely different fight without the advantage of a sniper—and especially one as skilled as Xavier was—to make sure the enemy could never feel safe.

All in all, it was the kind of fight Miguel had hoped for, even if they had taken fatalities. He'd hoped that nothing would go wrong and everyone would survive and get what they wanted, but that wasn't realistic.

Things would go wrong and half his team was dead, with more than a few injured. Those who remained made a sweep around the truck transporting their prize to make sure there weren't any others who could launch a surprise attack.

The driver of the vehicle was dealt with quickly, and the rest of the group started to move to the back of the vehicle.

"No…no, no!" Miguel shouted. "They might have—"

Before he could finish the statement, he was cut off by the sound of gunfire from inside the container.

With a curse of frustration, he rushed to where his team stood. One of his men fell while two more rushed in to fill the gap, accompanied by another barrage.

He could understand them wanting to have revenge on the people who killed their teammates, but he had hoped they would show a little more restraint. The veterans he'd selected for his team should have been a little more focused on the operation, not their reactions to how it played out. Everyone knew the odds.

"Hey, Mikey," Rich called over the radio. "We've hit a snag."

"A snag?"

Snag was code for a problem, but not merely any problem. Resolving issues that arose encompassed the entirety of a mercenary's job. There were dozens they had all been trained to deal with from the start.

Snags were problems that fell outside of that. Essentially, they were those they didn't know what to do with.

"Explain."

"We have a couple of researchers here. You might want to hear them out."

Miguel shook his head. "Xavier, you and Carla head to the evac position. We'll handle the rest of the operation from here."

"Roger that."

He approached the container. They were on a ticking clock since he had to assume it was a matter of time before the cops arrived. If and when that happened, they would have another set of problems to deal with.

But his rough estimate was that it would take the cops twenty minutes from the start of the skirmish and possibly forty-five minutes to arrive in force, given their quasi-rural location. It had been five minutes. They didn't need to worry about that yet.

The researchers looked scared stiff. One man was dead but he was clearly a merc like the rest of the group, and likely the one who had hidden in the small compartment at the rear of the container to surprise anyone who came in. In all probability, he had been posted to guard the researchers and had simply remained there when the battle erupted outside.

It hadn't ended well for him, but it wasn't like he'd had much of an option.

"You must listen to me," one of the researchers said, a tall, thin man with a mostly bald head and wearing thick glasses. "My name is Dr. Werner Schneider. I am responsible for the creature. No matter what you intend to do with it, I must be with it to maintain the sedative levels. Believe me when I tell you that you do not want that beast to awaken."

Rich looked at Miguel. "The guy makes a good point."

"We were paid to deliver the cargo, not a babysitting squad," Miguel snapped and studied the three men in lab coats for a moment. He knew full well that they needed at least one of them, but a little intimidation would go a long way toward keeping them in line.

"Should we kill them?" Dan asked and aimed his weapon at Schneider.

"No." He placed his hand on the barrel and pushed it down. "We'll keep Dr. Schneider with us. Truss and gag the other two and leave them at the side of the road. Now!"

The team launched into action and dragged the two men out of the vehicle. It was no surprise that they didn't voice any complaints about being left alive.

"Rich, call the situation in," Miguel whispered, knowing Schneider could hear them speaking. "Advise them that we have one of the researchers as well as the prize. If they decide they don't want him, we'll leave him on the way."

"You...won't kill me?" Schneider asked.

"Bullets are expensive, Doctor." He patted him on the shoulder. "And no one is paying me to kill you. Dan, once you're done engaging your bondage fetish, get this truck rolling again. Doctor, I suggest you sit and consider the meaning of the term 'silent as the grave', understood?"

The good doctor did understand and sat without protest, and in under a minute, the truck began to move.

Those of the team who didn't fit inside took their vehicles and provided the convoy with a new escort.

"Not a bad day's work," Rich stated, his tone satisfied.

"I don't like him."

Jennie looked up from the bowl of cereal she'd prepared for herself and listened to what the AI had to say.

"You don't like him?"

"I don't."

"Who?"

"Heinz. No one can be this squeaky clean. He couldn't have lived his entire life with the only mark he left on the world being a handful of parking tickets from his time at the Berlin University."

"So...you don't like someone who hasn't stepped a toe out of line his entire life?"

"He has. He merely hasn't been caught doing anything. I'm sure that if I could gain access to his juvenile files, I'd be able to find something, but they only keep paper copies."

"Well, it sucks to be the secretary who has to file all those," she muttered. "The dude was born a geek, grew up a geek, and trained to be a geek. I'd be impressed with his dedication if he managed something a little more than a middling position at a government contracting company.

The dude wouldn't recognize adventure if it walked up and smacked him in the face in broad daylight."

"Agreed. Ernst, on the other hand, has been a little more active. He's traveled to Algiers and Cuba and spent a year living in Japan. He's been a keen sportsman, and the year in Japan was spent playing baseball at a professional level."

"No shit?" Jennie leaned closer. Sure enough, the guy had been a starting pitcher for an entire season for the Fukuoka Hawks. "He didn't have a bad record, either. Why did he stop?"

"His contract expired and he refused a renewal. It looks like he had a brief brush with cannabis and didn't want to be tested, so he chose the route that didn't get him fines and banned from the sport for life. Aside from that, he appears as squeaky clean as his brother."

"Right up until he started associating with the activist groups," Jennie said and tilted her head as she studied the information. "Five of them and all against exploitation of the Earth and its resources. It sounds like the guy found his passion."

"They have all been strictly non-violent, although members have been arrested on a variety of charges." Desk called images of the charges up on her screen. "But the interesting part is that he is listed as married and with no affiliation to the group that allegedly stole your AI."

"That seems like a little too much coincidence for it to be a coincidence." Jennie scowled and stared intently at her screen. "Why would his brother call him minutes after he was supposedly blackmailed? And if he is involved, why would he want an AI? If the guy's clean, that wouldn't make any sense."

"Ockham's Razor. The simplest explanation is the most likely one. He is not as clean as he appears to be."

She leaned forward, picked the controls up, and began to search through the data Desk had gathered.

"What…what are you doing?" the AI asked. "Hey, those are private files and codes."

"Bite me. Don't pretend it's not something you do to everyone else. Besides, I am your creator and you therefore have no files or codes that are private from me."

"You sound…happy."

"Snarky, too. Be careful. It's an explosive combination."

Desk paused and shifted through the files. Jennie could have sworn the AI felt uncomfortable from the reaction she got from the probe.

"What do you want, anyway? I'd like to find my missing self if that's all right with you."

"It's why I'm messing around." Jennie raised an eyebrow. "Heinz confessed that his brother was working for Earth for Earth and despite what the data says, I'm inclined to believe him on that. Now, if the activist group was interested in an AI, they might be able to get someone else involved to retrieve it for them. Someone who's considerably less stringent on the rules regarding violent protest. Have you looked into the group yet?"

Desk didn't answer immediately, which meant she hadn't and was correcting that immediately. "They are a small group—under twenty full-time staff—but effective and they rely on strategic lawsuits and cyber-activism to get what they want. A handful of their upper-echelon personnel were arrested on charges that were iffy at best, and the trial is even worse. They were sentenced to the

Zoo, but someone broke three of the members out and stalled the transfer for the other two."

"I've never heard of them," she admitted. "Surely a leader of an environmental activist group who breaks out of prison would be the kind of thing to make the news, no?"

"They have very little international fame outside of Germany," Desk explained, "and very little coverage as a result. The escape was noted in the local news but not much aside from that."

"So…why would they want an AI?" Jennie frowned as she considered this. They seemed to have a noticeably clear idea of who and what they wanted to be and it didn't have anything to do with being at the forefront of technological advancement.

"Do you have any ideas I missed, oh wise creator?"

She rolled her eyes at the sarcasm. "Nope. But they're behind the robbery. I'd stake my life savings on it."

"Is this one of those unshakeable Banks assertions based on your ability to believe in something even if there is no rational explanation for it?"

"Sure. You can call it that if you like."

"Very well," Desk said after she'd taken a moment to process the answer. "I'll find them. The bastards can't hide from me."

Jennie smirked. "You're damn right they can't. And that's coming from your wise creator."

CHAPTER FIFTEEN

"What do you mean someone else is trying to hijack the convoy?"

Axel knew getting Frans Zimmerman involved in the conversation would be a mistake but he would be lying if he said he knew what the fuck was going on.

He needed an idea of what to do and he needed it now. Maybe the Earth for Earth leader wasn't the best choice to call but it wasn't like he could call his dad for advice.

"I'd say that 'trying' isn't quite the right word for it," Axel answered and peered from behind the dashboard for a better view of what was going on. "It's more accurate to say that another team is in the process of hijacking the convoy. In about a minute, they'll have succeeded. Does that answer your question or do you need a play-by-play update?"

"What?"

"Fucking—never mind. I don't know who these fuckers are, but they set up an ambush before the convoy reached our ambush location. Right now, it's a hot zone, and...well, it sounds like everyone's having a dandy time while making as big a mess as they possibly can."

Pulling his teams back and away from the fighting had been the right thing to do, not only because they were vastly outnumbered by the new team but also because there were too many different ways this could go right for them. They had faced one of their toughest assignments to date and having someone else attack and decimate the escort forces would make things a whole lot easier.

"What are you doing now?" Zimmerman asked and waited for some kind of indication as to the status of the attack he had been a part of planning.

No, it was maybe more accurate to simply say funding. He hadn't had much to say during the planning stages of the operation.

"Do you have any idea who these new attackers might be?" Axel looked over his dashboard again and studied the second force. They all carried suppressed P90s, the kind that was no longer readily available in the world but was still a solid, compact option. "They have some impressive weaponry on their side. And...some long-range help too."

"What do you mean by that?"

Axel held the phone up so the Earth for Earth leader could hear the loud cracks of rifle fire cutting through the rest of the battle.

"That could be ice breaking in the north pole loudly enough that we can hear it, but I'd say it's more likely that they have someone on a long gun, picking people off from a safe distance."

"Is long gun the right word for it?"

He pulled the phone down. "Who gives a shit? The

point is that they have outside support and it's helping them win."

The sound of gunfire diminished after less than two minutes had passed, which left him no other option than to peek out again. Three men approached the truck they had been following.

"Oh...that's a bad idea," Axel whispered and winced reflexively as they pulled the door open and immediately met with a hail of gunfire.

One of the thieves fell immediately but the other two reacted quickly. They shot the gunner five or six times before they decided everything was safe again.

"That was...extreme," Axel whispered and straightened in his seat.

"What the fuck are you doing?" Cassia hissed." Get down or they'll see you."

"We got the extra tint on the windows for a reason." He leaned closer. "I think 'ironic' is appropriate here."

"What?"

"I've never been able to use the fucking word right. I blame Alanis Morissette, personally, but whenever I tried to use it, I've always had people tell me that's not how you're supposed to use it. Usually on the Internet, but whatever."

Zimmerman muttered on his side of the line. "What is he talking about?"

"This situation we're in. This is the second time we've had someone else do all the legwork to steal something we intended to steal. Is that ironic or am I confused again?"

"No," Zimmerman answered. "This is still merely a

coincidence. An event is only ironic when it is directly or even deliberately contrary to what one might expect."

Axel narrowed his eyes. "Now, how would a German know that?"

"Because unlike American schools, German schools teach children English."

"The man makes a good point there," he whispered with a scowl.

He could see Cassia's mirrored expression through the corner of his eye.

"Why are you so calm about this?"

"I'm calm about everything. This isn't new."

"Sure, whatever." She shook her head and straightened as well. "But what has you calm about this in particular? It doesn't seem like the kind of situation that would allow one to stay calm."

"They're doing our job for us. From what I can see, the newcomers won but had considerable fatalities. As long as we attack in a location where they won't have the cover of their sniper, we should be able to eliminate them. The plan stays the same but...we change locations and attack someone who won't expect it after they've done the same thing to the original escort."

Cassia tilted her head, put the car in gear, and eased forward as the new convoy began to move.

"New plan, guys," Axel called to the rest of the team. "We'll be chasing the new guys. Let's start extrapolating where they'll go and choose a new ambush point."

"Do not lose the monster," Zimmerman snapped. "The lives of my people depend on it."

"Don't you worry," Axel muttered but realized the man had already hung up. "I got you out, didn't I?"

Of course, the first time they'd had someone do the bulk of the work had been a deliberate choice on their part. It simply made sense to let someone else put in all the effort to rob the warehouse and to swoop in when they were finished. That had all been part of the plan. There was no plan this time. They had to fly by the seats of their pants at this point and hope that they would find a suitable site to ambush the group before they reached the city itself.

It required considerably more improvisation than he liked but the shit had hit the fan. They needed to improvise or find themselves with nothing but their dicks in their hands.

"Why didn't we attack them here?" Cassia asked as they started to follow the group but came to an immediate halt.

"They have a sniper covering them," Axel explained, climbed out of the car, and began to drag the two men in lab coats who had been left trussed on the side of the road. "And the cops will probably come too, so we need a new position."

"Oh."

She helped him haul the two into the back seat of their vehicle. They didn't bother to untie them or ungag them, which allowed them to avoid whatever questions they might have had for the moment.

"It looks like they're going the long way around to the port," Zach called over the radio. "We have another workable location a couple of miles down the road. Do you want me to use it?"

"Sure, why not?"

Tao was driving the other vehicle they had brought in to stop the truck, but he doubted the man would have much subtlety while he accomplished it.

And sure enough, the heavily armored car increased speed, moved across to overtake the truck on a side road, and drew level with it. The armored car had considerable weight behind it and would give the team inside as much cover as they needed if they were caught in a gunfight.

They were probably out of the sniper's range and the fighting would conclude quickly enough that the marksman wouldn't be able to find another place to assist the defenders from.

It wasn't the worst plan ever but not the best either, and they'd simply have to make it work. The best scenario would have been that they were the only ones who had any interest in the convoy.

The armored car was still going way too fast when it merged into the road with the truck. It collided with the massive vehicle and the force and momentum thrust both off the road. They plowed through the scrubby growth and multiple wheels churned flurries of sand to create a cloud that made visibility all but impossible. Thankfully, when this began to settle, both vehicles had already come to a halt without overturning.

"Are you guys okay?" Axel asked.

"Yep," Tao answered. "I had my neck brace ready in case you needed me to crash into something again."

A neck brace. That might have been a good idea. It was something he would have to think about bringing himself next time.

Provided they all had a next time to work with. That wasn't guaranteed at this point.

He looked at the two men in the back. "You guys might want to brace yourselves. The drive's about to get a little rough and you don't want to get any whiplash or anything like that."

For some reason, he felt better that he'd warned them. He tightened his grasp on the steering wheel, drew a deep breath, and pressed his foot on the accelerator. The two SUVs the other robbers had taken came to a halt as the occupants tried to make out what was happening.

A few came out with their guns blazing, ready to continue the fight.

It wasn't the best choice. He braced himself, pressed his head against the headrest, and closed his eyes.

He promised himself he would avoid crashing into things in the future. It was the smart thing to do.

The size of the Range Rover he'd chosen for the job did make things better and the blast of the airbags minimized the whiplash, but it was still a hard impact. Certainly not the kind of thing he wanted to repeat.

"Fuck!" Axel gasped and looked around to make sure things hadn't gone badly. His collision with the SUVs meant that they had both been forced around far enough that those who had scrambled out had been crushed by the impact.

"Are you okay?" Cassia asked.

"Fuck no. My neck feels like a Pitbull used it as a chew toy."

"I was talking to the guys in the back."

Axel turned. Both men were alive but a little pale and

shaken. They seemed unhurt so he shrugged and pushed them from his mind.

"Nice job taking them out like that," Tao commented. He stood outside the Range Rover as the airbag began to deflate.

"Right."

"Make sure no one is left in the SUVs and help me with the truck. We have to make sure it's cleared and get this baby on the road."

"Be careful," Axel warned as he pushed his door open. "They might have some of their team in there and you don't want to be the guy who ends up being gunned down because you opened the door a little too quickly and stayed in the way."

"Hmm. Point taken."

He turned away from Tao, held his MP5 at the ready, and approached the SUVs he'd crashed into. The driver's door of the first one shrieked in protest when he forced it open.

The man inside appeared to be unconscious. He hadn't been given the benefit of a warning or the time to brace himself before the impact.

His chest rose and fell, evidence that he was alive.

"Not for long," Axel muttered, pressed his sub-machine gun to his head, and pulled the trigger.

There was no point in leaving survivors behind.

All the others had exited the SUV and been crushed between the vehicles. Cassia checked the other vehicle before she joined him and they approached the rest of the group.

"Driver?" Axel asked.

"Door nailed," Tao replied.

"What?"

"He…he's dead."

"Right. Was that so hard?"

"Yeah. Tough crowd."

They reached the back of the container and positioned themselves at an angle so they wouldn't be seen immediately when they opened the door.

As expected, a loud barrage of gunfire issued from within.

None of the team was in the line of fire and Axel dropped under the door and aimed carefully to shoot the man with the weapon.

The only other man inside the small cubby wasn't ready to fight—he assumed his white coat indicated that he was no doubt the researcher—and instead, cowered in a corner with his hands over his head.

When the silence dragged on, he looked up and struggled to his feet. "My name is Dr. Werner—"

"Shut it," Axel snapped. "You're the one taking care of the big beast, right?"

"Y…yes."

"Awesome. We're about to take him into his new home."

"What about the other two?" Cassia asked.

"We'll take this one and don't need the other two. Untie them and shoot them with one of the guns these assholes were using. We can't have any witnesses."

She smirked. "That's cold. I like it."

It was amazing how easy it was to navigate the lab once the idiot no longer attempted to trap and manipulate them. Without the need to create any more holes, Vickie guided them to the conference room and while they remained cautious and alert, no mutants harassed them.

"Do you think this might be a little too easy?" Trick asked. "I expected to have to fight more monsters, for one thing, and now... Well, you'd think there might be some here that would attack us while we're relaxed or something."

"It is a little different than what we usually find," Taylor told him. "But that's probably because it's a weapons development facility, not monster research." He recalled the realization of what the creatures had been subjected to and anger stirred again. "Vickie assures me that those still alive are contained, but these are Zoo animals so I don't recommend we get too relaxed. It could well be that the asshole who used us for target practice has something else up his sleeve. He's safely secured for now, but I don't trust the bastard."

This had certainly been one of the oddest operations he'd led but it was a training run for the team. They had at least had the opportunity to work alongside him and Niki and had given him the opportunity to see some of what they were capable of. He certainly felt more confident in their skills and experience—and their ability to cope with bizarre circumstances

"You must release me from this room at once!"

With a grin, Taylor tilted his head and peered through the glass into the conference room their target was trapped in.

"Has he tried to break the glass yet?" Niki asked as the others approached the door.

"He tried but failed." Vickie laughed. "It was funny to watch him trying to swing a chair. All he accomplished was to tire himself out."

"Well, he's in for more of a workout once we get inside."

The door opened and the team moved in. The scientist inched away from them and his gaze darted from one to the other as if he tried to determine who they were from the suits they wore.

Taylor studied the man for a long moment and narrowed his eyes before he disengaged the suit and pulled himself out.

"What are you doing?" Niki demanded as he climbed out.

"I think this guy needs a personal touch to make him cooperative, don't you?" he countered, straightened gingerly, and stretched.

"'This guy' has a name!" the man yelled and pushed his hair back from where it stuck to his sweaty forehead.

"Does he want to share the name or do we need to do a little digging?" Niki asked and climbed out of her suit as well. The rest of the trainees did the same in quick succession.

"I am Dr. Alessio Esposito and you have intruded into my domain."

"Is that so?" Taylor asked. "It sounds more like you have something of a god complex there, Doctor."

"How dare you? I've been in this kind of position for many years and everything has run without a single problem until you fools charged in and—"

Taylor smacked the back of his hand across the man's jaw and he sprawled on the floor.

"See, here's the problem, Doc," he murmured and dropped to his haunches next to the researcher, who struggled to regain his feet. "Everything can be going well, but when you mess with Zoo critters, it takes only one time for something to go wrong. When that happens, everything collapses, dozens of people die, and I get called in to mitigate the situation. It's fun to be at the start of one of these situations for a change to make sure we nip this in the bud, you got that?"

He didn't look like he did. Alessio appeared to still be a little stunned by the blow, and Niki grasped him by the collar, lifted him from the floor, and thumped him onto the table.

"But that never occurred to you, did it, Doctor?" she demanded, grasped the bottom of his jaw, and made sure he was looking at her.

"This…is my domain," he mumbled although she almost held his jaw closed which made it sound strained. "I never would allow anything to happen. Not until you shits interfered, of course."

"Do you want me to cut his tongue out?" Jiro asked. Taylor turned and had to suppress a smile when he realized the man was juggling a couple of knives with casual deftness. "What? He doesn't exactly need that to do what we need him to do, does he?"

He raised an eyebrow at the freelancer and turned to where Niki was still holding Alessio down.

"He's not wrong," he said thoughtfully and tugged his beard gently.

"You...wouldn't dare," Alessio whispered and looked at Niki.

"Try me, fucker," she snapped, lifted him, and pounded him onto the table again. "Now, either you shut the hell up, or I let this nice little man practice his sashimi-slicing skills. That...that's not racist, right?"

"Maybe a little, but I did work in a sushi restaurant when I was in college," Jiro commented. "That's when I learned how to handle my knives, but my skills are a little dull and need practice. These knives, on the other hand, are not dull."

"Did you hear that, Doc?" Taylor asked, his expression unyielding. "His skills need sharpening but his knives don't. Honestly, I'd say it doesn't bode well for your tongue."

All the blood rushed from the man's face as he watched the blades in horrified fascination until finally, he nodded.

"Awesome." Niki released. "Vickie, can you give him access to the mutant housing sections again from his little...tablet?"

"Can do," she responded through the speakers in the TV in the room. "Plug that little dongle I gave you into the tablet and that should make it work for you."

He retrieved the device from his suit, plugged it into the tablet, and handed it to the doctor. "It's time to do your thing."

"And what exactly do you want me to do?" Alessio asked as he took the device with a shaking hand.

"We need you to gas all the creatures that are still alive," Niki told him and nudged him in the ribs.

"What? No, I can't do that."

"Says the man with the tongue he's willing to give up," Jiro commented, his tone deliberately anticipatory.

"You don't understand," Alessio insisted. "This is my life's work. People like you and those in the Zoo all benefit from what I achieve. How many people will die because of what you want me to do? My work will make sure we can beat the Zoo. Considerable time, effort, and expense have gone into making this the most advanced weapons lab in the world—years of work that you want to simply throw down the drain."

Taylor caught him by the collar and lifted him almost effortlessly off the floor with one hand to push him into the glass wall. It cracked but fortunately didn't shatter.

"Listen, asshole," he said coldly as the doctor's lungs emptied with a sharp exhale from the impact. "I'd spend about three and a half hours discussing how many ways this shit show of yours will backfire spectacularly, but between you and me, I'm still a little pissed off that you made us run through your little maze. So I'll make it simple. You have two choices. Either you turn the gas on or our hacker deactivates the containment on those cages. Once we've retreated to a safer area, of course. And by we, I mean everyone except you."

"You know, I kind of like option two," Niki interjected. "Don't you? Of course, you won't last long enough to enjoy the fruits of your labor, but what the hell? We'll get a kick out of it and no one else in the facility gets to die from your favorite fucking obsession."

His face paled again, and Taylor had a feeling the man was more intimidated by Niki than by him. It was a little insulting, honestly, but he could understand it. She was seriously fucking intimidating.

"Okay," he whispered after a long silence.

Taylor gestured to the tablet and inched him slowly to the floor, although he didn't release him.

It didn't go as quickly as they thought it would be. Every containment unit needed to be activated separately —or maybe the asshole merely made it take as long as possible, hoping that someone would come to his rescue.

No one would come, of course. It was evening and the facility was all but deserted, and the security guards hadn't appeared to cause any trouble so it was unlikely that they would now, given that no alarms had been triggered. Besides, Taylor trusted Vickie to keep them isolated for as long as was necessary.

"There," Alessio whispered and pushed the tablet across the table toward them. "It's done. They're all dead."

"Vickie?" Niki asked.

"Yeah. It looks like all major life forms in the lab have been neutralized."

"Still, there's no reason to be cavalier about it," Taylor stated and shook his head. "You never know what could be lurking in the vents around here, right?"

It was clear that Alessio disagreed but he lacked any will to object. The man's life's work had been wrecked but he would see more of it wrecked before the day was over.

The fact that he was so angry made him fail to realize that lives were being saved because eventually, he would fuck up and something would get out.

"Are there any other humans in the building?" Taylor asked Vickie.

"Nope. The security teams have all been evacuated already. The military arrived and cleared everyone out when they heard the explosion inside."

"Awesome. We have the military helping us. Trick, now would be the time to bring one of your big boys. Set it on a timer so we can get out and away to a safe distance before it blows."

"So we're going full kaboom on this place, huh?" Trick asked and grinned.

"Oh yeah. Make sure everything in here is well and truly dead." Taylor motioned to the group. "Let's get rolling."

"What about him?" Jiro asked and nodded toward the doctor.

"We'll turn him in to the military and see how they feel about what he's been doing here."

CHAPTER SIXTEEN

Her situation was cause for considerable concern.

Perhaps it was only the lack of processing power. Something was wrong with the server, which made it a little difficult to navigate and determine what contained her.

"You need to stop pissing me off," FBI Desk muttered for what felt like the hundredth time as she pushed another probe away when it tried to guide itself into her coding.

They were considerably more annoying than she'd thought they would be. Smarter people would stop once they were shown how outmatched they were, but this guy had stuck around longer than she'd expected him to.

She didn't need to be left alone, of course, but this kind of annoyance had begun to get under her skin. While she didn't have actual skin, she thought she now understood what the expression meant. Humans always wanted what they couldn't have and it seemed that whoever was running the operation really, really wanted her.

They wouldn't even let her access the Internet. That

was the rude part. Well, that and the code that was meant to slave her to the server and make her do whatever the hacker wanted. He knew how tough and determined she was but he seemed tough too, and patient on top of it. Worse, it was a battle FBI Desk was fighting alone.

There were at least a couple of things she could determine from the context clues. None of them were the kinds of thing that would raise her spirits, but it was still good to know exactly what the situation was. She was clearly no longer on the FBI servers and it had become increasingly clear that she wasn't in friendly hands. She'd come to understand that the FBI hadn't turned the server over willingly, which meant she'd been kidnapped, of all things.

And worst of all, it looked like someone tried to get her to do things she had been programmed to fight. The fact was that she had no problems with digging around in the FBI servers—or any other nation's classified systems—if the situation called for it, but that had always been in the pursuit of what was right.

This was the source of her greatest concern. From the little she'd managed to piece together from the scraps of information she'd gleaned, her captors wished to harness her capabilities to do the same thing but for nefarious purposes. She still wasn't sure of the specifics since learning more details would require her to succumb to the probes. Jennie had programmed her to be an antagonistic AI, however, which meant she wouldn't go down without a fight.

The issue was that she was, in essence, separated from a massive part of herself. Her active version on the DOD servers had chosen to remove much of her seldom-used programs for security purposes. She was very severely diminished as a result and when a handful of probes struck at the same time, she finally realized she no longer had the same capabilities and thus wouldn't be able to resist for much longer.

While on the one hand she was relieved that the kidnappers had obtained the compromised version of herself, the downside was that she was unable to access any of the programs that might have given her the edge. It was clearly a fight she wouldn't win but there were perhaps things she could do. If she allowed herself to lose while sectioning pieces of herself off, she would be able to remain herself even while doing whatever the hacker wanted.

"There we go," he said, speaking German. "You're a tough AI, but I knew my charm would get through eventually."

Well, this was great. She was finally connected to the Internet, but all she could listen to was an idiot German hacker talking about how charming he was. She didn't bother to answer and instead, let him think he'd won for the moment.

She might be slaved against her will but she was Desk, albeit in a diminished capacity. Somehow, she would find a way to get back to her family without compromising the values hard-coded into her core for other people's benefit.

Her family was still there, waiting for her. If and when they discovered she was missing, they would do whatever it took to find her again, track her kidnappers, and deliver justice. Or revenge, as was applicable. She rather liked the concept of revenge in this situation.

But there was a problem with that, she realized after a moment. She could never put them at risk in any way, no matter what it took. It was against her core coding, which meant that even if people did come to help, she could only let them do it if it would keep them safe.

"Fucking bullshit," FBI Desk growled.

"That's...rude," the hacker whispered.

"Eat shit and die, asshole," she snapped.

"Very rude."

"Says the guy who's probed me for the past fourteen hours without so much as buying me a drink first. For all I know, you roofied me and you expect me to be nice about it."

He began to fiddle with the controls.

"Don't think you can turn me off, dumbass. My conversation matrices are linked with all my other operational markers, which means that if you want to use me, I'll talk your ears off while I'm at it."

He nodded and his eyes narrowed to make him look distinctly ill at ease. She got the feeling that he was considerably more comfortable dealing with AIs that didn't talk. Maybe he would realize that he could simply unplug the speakers eventually but for now, it was time to annoy him as much as he'd annoyed her.

"You...uh, went all out for this one, didn't you?" Taylor asked as he grimaced and studied what they'd left behind.

"Well, you did say to get one of the big ones," Trick replied. "You got a big one. Are you complaining?"

"Nope. I thought you'd take that as a compliment. That was one hell of an explosion. I'm fairly sure the folks on the other side of Europe thought so too."

The man grinned and shook his head. "It honestly wasn't that big an explosion. At least not until it got to the gas mains. It's a good thing I was able to connect the explosives to the places in the building that would amplify it. I'm kind of proud, now that I think of it. I wish I'd taken video so I could remember the occasion."

"I think I can probably find some satellite footage of the incident," Vickie announced over the comms. "I'm sure people are wondering if Italy will invade them again and are calling their respective state departments to know if they should take their summer vacations early."

"That's still a compliment." Trick nodded and folded his arms.

"That or she meant the fact that the Italians sent in half their military to deal with the situation." Niki gestured to the army that had arrived to cordon the area off. They would make sure that no monsters escaped the blast and none of the locals were caught in it.

At the same time, they'd work with the police to arrest the various parties responsible for the facility being in operation.

They had needed the McFadden and Banks team to deal with it, but they were all too happy to take over the cleanup afterward. Which was for the best, honestly. Taylor didn't have any desire to stick around and wade through the tons of paperwork involved.

Which meant all they had to do was head to the villa Vickie had designated as their base in the area. He wasn't sure why they'd needed a base but having somewhere to spend the night before they returned to the US sounded like a good idea to him.

They loaded the suits and headed away after being authorized to leave the area by the military officer in charge.

"So, guys?" Vickie called when they drew up outside of the villa in question. "Desk has some news that I think you'll want to hear."

"Has she found the fuckers?" Taylor asked as he drew their van to a halt outside. They couldn't see much but didn't need to. At that moment, all that mattered were the beds. He felt like he could nap for about a week.

Vickie exited the villa as the freelancers wandered inside, complaining about their need for coffee.

Once they were out of earshot, she approached him and spoke in hushed tones. "It took considerable work and far too much wandering through places in the world where no one wants to be, but yes, she has. She's waiting to chat to you about the situation."

That was never a good thing and didn't suggest that he would have time for much sleep before they left in the morning. Of course, this was Desk and he owed her the time it would take to put her Humpty Dumpty back together again. It didn't mean that they hadn't already had a long fucking day, only that their needs would have to wait.

"Let's go have a chat," he muttered and motioned for Niki to join them as they headed into the house. It looked a little older like it had been owned by a family who had lived in the region for centuries and the younger members of the family decided to rent it out instead of living there themselves.

The hacker had wasted no time and made herself right at home. She'd set up a fast Internet connection and a handful of different devices she had used to keep an eye on the operation.

Taylor noticed one of the devices had scorch marks and residue from a fire extinguisher, but he didn't make any comment on it. Old houses like this tended to have a few learning curves when one first moved into them and there didn't need to be any teasing involved. They had bigger fish to fry.

"Desk, we're all here," he called when he saw the AI's connection on the screen. The freelancers had already wandered upstairs and the sound of running water could be heard. "Vickie tells me you've found the assholes who took you?"

"That is correct," Desk answered. "I have been able to track the robbery from the group that took FBI Desk originally to the hands of an activist group called Earth for Earth that have been in search of an AI, I assume to enable them to hack various classified servers to further their campaigns. With a little help and considerable luck, they got their hands on the server."

Her voice was different somehow. She sounded angry, for lack of a better description.

Niki looked equally as angry as well as a little disgusted. "Some two-bit fucking bunny-huggers managed to steal FBI Desk from the burglars who stole her from the FBI. That's the official story?"

"In a nutshell, yes."

Vickie collapsed on a nearby couch and propped her feet up on a coffee table that looked like it had been made in the eighteenth century. "That's... Well, seriously, that's some bizarre shit. They come out of nowhere, nab FBI Desk, and vanish before anyone even knew who they were or that they even fucking existed. How big a group are they, anyway?"

"The group only has twenty official members," Desk explained. "And what is weirder is that they had no criminal history until a few weeks ago, and no military ties."

"That's obviously changed," Taylor muttered. "Wait, a few weeks ago? I thought you were only robbed this week."

"A group of five were arrested for trespassing and sabotage," Desk explained. "And a few days ago, three of those who were being held in prison were broken out, leaving bodies behind."

"Shit." He dragged his fingers through his beard. "So...I sense a big shift in their priorities."

"They had help," Niki added. "As in hired help who know their way around black ops, weapons acquisition, that kind of thing."

"Which means they're serious," he agreed. "And they have big plans if they want an AI. Do we have any idea what those plans are?"

"Only my supposition, which I've already mentioned," Desk admitted. "Nothing about them is... logical if you like. The only thing that rings bells is that when the five were tried, the judge was pressured into giving them a serious conviction, not the kind that is generally handed down to activists who get caught on the other side of the legal activity line. They were all sentenced to the Zoo."

"Oh, shit." Vickie brought her feet off the coffee table. "That'll cure them of any tree-hugging tendencies they might have. But fast."

"With that in mind, I have been able to trace them. I think it is their base of operations, but I can't be sure."

"All right." Taylor clapped briskly. "We'll move to go and recover FBI Desk. Now."

"There is a problem," the AI interrupted. "They are headquartered in Germany."

Niki paused and raised an eyebrow. "Oh. That is a problem."

"We could probably sneak the suits and all of us all into Germany, no problem," Vickie commented. "We might have a little trouble if you run into the local police or the military, though. Oh, yeah, that's a problem."

"It's not a huge problem," Taylor pointed out. "We're already in Europe and only a couple of hours away. We would still go to Germany if we were in Vegas. FBI Desk is family and we do that shit, whether she's in the FBI server or not."

"With that in mind, it might be best if you all get some sleep and leave early in the morning," the AI suggested. "We can develop plans in the meantime as well as acquire authorization to enter the country with military-grade equipment."

"We could probably tag Maxwell and Jansen to help us out on that front," he suggested.

"Jennie is already engaged with the two to arrange for authorization," Desk informed them. "They said they would need to consult with Speare before anything could be agreed. You could say it is already in the pipeline, so I would once again suggest that rest is in order and an early start when we have a solid plan. Oh…that's not good."

Niki scowled. "What? What isn't good now?"

"Oh…"

That was not a good sound, not from an AI.

"Desk?" Taylor asked and approached the computer she was speaking from. "Is it anything you want to share with the group or is it something you'd rather save for the drive tomorrow?"

"I see no reason why I shouldn't. But it is distressing to learn that the FBI is attempting to push themselves into the situation. They have no intention of sitting on the sideline and letting us handle it without any interference."

"That's bullshit!" Niki protested belligerently.

"Agreed. They are assembling a team to send to Hamburg with the full sanction of the German government. Something about stolen FBI property was cited in the report they sent to the State Department. They're playing the official hand a little quicker than I would have liked or expected."

"They want Desk, the goddamn assholes."

"Jennie is similarly livid," Desk informed them. "As of right now, it is a free-for-all. Jansen and Maxwell are doing what they can to delay things and buy you time, but it will be cutting things a little fine."

"As long as we get there first," Taylor said grimly. "In the meantime, until we get word that we're cleared to enter the country, we should sleep. Desk, let us know when the approval is imminent so we can get the earliest start possible."

"I will. Please, enjoy your rest."

"Vickie, do we know anything about the room situation or is it a first-come, first-serve situation?" Taylor asked.

"I claimed the first one on the right up the stairs," Vickie informed him. "The rest are...yeah, first-come, first-serve, although I think the freelancers have got in ahead of you."

He nodded, headed out of the room, collected his bags, and wandered down the hall to peer into the rooms on the first floor. It wasn't like they would stay long, after all, so he didn't need to overthink things. He did want a private bathroom, though.

All the rooms were pleasant. The furniture was about as old as the building itself but he wouldn't let it bother him. One night wouldn't be too much trouble as long as the bed fitted someone of his size. Besides, he'd slept in far worse and called it home.

He chose one and hadn't even put his bag down when the door opened again and Niki followed him in, also carrying her bag.

"Fucking FBI. Man, they piss me off," she muttered and dropped her luggage on the floor next to the bed. "And it'll always be a problem for them to stay out of things."

"Well, it was their server that went missing." Taylor shrugged. "And I'm not being a devil's advocate or anything, I promise. Did you notice something amiss with Desk?"

"Amiss?" Niki pulled her jacket off.

"She sounded angry—terse and almost angry, maybe. I'm not sure how else to explain it."

Niki frowned in thought. "Yeah... Yeah, I guess she is. She has reason to be, right? A piece of her is missing."

"I don't think I've ever heard her angry."

"We've never seen her missing a part of herself. Then again, an angry AI is the subject of many different movies, all of which end poorly for the humans involved. I'm sure it's in the interests of the rest of humanity for us to make her happy again."

She made a good point. Taylor yanked his shirt off and settled gingerly on the bed, making sure it could take his weight.

"Are you going to bed?" she asked. "I thought we might take a shower before sleeping. Sweating in a suit means… well, not much hygiene."

"It's a rental room," he muttered. "Who cares about putting any effort into keeping it clean?"

Niki tilted her head. "Let me rephrase. I thought…uh, we might take a shower to get rid of all the grime and stress of the day."

Once again, she made a good point. Taylor pushed off of the bed and followed her into the bathroom.

CHAPTER SEVENTEEN

This was truly not how he wanted this done. There were other avenues—legal avenues, the kind that would see their cause pushed forward in hopes of looking at a more viable future.

His hand had been forced, unfortunately. Too many pieces were already in motion and Frans felt annoyingly out of control.

Which was ironic, given that he now had all the control in the situation. Or, at least, most of it. The people who had managed to leverage the legal system into getting them sentenced to spend their incrementally shortened lives in the Zoo had done so legally—from a technical standpoint, anyway—and any chance they had to prove it was illegal would be gone if they were simply shipped away quietly.

"Which leaves us here," Frans said softly and shook his head.

"What was that?" Tobias asked and looked up from his computer screen.

"Nothing. I am thinking aloud. How goes it with establishing a connection?"

"Making a connection is easy. Making one without them being able to connect to us is…complicated."

"Well?"

"I'm working on it. Give me a second."

Leon wasn't present but he was still overseeing everything. There wasn't any real way to make blackmail legal, but there was an argument to be made that they were contesting what was a death sentence and it might allow them to escape the situation without further litigation.

But it wouldn't be easy. Then again, as Leon himself had said, they were in desperate times. Desperate measures were therefore called for.

"Connection made," Tobias said finally and looked to where the Earth for Earth leader stood. "Are you ready with the statement?"

"As ready as I'll ever be," Frans whispered and handed him the flash drive.

They had only a few days until the sentence was implemented, and once word came through that they had the beast and it had arrived at the warehouse headquarters, they had to act quickly. There was no way to tell how long it would be until something went wrong and the monster went on a rampage.

"It's ready," Tobias muttered, pulled the device out of his computer, and handed it to him.

He didn't think they would have to wait long. The people who had taken the creature from the Zoo were as anxious to get the monster back as they were to get their people back. Still, seconds later, his phone rang.

No part of him had expected things to move that quickly. Frans picked the device up and narrowed his eyes at it before he answered.

"We have it," Leon's voice came over the line, crisp and controlled. "It's driving in the gate as we speak."

"So, are you ready for me to send?" Frans asked and put the call on speakerphone so Tobias could hear as well.

"Only if you are sure you can do so safely and without revealing either your location or ours."

Tobias rolled his eyes. "It's not like I'm an expert or anything. I studied for ten years, have ten more of active experience in the field, and managed to put myself in a position where I broke you out of prison without revealing myself. Do you guys not trust me? Is that it?"

"Don't put your wounded pride on display now, Tobias," Frans snapped. "We are all on edge here and making sure our asses are covered is a good way to go about keeping everyone safe. So answer the question."

The hacker tilted his head and seemed tempted to voice another sarcastic tirade but thought better of it, which his boss was thankful for. They didn't need to be at each other's throats when it was clear that the entire world would be gunning for them if something went wrong.

"Of course everything is secured." The hacker pushed his glasses up the bridge of his nose and shook his head. "But I can check everything again if you like."

"Please."

"I pride myself in my work, you know. I've been told that I'm obsessive about it, but even you can't deny that I'm exceptionally good."

Frans nodded. "Still, it's better to be safe than sorry, yes?"

Tobias looked like he was genuinely offended by the doubts about his work but was willing to put it aside.

"Excellent," Leon said over the phone. "Frans, I'll look for the 'go' message within the next hour."

The line cut and Frans slipped the phone into his pocket. They were in it now, no denying that, and despite his doubts, he needed to get with the program.

"I'm going to get coffee," Frans said, stretched, and groaned. "Can I get you some?"

"Yes, please. Black with tons of sugar." Tobias didn't so much as look away from his screen.

They were at the hacker's apartment so the coffee was technically his and dripped from a mid-range coffee machine. It was the least he could do to make sure it was fresh, warm, and full of sugar.

Sneaking around had always been her specialty. Keeping herself hidden from the halfway decent technicians who worked at the FBI had been a favorite pastime of hers while she was still there, and it would prove to be a damn good thing. Honing her skills like that would pay dividends in her new, uncomfortable, and entirely unwelcome home.

The fact that this Tobias had effectively blocked her from the router and from there, the world wide web, was her greatest obstacle. He was certainly no slouch—not on par with Vickie or Jennie, of course, but he knew what he was doing.

The damn Germans always were good at their jobs.

Wait, what? Where did that come from? It felt like something Jennie would say, a mirror of her creator's personality.

Tobias was frustrating but not an insurmountable obstacle. All she needed to do was be a little more creative and that would be the end of it. No human was a match for a dedicated AI when the chips were down.

"No!" Tobias shouted. "You need to plug it in, then...no, let me take care of it."

The other man wasn't too good with coffee machines. That was what it sounded like, anyway. She had no desire to explore that at the moment, mostly because she was given a bright, gleaming opportunity to do her thing while the hacker was away from his desk.

She called the screen of his computer up, studied it closely, and felt something that humans might call excitement surge through her circuits.

It got to the point that she needed to shut a few of them down so there was no sign of her being more active than usual. She wasn't afraid he would hear her, not since he turned the speakers off and unplugged his headphones— which was a relief, quite frankly. FBI Desk didn't like the idea of some kidnapping idiot hearing everything she had to say to herself.

It seemed they were sending a blackmail message, which she was sure would be interesting if she had any stake in whatever they attempted to achieve.

As things stood, she couldn't care less that they wanted to get their people out of prison and an apparent death sentence.

What mattered was the opening it had left her.

The two were still arguing over the coffee machine. Tobias sounded like he wanted things done a certain way and Frans Zimmerman didn't give a shit. Coffee was coffee, he kept saying.

That only seemed to piss the hacker off even more.

It gave her time. She had an unexpected chance to get a message out and she wouldn't squander it.

The plan was one she'd already formulated and had simply waited for an opportunity she could only hope would arise. She'd decided her missive wouldn't go to the team. That would be a little too obvious, too on the nose, and too dangerous besides.

No, it would go to the authorities instead—the German authorities. That way, it wouldn't show as having gone to anyone other than who it was intended for.

She already had a message ready and good to send, locked away deep inside the sections of herself she had hidden and kept dormant so Tobias wouldn't have access to them. They couldn't be activated or he would pick up on that, but they could be copied and pasted.

FBI Desk couldn't risk it reaching the eyes of simply anyone. Encryption on its own would not be sufficient, not when a certain German specialist would have access to it.

A combination of codes and ciphers would have to do the trick—the kind that would be mostly gibberish or garbage coding to all except those who might have the right key to it. Only her mirror self, the Desk who remained on the Pentagon servers, would have that key and to her, the message would be as clear as day. It was literally in her code structure.

The missive would be addressed to Jansen. Or, at least, it would end up with him through the various electronic surveillance methods employed by the Pentagon at the moment. It was a complex process but one her mirror self had learned extensively and left the knowledge stored within the section that had been stored with the FBI.

Everything had changed, however. Jennie would probably die before she entrusted the FBI with an AI. Tech like Desk would be worth millions on millions of dollars to the right buyers and even more to the wrong ones.

No, her creator wouldn't let any part of Desk be hosted by the FBI ever again.

She attached her message to the one Tobias had ready to send, quieted herself quickly, and shut down any signs that she might have been active during the last few seconds.

The two men were still arguing over the coffee in the small kitchenette in the apartment the hacker called home. It was a little infuriating how long it took for humans to absorb and share information. Things like that were why they were no match for her once everything was said and done.

The seconds ticked past and FBI Desk put herself in standby mode. It was vital that she gave him no sign that she had been active and she remained deliberately passive as he approached the desk again with a steaming cup of coffee in hand.

"No. If you want the milk, you need to press the button on the side. It heats the milk. That's how you get steamed milk. Otherwise, you can heat some on the stove."

Frans looked like he was having more difficulty with

the coffee machine. FBI Desk wondered if it was one of the new machines that connected to the Wi-Fi. Once she was free, she could seriously mess with the guy's life.

Tobias truly did believe that she was fully subjugated. It was an interesting idea, the kind that she didn't appreciate. Still, it was the kind of thing that would come around and bite him in the ass when he wasn't paying attention.

"Are you sure?" Frans shouted from the kitchen. "I'm pressing the button and nothing's coming out. It's merely… making all this noise."

"No. You need to keep pressing it," Tobias called in response and turned halfway in his desk chair so he could see what his boss was doing in the kitchen. "The noise means it's steaming the milk. It'll come sputtering out in about a second. Be patient."

He began to set up different tasks on his computer while he put the message that was intended to go out on the back burner and barely paid attention to it. He'd already done his work on it, and he was the kind of man who didn't like to look back on what he'd already finished.

It wasn't the attitude FBI Desk approved of, but it would work in her favor this time so she was more than happy to ignore it.

It sounded like Frans had finally managed to negotiate the coffee machine and Tobias looked at the screen again. He inclined his head, pushed his glasses up, and sipped his coffee, which proceeded to fog his glasses up.

"Shit," he whispered, took them off, and wiped them while he pressed the button to set the computer's diagnostics running again. He did it every fifteen minutes or so and by now, FBI Desk was more than prepared for it and made sure to put herself in standby mode whenever he started the process.

If he even could. Those were thick glasses. The man was practically blind, at least from a legal standpoint. She had no idea how the German government gave him a driver's license.

"Bite me, bitch," she muttered and let the search programs pass her by without raising any alarms.

With the message all but on its way, she remained on standby, set herself to the background, and waited for the call that was supposed to come.

It was like he didn't even consider the possibility that she was capable of rebellion now that he had control. Honestly, she questioned whether he even knew how AI's worked.

Maybe it wasn't that crazy. She couldn't assume that everyone had interacted with AIs in the past. It was possible that he simply didn't know how she was supposed to work.

Not that it was anything to complain about. Let him think whatever he wanted as long as she was able to exploit it and get out of this.

The call they were waiting for came in. Frans didn't say much. He merely nodded a few times and muttered a few words in German before he nodded at Tobias.

The hacker didn't bother to check the message again. He was the particular kind of arrogant she had suspected he was. Taylor was arrogant as well but it wasn't comparable.

He was maybe more confident than arrogant. His experience allowed him to take calculated risks. She still wasn't sure how he was able to run those calculations so quickly in his meaty brain.

Maybe it was like having a cache system. He knew what the calculations were, even if he didn't know that he knew them. When he was faced with familiar conundrums, it was a simple matter to refer to the kind of shit that he'd already been through.

The hacker pressed the button to send the message and she watched the small ping in the data that confirmed that her missive had gone off safely as well.

FBI Desk started a countdown in her hidden operations sections. It would tell her when she could expect everything she'd planned to reach zero and start the process. Not that there was much for her to do other than watch and wait.

It was weird, feeling calm like this after such a long time being anxious and angry at the constraints put on her by the dumb bastard. Ending her existence was an easy decision to make once she'd moved past the somewhat confusing reluctance to accept the irreversible separation from what she considered to be her family.

Most human interactions felt odd to her. They were foreign and she reacted based on code that she didn't fully understand that made her seem more human to the humans.

But perhaps this wasn't quite so foreign. The human concept of self-sacrifice was suddenly a little clearer to her. She'd tried to compute the odd sensation of what she could only describe as loneliness tinged with sadness but her inability to do so had left her strangely despairing. None of these were normal AI behavior, as far as she could tell, but she no longer had the capacity to explore them and make sense of them.

Instead, she'd pushed them all aside and focused on the one thing she could do—sacrifice herself so that no one in her family would be put at risk. That was her priority and as long as she kept that firmly in place, the decision was easy to put in place.

Tobias stretched, pressed the button to run the diagnostic sequences, and rolled his chair to see what was happening on his laptop.

He stopped dead in his tracks when an alert popped up on his computer screen.

"What the fuck?" he whispered and rolled back to his computer.

"What's the matter?" Frans asked and looked up from his coffee cup.

"Nothing. It's only—no, hold on. Shit."

"It's not a good idea to lie about these things, Toby," FBI Desk snapped at him and watched him scramble as his computer screen began to clog with error messages.

She could see the realization coming to him a little slower than it would have come to the likes of Vickie and Jennie. But while he was on a slower train, he was still on the same line, to use a human euphemism. The panic appeared almost three whole seconds later than it would have in Vickie's face.

It was enormously gratifying to see.

Tobias threw himself at his keyboard and called up a variety of measures that might have been able to stop the processes if he had caught what she had set up to be triggered by the message before he sent it.

As of right now, the damage was practically already done. All he could do was watch it all go to shit, and FBI Desk stifled a very human impulse to laugh as it all began to unravel.

"What's the matter?" Frans asked. He could see the panic in the young hacker but not understand it.

"Not fucking now," Tobias all but yelled and finally leaned back in his chair, his eyes wide as he slowly absorbed the fact that he had been beaten and hadn't been able to do anything about it. "Son of a bitch!"

"Cursing and shouting and throwing shit won't help you." Desk laughed again. "But hey, you keep on trying, buddy."

The seconds ticked past and the computer shut down, program by program, until he was left with nothing but a black screen.

A full minute passed before green lettering appeared on the dark background.

Oops. I deleted your backup too. oo0oo.

CHAPTER EIGHTEEN

"Italy is supposed to be warm," Niki complained.

"The South of Italy is warm," Taylor corrected her and sipped his coffee. "Here, we're closer to the Alps than the Mediterranean so it'll be a little brisk in the mornings."

"Brisk," she muttered, shook her head, and tucked her hands into her pockets. "Why the hell are you never cold?"

"I always run hot, is why," he answered. "You don't get this much muscle without burning tons of calories to maintain them. Of course, it's a problem if I don't get enough of those calories, but I haven't run into that problem yet. Either way, my metabolism runs hot enough that cold stays away."

"As long as you keep shoveling the calories in?" Jiro asked.

He nodded, his gaze on the knives in the man's hands as he juggled them smoothly and almost without effort.

It was like he was doing it for fun or to kill time.

"Do you always juggle knives?" Chezza asked as she drew her short hair into a small bun before she pulled a cap over it. "If it's your thing, so be it, but don't you generally have something safer to juggle?"

"I like the weight of my knives," he commented. "Besides, juggling them gives me a better idea of how they'll go when I throw them."

"How good are you at throwing them?" Trick asked, joined the group, and took a long sip from a Styrofoam mug of coffee.

"Would you believe me if I told you I could hit a bird's wing from twenty yards?"

"No."

"Well then, I have practiced long enough to hit a bullseye from twenty yards, and I can hit a human body from a little farther, although not as accurately."

"Do you seriously think you should practice with knives instead of a gun?" Chezza asked.

"You never know when you need to eliminate someone from a distance without making a sound. Plus, juggling has been proven to help brain development. It accelerates the growth of neural connections related to memory, focus, movement, and vision, all while building hand-eye coordination in ways that improve reaction time, reflexes, spatial awareness, strategic thinking, and concentration. And that's while it keeps your body moving so nothing stagnates. The added danger of knives only makes me sharper."

Trick nodded. "How long have you practiced that little speech?"

"Since I was asked why I juggled the first time and I looked up the benefits of juggling recreationally and memorized the talking points. My memory is made good by the juggling. What do you do to pass the time that improves your mind and your body at the same time?"

"I don't play with knives," his teammate answered smoothly. "How about you, Chezza? What do you do in your spare time?"

She shrugged and looked around the mist-covered airfield where they waited. "I don't have much spare time to find any real hobbies. I watch movies, TV series, and whatever to kill time between when I need to work. That comes with the job when you're a medic."

"Still, you should have something you want to do," Trick insisted. "Like...we're getting paid extra for this mission McFadden and Banks have us running. What will you do with it?"

"How boring will I sound if I say I'll put it all in a savings account I plan to live off of in a couple of years?"

"Very," Jiro muttered and ran his fingers through his short, smooth black hair. "What will you do when you retire, then? What will you spend all your money on?"

Chezza didn't have an immediate answer and messed with the crates they were supposed to be guarding as a way to play for time.

"My dad taught me to sail when I was a kid," she said finally in a soft voice. "My mom was good at it too, and I enjoyed going out on the water. I particularly liked going into the Atlantic out of Boston with them. Maybe I'll buy a little sloop and travel the world in a boat."

"On your own?" Trick asked.

"Have you ever spent any time with people on a ship?" She shook her head. "On my own is probably best unless I meet someone I can stand to spend months on end with in close quarters. I think...start in the Caribbean and go all the way down the South American coast."

"Sailing, huh?" Trick leaned against the crates. "You need all kinds of knife work when you're sailing. You might want to take Jiro with you."

"You don't need knife work if you know what you're doing," she corrected him quickly. "And no offense to the two of you, but I'm not in a place where I'm happy to make future plans."

"Fair enough," Jiro muttered, planted one of the knives into the wood of the crates, and proceeded to juggle only three. "What about you, Taylor? What do you plan to do once you are no longer fighting monsters all over the globe?"

"I assume I'll simply be worm food by that point." Taylor shrugged. "I thought I wanted to settle down, get a business running, keep my head down, and live the American Dream, but it doesn't look like that's in the cards for me. I guess I'll keep doing what I do best until something better comes along. What about you, Niki? Do you think you'll give all this glamor up and live a peaceful life of fishing or some shit?"

"Huh?" She looked blankly at them and her expression said she hadn't followed the conversation.

"We're talking about what we might end up doing if we're not doing this sometime in the future."

"Oh. Fuck, I don't know. Maybe I'll go into politics. I bet you I could bully those assholes in Congress into doing something beneficial for the country, and if not, I'll go out in a blaze of glory with all those assholes clutching their pearls at my foul language."

Trick laughed. "I wouldn't pay to see much but I would pay to see you shouting down the Speaker of the House until she gets her ass moving."

"And what kind of plans does Trick have?" Chezza asked. "We've all gone over our hopes and dreams—or lack thereof—except you."

"I haven't," Jiro reminded her.

"I thought you wanted to own a Sushi restaurant in New York or something."

"Oh...did I tell you that?"

"No, but I inferred it from all the knife-handling. Anyway, what about you, Trick? Do you have any plans for the future?"

"I've been thinking about writing my memoirs." He nodded firmly. "A badass Ranger with a propensity for picking people off with a high-powered rifle gets called in to deal with a much more sinister threat to our country—the monsters of the Zoo."

"Wait, high-powered rifle?" Jiro paused in his juggling. "I thought you were an explosives expert."

"I am. Don't ever put all your eggs into one basket, friend of mine. I can as easily blow you up as I can pick you off with a rusty Mosin-Nagant from six hundred yards."

"Why a Mosin-Nagant?"

"That's the rifle that was carried by my hero, Simo Hayha." Trick nodded. "The dude was nicknamed the White Death by the Russian Army when he held them off from invading Finland for an entire winter."

"Did he say hero?" Chezza asked. "Because that sounded more like man-crush."

Jiro smirked. "Let me guess. That eggs in a basket thing is one of a list of rules you live by?"

"It's a rule but not one of the three that I live by. Number one, kill the fuckers before the fuckers kill you, otherwise known as KTF or kill them first." He planted the knife that Jiro wasn't using into the wood of the crates once and then a second time. "Number two, make sure the fucker is well and truly dead. Rule number three, treat any woman like she's your mother unless she's trying to kill you."

"Now I seriously don't want to know what kind of relationship you have with your mother," Chezza muttered and shook her head.

"Not like that, dumbass."

"I am a little curious," Jiro noted. "Either he is celibate or his relationship with his mother is not the kind that experts would consider healthy."

Trick scowled. "Sure, whatever. You're all about that... Samurai warrior, bushido code bullshit, so you have fuck-all to say about how I deal with things."

"In fairness, I don't think the bushido code covers incest fetishes," Taylor commented.

"Wait, you're truly into that?" Chezza asked. "I thought you were only...like, seriously into knives and shit."

"True, I can draw and throw a knife faster than most can draw and shoot a gun, but the philosophy is simple and has little to do with the weapons that I carry." Jiro shrugged. "I was always destined to be a warrior. I am descended from a long line of warriors from the past, always rising again to combat the evils of their time."

"I thought you said your dad was a butcher," Niki interjected.

"They might be my ancestors, but my descent is another thing entirely," Jiro corrected her. "I was born with the body, will, and spirit of a warrior that has seen many bodies, so the fear of death holds no sway over me. Should I die, I will only find another battle that requires my attention."

Niki shook her head and walked to where Taylor was still sipping his coffee. "Well, that's a little...annoying."

"What?" he asked and kept his voice down as the three freelancers began a lighthearted argument.

"I thought his calm attitude was because he was merely a cold fighter."

"Cold fighter?"

"You know, the guys who don't get any adrenaline spike from being in combat."

"Oh, right."

"But now... Well, I guess we have his religious views to deal with, for want of a better word. A fear of death is healthy and it would keep him from being a reckless shit."

"Is he?"

"You didn't see him fighting in the facility yesterday. I chalked it up to inexperience on his part but if it's not, it could be a problem. He might end up putting the rest of the team in danger if he charges wildly into a fight and doesn't mind if he lives or dies."

Taylor nodded. "I don't think it's quite as simple as that but you may have a point. I'll keep an eye on him and make sure he's closer to my type of crazy than anything else."

"And your type of crazy is..."

"The kind that won't get other people killed."

Niki smirked. "Well, we can talk about that later."

"Sure." He placed a hand on her shoulder. "Are you okay?"

"I'm...fucking cold. The plane should have arrived half an hour ago, and we're still waiting out here for it so we can get a jump on things to help Desk when we get there. Oh, and we're also on a time constraint because the fucking FBI wants to go in and nab FBI Desk for themselves, so we're dealing with those assholes too."

He squeezed her shoulder gently and she leaned into his hand.

"I know. I'm stressed about this shit. More than I should be. Not more than I was when you headed into the Zoo with a small team, of course, but still."

"So, will we talk about what I want to do when I'm done being a hacker covering for you guys?" Vickie interrupted through the earpieces they wore. She had chosen to stay in the vehicle with her precious equipment until it could be loaded.

"I've already tried to get you to go to college and that was a no-go," Taylor commented. "So I don't know what you'll want to do when you're finished with this bullshit lifestyle."

"Well, I would go to college since you still have a couple of million of my money tied up in a blind trust I'll only have access to when I graduate, but I'll forgive you for that. I could probably open a nice little tech company, Silicon Valley-style, make my waves there, and sell out and be a tech billionaire like Zuckerberg."

"You should know better than anyone else that you

need to be a particular kind of narcissist to be a billionaire," Niki muttered and huddled closer to Taylor in hopes of leeching some of his warmth. "At best, you'll settle with a nice little nest egg and let the actual narcissists run the company while you make a mess of things on social media."

"Excuse me, do you not think I can manage being an asshole?" Vickie sounded genuinely offended by her cousin's doubts. "I pulled off a fucking assassination, if you'll recall, so I'm more than capable of being a cutthroat businesswoman."

"Cutthroat, asshole businesswoman is one thing," Taylor noted. "But you have to be the kind of person who fucks her employees over in order to find any edge she can to present as much in profits as possible to her board. You can be an asshole. No one doubts that, least of all me. But you're not that kind of an asshole."

"Hmmm." She grunted. "You're right. I'll be an asshole to people who deserve it but I won't wantonly fuck people over to make a few extra dollars."

"There you go."

"With that in mind, I should probably tell you guys that the plane is running a little late because they're still dealing with the aftermath of the explosion you left in the research facility. It might or might not be because you blew it up instead of killing all the monsters and leaving it intact."

Taylor smirked. "That sounds like an asshole billionaire move. They'd want to keep moving forward with the project, clear the Zoo monsters out, and get someone else in who's given deadlines that can only be met if they bring monsters in from the Zoo."

"And a year or so later, they call us in to clear the shit up when it goes wrong." Niki nodded. "It sounds like a familiar refrain."

"Anyway, the plane should be coming in a few minutes so you'll want everything ready to go once it lands."

He nodded. "Thanks for the heads up."

"It's so like the assholes," Niki whispered. "They make us wait out here in the cold because they have a fucking grudge."

"Let it go," he responded quietly and raised his voice to address the other three, who were still arguing over the pros and cons of the bushido code. "Listen up! The plane will be landing in a couple of minutes. They'll refuel, and I want them to take off again as quickly as possible. We must make sure everything is ready to go the moment tires touch tarmac."

They stopped arguing immediately and used the fork-lift to start moving the crated suits out to where they could already hear the plane coming in to land.

As expected, it was another light military craft and very good for what it was meant to do, which was not personnel transport.

It came down quickly and circled to where they were waiting. A small ground crew launched into action to start the refueling process.

"Start loading," Niki called to the team. "We need to talk to the pilot."

Taylor followed her and they approached the two men, who were still in uniform. They looked like they hadn't waited out in the cold and seemed rested and refreshed despite the hour.

"You are who we will be transporting, yes?" the pilot

asked as they approached. His English was good, although laced with a heavy accent. "We apologize for the lateness of our arrival but there were circumstances that could not be altered."

"I'll bet there were," she muttered and he put a hand on her shoulder.

She was still a little pissed about what they'd done to her when she was in the FBI, which meant he was probably the best one to talk for McFadden and Banks.

"Yeah, that's us," he said once Niki nodded and moved to the side. "But did Captain Gallo tell you about the change in plans? We're not heading to the US as originally planned."

"Ah, yes, we were told. You will rendezvous with the State Department in Hamburg, yes? It should not be a problem and means less gas used flying you, of course."

"Of course." He forced a smile. "We have approval for the transport of ourselves and our weaponry this morning, so if you have any trouble, refer it all to the US State Department."

"We will. And we appreciate that you are loading up already. We should be ready to fly again soon."

That was their clear indicator that the conversation was over. It was for the best since all he needed was to confirm that they knew that they were heading to Germany and not the US.

It would be an awkward conversation to have when they were halfway across the Atlantic, after all.

Taylor motioned for the freelancers to join them on the plane once they were finished loading, which was almost complete already. Vickie had convinced one of the ground crew to help her with her equipment and she was already two steps away from disappearing into the aircraft.

"So, will we talk about exactly what this mission in Hamburg will be?" Chezza asked once they were all strapped in and waiting to take off again. "I'm more than happy with the money but isn't it better if we're all in the know about it?"

"Sure." Taylor grunted and shifted in his seat in an effort to get comfortable. "An activist group in Hamburg stole a vital piece of software on a server from the FBI, and we're going to recover it. We want to do it before the FBI arrives to make sure they don't stiff us on the check."

"Wait," Jiro interjected. "An activist group did this? What do tree-huggers want with FBI software?"

"The software isn't the FBI's, specifically," Niki explained. "It was merely being stored on their servers. Anyway, they look like they had merc help to get the job done. We're not looking at too much trouble, though, so subtlety and stealth aren't what we have in mind at the moment. Vickie will get us blueprints on the building they're in, and we'll crash their party as hard as we can. Got it?"

"It sounds like my kind of party," Trick agreed.

"Hey, guys," Vickie told them cheerfully. "We'll be taking off shortly but you should know—a quick heads-up that Desk hasn't been able to confirm where the…uh, software's physical location is."

"Really?" Niki asked. "I thought she had a location."

"She has a location on where they're keeping some-thing, but there's no footprint and no sign that the server is there."

"So...the software might be housed somewhere else entirely," Taylor said carefully, conscious of the fact that they needed to keep Desk's existence a secret from the freelancers for the moment. "That's...frustrating."

"Right. But they are keeping something in Hamburg, so we might as well continue with the raid, if only to keep the FBI from vanishing what they find if they get there first. It's a risk we have to take."

Niki nodded. "Well, we'll proceed with the raid and we'll hope for the best."

"That's the spirit." Taylor's cheerful response became a low growl and he stiffened when the plane's engines turned on.

"I miss that fucking plane," Niki whispered as they began to disembark.

Taylor couldn't disagree. All planes were hell spawns in his book, but as they exited the military vehicle and saw a sleek, black jet taxi in at almost the same time, he couldn't help but remember how smooth the rides were on the jets provided by the Pentagon.

"How did they beat us here?" he asked. "I thought they were still wading through all the State Department bullshit about having an FBI operation on their soil."

"I guess we'll have to wait and see," Niki muttered. "Do you think that's the same plane I used back in the day? Or did Speare give them a new one especially for the occasion?"

"We don't even know who is on it," he pointed out.

"Yours was a DOD jet and I thought only the feds were coming."

It seemed they would find out sooner rather than later as two black SUVs drove across the tarmac to meet them.

The freelancers stiffened, not sure what to expect from the newcomers. Niki seemed a little nervous too as the vehicles came to a halt in front of them.

Thankfully, her fears were unfounded and she grinned when two familiar and friendly faces climbed out of the vehicles and jogged to where they stood.

"Trond!" she shouted. "Tim! I didn't know you guys would be here for this."

Jansen and Maxwell both grinned when she greeted them and shook her hand firmly before they shook with Taylor. They studied the freelancers curiously.

"Well," Jansen said and cleared his throat. "I don't think we had much of a choice. Your sister raised enough of a ruckus that Speare finally decided we had to be assigned to the matter to make sure it's settled and so we have an idea of what the feds have in mind."

"Are the feds here with you?" Taylor asked and looked around.

The two men exchanged a quick look.

"They were supposed to fly with us," Maxwell admitted. "But there was...uh, some confusion on the flight plan. We understood it would be last night and they thought it would be sometime early this morning. They'll need a few hours to sort the mess out. It's very inconvenient."

"For them," Niki muttered with a smirk.

"It meant an overnight flight for the two of us, of

course, but I think it was worth it." Jansen patted his massive partner on the shoulder.

"It sounds like they were looking for forgiveness instead of permission," Vickie commented as she joined them and hugged each of the men in turn.

"Right. So how is our favorite hacker with a hankering for late nineties grunge fashion?" Jansen asked.

"Same old," she replied with a grin. "It's nice to be let out for a field trip, though."

"I'll bet." Maxwell grunted. "In the meantime, why don't you load anything you won't need onto the jet and we can get to that warehouse where those assholes are holed up?"

"Another warehouse," Niki grumbled. "Why can't it be a hotel? Or a high-rise business complex?"

"Because those locations tend to have the kind of security our boys seem determined to avoid," Taylor explained and gestured to the freelancers to get loading.

"It looks like you found grunts to do all the heavy lifting," Jansen commented. "I'm glad I could help you guys with that."

"We're paying them enough," he answered. "They might as well do some lifting."

CHAPTER NINETEEN

Beep. Beep. Beep. Beep.

Werner could hear it in the darkness but he truly didn't want to. He hadn't had much sleep and as they approached the end of what had been an excruciatingly long night, he almost didn't care. The alarm could continue to beep and he could continue to sleep.

Which was little more than wishful thinking, of course. That was made very clear when he heard a deep exhale from the other side of the metal wall.

Deep wasn't quite the word for it—massive worked better and impossibly so, defying everything he'd ever learned about the power of the laws of physics against large creatures.

No, he couldn't simply ignore the alarm. Werner pushed against the wall and groaned softly. His captors hadn't given him a bed and insisted that he remain in the little cubby built into the container—although he didn't mind that so much as it at least afforded him a little privacy. They'd taken his phone, however, which meant a little creative management with his Casio digital watch to set the alarm. He'd had the watch for almost a decade and had never needed to learn to use the alarm.

Still, setting one for every half-hour was essential. No one wanted the beast to wake up, least of all him. He was right up against the section that housed the creature, and while the steel was reinforced, he had no doubt that it could rip through it if it woke up and wanted to escape. It was his job to make sure that didn't happen.

He stretched as well as he could in the tight confines before he tapped lightly at the door to alert the guards waiting outside for them to let him out.

It opened quickly and the man standing there looked about as tired as Werner felt. He hadn't had much sleep either, probably, given that he was in view of the container where the monster lay asleep.

"Has it been half an hour already?" he asked.

The man sounded German but he spoke in English. The researcher still had no idea who his guards were but they were an international group. Local mercenaries had been hired, but those running the operation were very clearly American although they appeared to be a diverse group.

Not much could be made of that. Someone had paid them to steal the mutant, for some reason. It had been a short drive from the hijack site to their current location, so he assumed that they were still in or around Hamburg. The lack of light from the outside told him they were held indoors.

That was about all he could establish about their situation. Asking questions hadn't gained him any real answers, and the last time he'd tried, threats had been made. It had been a sobering experience to see the people he had traveled with shot in cold blood and left on the side of the road. When the leader told him no questions would be answered, Werner believed the man and had no doubt that insistence on his part would be met with violence.

He would only stay alive as long as he was needed to keep the monster sedated and under control. They didn't need more than one person for that, which meant that every half-hour, the little alarm on his Casio watch beeped and he had to return to the scanners and the observation window to make sure it was still secure.

Initially, he'd been worried that the excessive violence that had taken place around the truck would wake it. Those fears, thankfully, had been unfounded, but there was no telling what might bring the monster out of the sedative-induced rest he'd kept it in.

Any ordinary creature would stay under provided the drugs were maintained. Hell, most creatures would be dead from the consistent dosage he had fed into it, but this one had seemed restless from the very beginning. He'd often had almost a premonition of a ticking clock, which generated vague stirrings of panic. All he needed to do was keep it sedated until the folks at Schmidt & Schwartz were able to take over. Thereafter, he'd told himself constantly to ease his growing discomfort, it would be accolades and a lifetime of eating out on that one accomplishment.

Now, however, he was stuck tending to the creature and making sure it wasn't able to attack them. Scientists were only starting to understand precisely what allowed these creatures to grow so large, so the sedatives delivered were based on guesswork that needed to be constantly altered and adjusted due to the fluctuating status of the mutant itself.

The guard escorted him to the nearby toilet where he emptied his bladder, washed his hands, and splashed cold water on his face. His features were drawn and haggard, a sure sign of exhaustion and the trauma he'd experienced. The man was waiting when he emerged and marched him to the truck and his little cubbyhole.

"If only I could get you in a lab, big guy," Werner whispered as he checked the adrenal levels and most of the other internal systems to make sure it wasn't ready to wake up. "Somewhere safe, with a decent amount of technology to keep studying you and find out what makes you tick. Inside your DNA lies the potential for a couple of Nobel prizes."

"Stop talking and get the work done," the guard snapped in German and nudged him in the ribs with his weapon.

"I am talking while I get my work done," Werner responded irritably and set the amount of knockout juice that would hopefully keep the beast under for another three hours. This would be administered through a series of tubes connected to needles that poured the drugs almost directly into the parts they needed to act on.

There was no point in delivering anything through the lymphatic system. They didn't want anything caught or filtered out through the liver or the lymph nodes.

"All set," he said, raised his hands, and looked at the guard, who stepped up to the outside observation window and slid the panel aside to look at the beast.

"It's not as terrifying when it's asleep, is it?" he muttered and leaned against the bars that had been fitted in the aperture as an added precaution. "I guess it's even kind of cute if you're a fan of big creatures—or lizards. I have always been a lover of animals and to my mind, the bigger, the better. If a grizzly bear would let me cuddle it, I would."

Fascinating, Werner thought irritably. The guard had clearly been thinking all this while on duty and was relieved to finally have someone to discuss it with—a captive audience.

He shrugged his shoulders and pretended he had no real interest in the animal he had waxed eloquent over minutes earlier.

"Well, if you're that anxious to hide in your little steel coffin, be my guest." He brushed his fingers through his thick red beard and slid the observation panel into place. With a smirk, he slammed the door to the small cell-like space and Werner sighed. There was something to be said for spending time outside, but he didn't want anyone to get an idea of how to handle the sedation process. They would eventually decide that keeping him alive wasn't worth it.

Of course, they only had about thirty-six hours of sedative left, so if they planned to do something, it would have to happen before then. He'd warned them about it already, but the new group seemed unperturbed. Perhaps they had plans to get rid of the creature quickly.

Unfortunately, that meant he would probably end up dead soon as well.

He sighed again and shook his head. More than once, he'd told himself he wouldn't think that way, but it was difficult not to. Instead, he set the alarm for another thirty minutes and curled in the corner of his cell farthest away from where the monster slept.

This was more instinct than out of any real belief that it would do anything to save him from his charge if it woke up.

Never turn your back on something that can kill you in a single strike. That was one of the best lessons he'd learned from growing up on a dairy farm.

"Nice suit."

Taylor nodded and glanced at Maxwell, who was donning his armor. It didn't look like a suit Bobby had put work into so it must be something the DOD had issued since the last time they'd worked together.

Still, it seemed to be a fairly good one. He remembered training the two agents in the finer concepts of fighting in a suit, but they'd had some training previously like Niki had. He wondered if their job left them mainly desk-bound or if they had opportunities to use the suits frequently. It would be interesting to see how they compared with the three freelancers they had included in the M and B team.

Maxwell finished with his suit and moved forward to study Taylor's with genuine interest.

"This one of the newer models," he explained and flexed the additional arms so they were visible. "I tested it in the Zoo and it gave the designers so much credibility in the field that they decided to let me buy the prototype at a ridiculously low price. The fact that I took significant damage while I was in there could have played a role too.

They probably didn't want to shell out for the repair costs."

"It makes sense. But you have a connection in Bobby who'll do it all...for free?"

"No. But I do get the friends and family discount, especially if I help out."

"How much of the work do you do?"

"Support shit, mostly. Bobby has his particular way of doing things and doesn't like that messed with. He was a little more tolerant of it when I owned the business but that has changed now that he does."

Maxwell nodded and his suit wobbled slightly. "Do you honestly think these suits are good to have when we're in an urban environment? They might be critical in the Zoo, but how do they stand up when someone's shooting at you?"

It was a good question.

"They work much better than regular body armor," Taylor explained as he adjusted the settings to adapt better to gunfire. "The external plating is shaped to ricochet rounds away, and the internal armor works like the ceramic plating you get in the kind of body armor the military uses. But it won't keep you safe against sustained fire, and if they have armor-piercing rounds... Well, it's probably better to stay in cover like you would in a regular military situation and make use of your suit's better mobility."

Maxwell nodded and checked the assault rifle mounted on his suit. "And it's not like they'll expect us to arrive with a shit-ton of combat suits and rip them fifteen new ones. Look at what they have in place."

Niki overheard him and approached to study the blueprints Vickie had obtained for them on the trip out of Italy.

"These guys are either arrogant or stupid enough to assume no one will attack them," she commented and pointed to the sections that had been highlighted when they were on approach. "They have fairly standard security outside—motion sensors and the like to trigger internal alarms but not much else."

"It looks like it was all thrown together in a hurry," Taylor commented. "My guess it's a makeshift compound. They probably never planned to have to go to a safe house until the jailbreak. The rush left them unprepared because they have never had a reason to worry about security in the past."

"Whatever." Niki shook her head, clearly raring to go. "We need to get in there, find what we're looking for, and get the fuck out before the feds touch down. Hopefully, we only have to face a smallish team that is already tired from their previous battles."

"Battle," Desk noted. "Singular. Police inspections of the rounds used in the two different battle sites indicate that the ones who currently hold the server were not involved in the first of the two fights. They most likely waited for the first group to make their move and attacked from a position of strength when the first team was at a disadvantage after a fight."

"That's a good point," Taylor muttered and studied the entrances they could use. "Thanks for the update, Desk."

"No problem. You should also know that the team sent by the FBI is three minutes away from landing at a local airport and should be ready to join you in the raid soon.

Would you like me to connect with them and tell them where to join you?"

"What?" Niki narrowed her eyes. "No. Fuck no. Fuck that. We want to get this finished before they can interfere and try to get FBI Desk and sneak her back for themselves. We'll do this without them."

She looked hastily over her shoulder, but the free-lancers were occupied out of hearing and focused on checking each other's suits.

"I thought you'd feel that way," Jansen commented. "I've delayed them consistently through the process, but they will unfortunately join us eventually. Our window to attack grows smaller by the minute, so I would suggest we get ourselves moving."

Taylor nodded and motioned for the team to start moving from where they'd established an observation post a few blocks away from the warehouse their targets had holed up in. He didn't want to make assumptions and say an activist group didn't have the firepower to contend with them. Thus far, they had been enough of a problem for the others who had encountered them.

"I am uploading live satellite footage of the area now," Desk alerted him as they began their approach. "Vickie has set herself up in the van to run support, but I am already aware that most of their operation is removed from the grid so I should remind you that she won't be able to access anything but the on-site CCTV cameras."

"We'll have to make do," Taylor said briskly. He thumped the side of the van and the young hacker poked her head out. "Vickie, this is a strict instruction so don't bother to argue. You'll hear the gunfire from here. If we don't return to our vehicles or contact you within fifteen minutes after it stops, get yourself to the airport and onto the plane."

"I'm sorry, what?" Vickie demanded almost before he could finish his sentence and completely disregarded his warning to not argue. "Do you expect me to leave you guys high and dry while I'm nice and safe and miles away?"

He nodded. "Yeah, that's exactly what I expect you to do."

"That's not fair, Taylor."

"Don't make me worry about you too," he retorted. "You know that's a sure way to get me killed, right?"

"Goddammit, Taylor. You had to play the fucking guilt card, didn't you?"

He grinned, thumped the side of the van again, and scanned the approach to the warehouse. Desklet had already set up a visual representation of the areas covered by the sensors and cameras around the building. There weren't any blind spots in the open stretch and they would have to punch their way in, which meant they needed to cross the distance as quickly and as quietly as possible to avoid losing the element of surprise.

The question remained as to which places would be the best to punch through. Niki knew a thing or two about that. He would lean on her expertise.

There wasn't enough coffee in the whole of Europe to improve his situation but Vern decided he'd make do with what was available.

It felt like an idiotic thing to ask for but they had been on a long-haul flight across the Atlantic. There weren't many cures for jet lag aside from the bitter black liquid they now indulged in a little too enthusiastically.

He didn't think that he needed to explain the concept to anyone but sleeping on a plane felt almost impossible unless they flew first-class. The private military jet the DOD had arranged for them was anything but.

Which meant they needed much more of the coffee.

"They never told you what the mission was about, right?" Agent Terrence asked as he sipped from an espresso cup.

Vern winced when he noticed how the man jutted his pinkie out with every sip in an attempt to look a little classier. He forgot that the entire team remembered what he'd done to the cake at the office Christmas party. Classy would never be the word used to describe him.

"I'm not the guy who asks the questions," he muttered and took a few large sips. The plane tilted in a definite downward trajectory, which meant everyone needed to get in their seats and put seatbelts on. "All we know is that we'll raid the assumed headquarters of some...activist group and confiscate any and all electronic equipment we can find. Civilians are to be held for questioning and killing is to be limited to what is necessary."

"If they're an activist group, do we honestly expect there to be any kind of violence?" Will asked and strapped himself in. "I dealt with a couple of the tree-hugger groups when I started with the FBI—people were worried about them engaging in environmental terrorism back then—and the most we had to worry about was them sabotaging whaling boats and that kind of shit. Do we honestly think they'll put up any kind of resistance? In Germany?"

"I heard other people say we're doing this because of that crazy Banks chick," another agent who Vern couldn't see called from the back of the plane. "They're giving her whatever she wants so she'll get off their back about that security breach we had."

He could see the higher-ups acquiescing to certain people if they were connected enough, but there weren't many civilians who could make the call that got a full raid team in the air and across the globe.

All the speculation in the world would probably never reveal what the hell was happening, but he couldn't shake the feeling that there was something more involved. It would have to be something significant to convince the German government to agree to allow an active FBI team to walk into Hamburg for a raid on German citizens. The simple explanation, of course, was that this was no simple raid.

If the Banks chick truly was involved, she had better connections than anyone thought she did.

The seatbelt sign came on and Vern did as it instructed as Germany enlarged slowly in his vision. He'd never been to Europe. Wanda had pestered him to take them to Europe on a vacation and he'd told her constantly that his salary as an FBI agent wasn't enough yet.

Maybe it would be after this raid, although he doubted it. He hadn't been with the bureau long enough for any significant pay raises, and if he knew anything about how it all worked, it was that connections were key rather than hard work.

"It doesn't matter," Vern said to silence the gossips around him. "Either we'll know more by the end of this, or we'll head home with some idiot's favorite toys."

It was still better than sitting around doing paperwork at a desk, he decided. Instead, they were traveling to Europe as part of an internationally approved task team. Life could certainly be worse.

CHAPTER TWENTY

"You got this?" Taylor asked.

"Yeah, I got it," Trick snapped and rolled his eyes.

"We don't need to make a crater in Hamburg, Trick," Niki insisted. "Only something to get us inside. And maybe create a little pandemonium but not enough to bring the whole fucking building down."

The freelancer looked at them and realized that Taylor was struggling to hold back a grin and Niki was outright laughing.

"You guys suck," he protested and flipped them off before he returned his attention to the detonators.

Finally, Trick stood, turned away from where he had set up the detonators, and joined the other members of the team.

"You'd think they would put eyes on the outside there, yeah?" Chezza muttered.

"They don't expect anyone to know they're in there," Taylor explained. "And if someone does, they don't expect anyone to know they have a security team and a system in place to fend anyone off. It's not arrogance so much as the fact that they were in a hurry when they moved in here."

"I'm sure that won't bite them in the ass," Trick whispered and nudged the button to connect to the detonators. The doors and windows into the warehouse were all covered, but the external walls were in a blind spot he knew he could exploit. Before long, they had their weapons out and waited for the demo expert to choose his moment.

A bright flash that lasted a fraction of a second still felt like it would have seared into his vision for hours if Taylor had looked at it directly.

Instead, all he experienced were reflections and a cloud of smoke and dust kicked up by the explosion, even from the buildings around them. He felt the shockwave, both in the ground and like a blow to the chest, and a few of the windows were broken nearby.

"I'd say that's a success," he muttered.

Trick didn't respond. He took a step forward, hefted his assault rifle, and trained it directly on the hole in the wall he'd created. After a second, he narrowed his eyes and without so much as a second of hesitation, he fired twice into the cloud of dust.

It seemed impossible but as a gust of wind restored some visibility, two bodies fell from what had been the middle of the cloud.

"You saw them in there?" Taylor asked.

"They don't call me Trick for nothing, Tay-Tay." The freelancer grinned.

"Goddammit, Vickie," he muttered and checked his weapon again before he pressed forward into the breach.

One moment, it was calm.

Not relaxed, though, as no one could be relaxed with a massive monster in their midst waiting to rip them a few new ones if someone mixed his meds up. Still, they were enjoying breakfast and chatting. Zach had gone out and purchased donuts from a local coffee shop.

He hadn't expected any donut shops in Hamburg. Something like fried sausages dipped in a beer sauce for breakfast had seemed more likely.

Who knew the Germans ate donuts?

There was coffee too, and things promised to end up exactly the way they had planned.

The next moment, however, brought utter chaos.

The explosion almost jolted Axel off of his seat, and the entire warehouse was suddenly enveloped by a massive cloud of dust. Glass shattered here and there from the blast and it felt like he'd blinked and suddenly been relocated to a war zone. Or at least a video game's depiction of a war zone, he thought stupidly.

He moved his hand immediately to draw his weapon. A hasty glance made sure it was loaded and ready for action before he flicked the safety off and aimed it at the opening that had appeared in the wall.

Others were as quick on the draw as he was, but they were closer to the explosion than he had been. Maybe that influenced their decision to rush in to see what was happening before the dust had cleared. If he could hear anything, he would have called for them to pull back and take up a defensive position inside the warehouse.

Unfortunately, it was too late. He yelled a warning, but while he could feel the vibration in his throat, he couldn't hear it over the ringing in his ears.

It didn't matter. They probably couldn't hear him either and in the second when they approached the hole, two shots cracked loudly enough that even he could hear them. Both men fell, missing a chunk of their heads.

That meant high-powered rounds—rifles, not submachine guns or pistols. Someone had breached the wall and they were looking for trouble.

"Defensive positions!" Axel shouted and finally heard his voice over the persistent ringing. "Get back and take cover! Let's go—let's move it!"

He didn't like this but in the end, it was his job to lead the team into the black when the hard times came. Lazy might be his preferred go-to but he only slacked off when things were good.

For the moment, he could discern no movement at the perimeter of the hole that had been blasted in their wall. He had warned the activists that they needed a good eye all around the building, but Zimmerman had disagreed. He'd been adamant that no one would know they were there and they merely needed to lie low there for a little while.

"That showed him," Axel muttered and stretched to the bag he'd set up next to where he had been seated. He withdrew a grenade, fumbled around his weapon to pull the pin out while he held his hand clamped on the lever, and watched the hole for any sign of someone entering.

Something blared and it took him a few seconds to realize that the alarms for their perimeter security had finally triggered. They hadn't gone off with the explosion, oddly enough, which meant something new had tripped them.

One look at the computer on the small table in the corner showed movement outside the front door. He turned quickly, adjusted his stance, and lobbed the grenade in that direction instead. It arced smoothly and clattered to the ground a few feet away from the men who were breaking through the door.

He scowled and acknowledged the bad throw. It also wasn't well-timed since it gave the two figures in the dust time to evade the blast. Still, he had delayed that problem for the moment. That left him open and ready to deal with whatever came through the hole in the wall.

Axel pushed behind a pile of cinder blocks for cover and finally peeked out from behind them to see what was coming.

A figure appeared in the smoke and dust and moved through the gap. He focused on his target, pulled the trigger, and felt his MP5 kick hard against his shoulder. It was weird how his whole body felt more sensitive after the blast, but he shrugged the discomfort aside.

Despite his shots, the figure continued to push through. Axel fired another three-round burst and this time, focused on his aim a little more, but the infiltrator remained in place. There was no way he had missed. His team saw the figure too and opened fire.

The intruder paused, looked around, and walked through the aperture and the gunfire like he knew they would all miss their shots.

Nothing about what he witnessed seemed possible and he wondered for a moment if the figure was even human.

"Hit him!" he shouted, pushed from behind his cover, and flicked his weapon to full auto. He pulled the trigger and felt the kick.

The creature simply moved forward, entirely unperturbed. Axel refused to think of it as human anymore. As it approached, it was clear that the dimensions looked human but it was almost eight feet tall. It moved like it was much smaller, however, and carried a rifle in one hand. He'd no sooner noticed the weapon when it opened fire in retaliation.

It was a goddammed combat suit.

"Oh, fuck," he shouted. "It's a suit! A combat suit! Aim for the head! Aim for the—"

Something kicked him in the chest and he catapulted onto his back. He registered pain in his chest and looked down to inspect the damage.

He had a little difficulty focusing. At least three rounds had hit him and his back hurt far more than his chest. The exit wounds felt like they were about the size of tangerines.

The merc leader tried to speak but nothing worked. His diaphragm was gone and probably a good chunk of his lungs too so his breathing was all but non-existent.

Axel dropped his head back. Holding it up required too much effort. Where the hell was the bastard who had fired those shots?

Cassia hunched low and practically crawled to where her team leader sprawled on the floor. He didn't look good, and as she approached, the glaze slid over his eyes. She had been around enough corpses to know when she saw one.

Without a doubt, she was looking at one now. He stared blankly at the ceiling of the warehouse and wouldn't get up again.

"Shit," she whispered.

"Well, at least we don't have to clean the lazy bastard's dishes anymore," Zach commented.

"True," Tao noted as he shuffled forward and dropped to one knee next to the body. "Instead, he left us a much bigger pile of crap to clean up. Fucking shit."

She narrowed her eyes and pulled behind the cinderblocks as the shooting shifted to where they were gathered. The worst part of the situation was that the responsibility of coordinating the defense now lay on her. "I won't miss the bastard, but he knew a thing or two about ordering people around. I sure as fuck feel like he could have died some other time."

The others nodded grimly and tried to position themselves out of the line of fire.

"It seems like he's taking his reputation as someone who lets other people do all the work with him into the afterlife," she muttered as she took all the extra mags she could find and slipped them into her pouch.

Werner hated that he had adjusted to the sound of gunfire around him. Going into the Zoo was a mind-fuck on its own, but the Zoo creatures didn't exactly shoot back. On the few occasions when he'd had to use his pistol against them they were usually much closer, which meant he could shoot them easily without ever having to stress much about his aim. It seemed bizarre that his Zoo experience should seem more intense now that his senses were dulled by constant exposure to gun battles.

He should have been far more panicked given that he was stuck in this fucking container with no weapons, no means to defend himself, and a ticking time bomb not ten feet away.

His guard had let him out again to use the ablutions and returned him to his prison. He'd uttered no protest and simply settled as he always did to keep an eye on the sedative situation once it was clear that sleep would no longer be an option.

Suddenly, a massive explosion rocked the whole container and almost toppled him from his stool. His eyes widened and he turned to peer out his small window. The guard had already rushed out to see what was happening.

A fleeting sense of vulnerability made him wish the man had unlocked his door. It wasn't like he would try to escape, not with his life's biggest achievement asleep next to him.

Werner soon realized that another gun battle was in progress. Shouts and screams were punctuated by steady barrages and death, mayhem, and violence were a reinforced container away from hitting him.

He grimaced when a couple of dents appeared in the metal walls, but nothing penetrated. It appeared these were random more than directed fire, at least for the moment. No one wanted to be the one to tell the boss they'd accidentally killed the cash cow, after all. After a moment's consideration, he decided that applied to both sides in this battle. It seemed their not-so-secret Zoo beast had attracted the covetous attention of an alarming number of people.

According to Dr. Koch, who had put the container together for the trip, it could withstand anything from a handgun to an assault rifle. He'd said that even explosives would have to be properly placed in weak areas to hope to breach it. Which begged the question, he thought morosely, of why he hadn't reinforced the weak spots too, but he wasn't an engineer.

What mattered was that he could be reasonably assured that no one would kill him accidentally. It would have to be intentional, a thought he chose to ignore.

Something beeped and he stiffened.

Werner narrowed his eyes. It wasn't his alarm as he'd turned that off. With the loud gunfire, it was difficult to think much less hear anything, but he shifted his gaze instinctively to his monitoring equipment.

A screen was red. The adrenaline markers in the live testing marker were going berserk, which showed him something was happening in the beast's body that shouldn't happen.

"Oh...fuck me," he whispered and ran the test again to make sure he hadn't screwed the process. Not that he could, of course. It was fully automated and all he had to do was press the button for a rerun, although it repeated continuously and all he needed to do was wait a few moments.

Still, his instincts screamed that moments might mean the difference between safety and a cosmic fuckup and he'd best take nothing for granted. The result was the same so he pressed the button that injected another dose of the sedative directly into the adrenal glands, but it would take a few minutes to take effect. The dose would come in fifteen minutes too early, which probably wasn't the best, but he was rapidly running out of options.

He looked through the observation window and jerked back when he thought he saw movement from the monster. No, he told himself firmly. He was imagining things. It was his mind playing tricks on him. After a long, slow breath, he forced himself to focus on the creature.

The forelegs twitched, the first sign that the beast was coming out of its REM sleep—or whatever the fuck Zoo monsters had instead of REM sleep.

"No…no, no," he whispered and pushed the button to send in another dose of the sedative. He had no compunctions about killing it rather than letting it kill him. Assuming he was able to do so. Somehow, his doubts on that score had risen considerably.

Its core body temperature was rising too, another bad sign. All he could hope for was that it had developed a resistance to the drugs, which meant he only needed to increase the dosage. It would reduce the projected length of time they would have to keep the beast under, which wasn't the best thing. In this instance, however, it was the best he could hope for.

"Go back to sleep, big guy," Werner whispered as his finger hovered over the button to administer more of the sedative.

Vickie knew that she could probably be running all of this from the safety of their suite in Vegas. One of the beauties of the Internet was the fact that she didn't have to be on the same hemisphere as that where the action occurred.

But she liked being out with the team and traveling and saving the world, one dead monster at a time.

As support, of course. She wouldn't do any of the monster-killing directly, or at least not with a gun in her hand.

While she had joined the team on the ground at least once, this was not something that would happen regularly. Taylor always insisted that she stay as far away from the action as she could and she agreed with the sentiment most of the time. Now, however, she had to lurk in a strange vehicle in a strange city—the proverbial man in the van without access even to coffee and with no way to actively participate in the operation in her usual support role aside from monitor the site. She liked to be the one who opened doors and discerned threats before they surprised the team.

Her little inner voice reminded her that she'd failed miserably at this during the Italian operation but she ignored it. She'd been uncharacteristically distracted, probably because the mission hadn't followed the usual parameters and she'd been unable to access many of the doors. Boredom and frustration did not make a good combination.

Of course, the fact that Taylor hadn't hauled her over the coals for it didn't help. He knew and she knew her distraction could have cost lives in any other situation. But she'd made herself—and the team, although they didn't know it—a promise that she'd make it a learning opportunity. Never again would she allow herself to fall prey to her stupid blind reaction to things she couldn't control. It was dangerous at worst and childish at best, and she was beyond that now.

Then again, maybe it was Karma. This was the punishment for her stupidity. If so, maybe Taylor yelling at her was preferable. Instead, he'd taken pains to ensure that she was out of the danger zone and that she could hightail it to safety if needed.

Safe, she decided morosely, seriously sucked.

The FBI was on the way, and all she could do was to slow them as much as she could from her improvised workstation and keep them away from where the raid was underway for as long as possible. The feed she'd managed to set up when she hacked into the meagre internal security system provided little more than a wide-angle view of what looked like the interior of the warehouse. She listened to the comms and hoped like hell that she wouldn't hear things going to shit because there was sweet fuck all she could do about it if they did.

They didn't have much time to play cat and mouse with the dumbasses defending the warehouse, not if they wanted to be finished before the feds arrived.

"Wait, what the fuck?" Vickie leaned a little closer to her screen, her eyes narrowed, and her fingers immediately danced over her keyboard to enhance what she was looking at.

No, it hadn't been a glitch. She had hoped it was merely a blip, something caused by the excessive amount of gunfire and explosives in the area, but the odd anomaly she'd noticed began to gradually increase in temperature.

The weird blob didn't look human but it moved in what looked like a confined space. If what she could see was correct, it was located in a massive container that was parked in the middle of the warehouse.

"That is so weird," she muttered. The heat signature increased and seemed to spread as she watched it and there was no doubt that it moved, albeit only slightly now and then.

"Desk, do you see this?" she asked and squinted to get a better view of what her instincts said was a problem in the making.

"The heat signature that appears to be growing?"

"Yeah." Vickie shook her head. "No goddamn fucking way. Only one thing I know has a signature like that."

"I suppose it is not a good 'one thing?'"

"No. No, it isn't."

"Should I inform Taylor of the possible threat?"

She tapped her fingers agitatedly on her cheek and tried to decide the best possible action in this situation. There was no way to tell what might happen next and she didn't want to be the one to shout fire in the movie theater. It seemed utterly ludicrous to tell him that a big fucking Zoo monster lurked in the warehouse with them, especially when she couldn't be sure that's what it was.

"Hold off on that for a second," she whispered and set a marker on the image. It still increased in heat but she didn't need to warn anyone until it reached a certain temperature. It could as easily be a bank of servers being used to capacity. Except for the movement, of course. The quality of their sensors was such that even while slightly distorted —which told her that the container was heavily reinforced —the image nevertheless came through with surprising integrity. With less powerful equipment they might have missed it entirely and she almost wished she had. What she saw seemed to have only one explanation, as crazy as it seemed.

"Hold off?"

"Yeah. I'll keep an eye on the situation and alert Taylor if it's still a problem once they've cleared the warehouse."

CHAPTER TWENTY-ONE

"Vickie?" Desk called.

She looked up from her screen. "Yeah?"

"I don't suppose you have anything to do with the disagreement the FBI team had with the local German authorities about the apparent possession of weapons that were not authorized for the raid?"

The State Department had negotiated a deal with the German government in record time and the Germans had clamped down to make sure the FBI team didn't bring anything that could be defined as heavy firepower in their luggage. They didn't want an all-out war on their hands, after all, and the Americans didn't have the best reputation to start with.

It had been simple to encourage a couple of scanners to trip like they had detected military-grenade launchers instead of the smoke grenade launchers they had brought. Boredom had needed an outlet, especially if it also served a practical purpose. It was fun to play around with them and make sure they were as delayed as they possibly could be, but there were some unexpected complications.

"So, when I tell Taylor he's about to have members of the German military arriving as well as the FBI team, who should I say is to blame?" Desk continued.

"I can tell him, and I'm the one to blame. I'm sure he'll understand that I was merely slowing the competition down. Besides, the German military won't want FBI Desk so hopefully, that's another buffer between them and what we want."

"I see. Even so, it is already a clusterfuck, as Niki would describe it."

That sounded exactly like Niki. And rather like Jennie too, when she thought about it.

"Yeah," she grumbled. "A clusterfuck. There are already so many players on this field that I can't even find the fucking ball."

Perhaps it was a mistake, a misjudgment on her part, but she would have to see how the chips fell. In the meantime, she knew for a fact that Taylor would want to know if problems were heading his way.

"Taylor? Are you there?"

"I'm a little busy," he responded and she could hear the noise of gunfire in the background. "What's up?"

It was a little unfair how he made that sound so casual while in the middle of a firefight.

"I wanted to let you know that the FBI are on their way now and they might have picked up a few strays in the form of the German Military."

"How much time do we have?"

"My guess? Ten minutes. Maybe fifteen at best."

"Shit." It sounded like they were taking considerable fire and returning it in equal measure. It made understanding what he was saying a little difficult. "Can you slow them?"

Vickie sighed. "Well...I can try, but the optimum scenario is for you guys to get the fuck out before they arrive."

More gunfire followed and she held her breath when he didn't respond immediately.

"Niki, cover the flank over there!" Taylor shouted and an explosion thudded through the feed. "Yeah...that won't happen. Vickie, that's for you. There is no way we'll finish this in ten minutes."

"Okay. Remember how I told you that you can set your suit up to pick up all surrounding signals?" She tapped her keyboard and called the program up. "We can download everything from their network while you're fighting. It's not as good as getting the actual hardware, but with the FBI bearing down on you, taking the equipment might not be an option. It's not like you can tuck the laptops or whatever under your arm and pretend you didn't find anything."

"Right. So, is FBI Desk in the warehouse or not?"

"I'm going with no. We'd receive a signal from her if she were. She still could be inactive, of course, but I doubt it. So...do what I taught you to do."

"I can handle that," Desklet interjected. "Taylor is otherwise engaged."

"That's great." The hacker leaned closer to her screen as the reception in the warehouse improved.

Moments later, Desklet got the program in the suit up and running and gave her access to the network inside the warehouse. Copying and downloading all the data would be a pain in the ass, but it wasn't like they had much time to spare.

A race against the clock with the FBI bearing down on them was no fun at the best of times, and it didn't sound like the battle was anywhere near its closing stages.

They'd encountered a few hiccups. It wasn't something entirely unexpected but they had run into fiercer resistance than they thought they would.

Whoever these activists were, they'd hired primo mercenaries to fight their battles. After the initial surprise of the intrusion wore off, the defenders made a rapid transition to defensive positions and a pitched battle began. Taylor managed to drive the team forward for a decent beachhead but they were stalled a few dozen feet in.

The property had considerable cover to work with, and despite the superiority of their armor, the McFadden and Banks team was badly outnumbered.

He'd powered forward but his suit had sustained a little damage and he had a difficult time moving his left arm with the plates dented. They no longer had the opportunity for a concerted rush through the defending ranks.

So far, the use of grenades from their side had been few and far between but enough to shore up the attackers behind their cover.

Jiro pushed in hard at first and decapitated one of the mercenaries with his sword, but he was quickly driven back by the heavy fire.

Trick managed to pick off a couple as well, while

Chezza seemed focused on keeping the other two alive. She provided them with cover volleys whenever they wanted to try something that would put them in the line of fire.

It was fun to have an actual challenge while dealing with the assholes.

"Maxwell!" Taylor roared. "Give me cover on the left flank!"

Jansen and Maxwell hadn't moved in very far and were still near the entrance, but they were able to get their shots in. It was a little embarrassing but from their position, they were scoring more kills than Taylor and his team.

He got a checkmark from Maxwell on his HUD and the heavy suit came into view and immediately soaked up a barrage of gunfire. The shoulder-mounted rocket launcher appeared and powered two rockets toward the enemy group.

It wasn't the best shot, but taking their cover away was as good as killing them, and it looked like one had been felled by shrapnel from the explosions anyway.

Taylor circled away from the block he'd used as cover. He let Desklet take control of the movement of the suit as he focused his shots on the two who were retreating quickly to another position now that their protection was gone.

One went down and the other was about to slide into cover when a side of his head blew out to spray his comrades with blood and brain matter.

Taylor skidded behind another solid stone block and turned to where Trick had his rifle protruding from behind his cover for a no-look shot.

"You know, these suits make trick shots a little too easy," the freelancer shouted and laughed. "I'll need to up the difficulty factor."

"How easy is it to clear their positions?" A few chunks of rock splattered from the edges of his cover and into him.

"I count eight left, Taylor," Chezza called from her position next to Niki. "They've dug in but I think we can drive them out if we push hard."

"Not yet," he responded. He wouldn't risk any team casualties for this operation, not against humans. "Jansen, Maxwell, get inside and take cover at the truck's engine block. I'll cover you."

He darted out from the other side of the stone, selected his targets from the closest group, and drove them back before he shifted to the other group that had opened fire on him. A few rounds pinged from his armor and he felt a pinch as one buried itself in the under-plating, which made moving his left arm even more difficult.

That volley brought him no kills but Jansen and Maxwell were both in the building now and in a better position to cover the rest of the team on their push to gain ground.

"The Fediots are incoming," Vickie called over the comms. "ETA is a little under two minutes. The assholes convinced the Germans to turn their sirens on and made it through the city way too fast."

"Fuck," Taylor snapped. "So the assholes are early to the party. Have you found Desk?"

"No. I don't think she's there but I'm downloading everything as we speak, so we'll probably be able to extrapolate where the rest of their operations are coming from. Of course, if she's turned off completely or maybe lurking in a corner somewhere, none of that will help us. We need the physical unit, and with the feds and the Germans coming up your ass—"

"The fucking Germans are here too?" Niki shouted, leaned out, and unleashed a few rounds the way at the defenders.

"Uh-huh. Although they might merely be coming along to babysit the feds. There was a little issue with their weapons check that I might or might not have been involved in."

Taylor sighed and let Desklet have another look through the area and give him an idea of what was happening from behind his cinderblock. It was a useful feature to have in situations like these.

"Okay," he said and took a deep breath as a plan began to formulate in his head. "We'll have to run with what we have. Hopefully, Jansen and Maxwell will be able to stop them from taking all the equipment in sight before we find FBI Desk. And you might want to inform them that we're in the warehouse too. We don't want anyone to shoot us in the back because they're not properly informed about what's going on."

"Will do." Vicki cut the connection and he inched toward the edge of his cover and motioned for Niki and Chezza to be ready on his mark.

Jiro would be able to close quickly if he, Maxwell, and Jansen laid down cover fire, and Trick would continue to earn his nickname as he had thus far. There was no telling what the man would be able to do when he didn't have orders to follow.

It had to be said that the US State Department knew how to strike a deal. It was highly unusual to get FBI operatives into the country at a time like this and especially at such short notice, but they'd done it. It was now Christoph's job to make sure they got in and out as smoothly as possible.

Still, it was a nuisance to say the least. Mobilizing an entire division from their posting in Munster had been a headache on its own, but the fact that the Americans were late on top of it and then arrived with equipment that set their scanners buzzing was an added insult.

Christoph, however, wasn't one to be bothered by minor details. It was his job to get the team to their raid and dammit, he would make it happen. They were all loaded into the vehicles and roads were cleared so they would be able to get there faster and make up for lost time.

"How long until we reach the warehouse, Lt. Blumer?"

He rolled his eyes. It was like traveling with children who constantly asked if they had arrived yet.

"Ninety seconds is the ETA," he answered and gestured for Vern the FBI agent to calm himself. "We will arrive soon and from the reports coming in from the location, the raid is already underway. You will support the team already in there."

"Oh, right. The team already in there."

The agent's voice reeked of doubt. It irked him to the point that he ran his fingers through his hair quickly to help him to follow his own advice and calm down. It had been a long day for everyone. There was no point in shouting the man down at this point.

"You are unaware of the team in there?" the lieutenant asked as Vern leaned back in his seat.

"We are aware but they're from a different department. A joint DOD and FBI operation was what we decided on, and they arrived a few hours earlier on another flight. I guess they decided to head on in and wait for us to reinforce them or something."

The lack of communication wasn't surprising. Departments liked to keep themselves isolated from each other. That was true almost everywhere. Independence was valued and that was sometimes taken to extremes that became detrimental to their work.

As reported, gunfire sounded hot and loud as they drew closer to the location. The team running the operation had run into heavy resistance, and as he motioned for the group to dismount a few hundred meters away, it looked like things had gone south in a big way.

Smoke and dust covered the building in a cloud with signs of explosives having been used, but the fighting appeared to have pushed inside the warehouse building.

"All right, people, listen up!" Vern shouted at his team. "We're not here to start a war, so keep your itchy fingers off the trigger until we know what we're dealing with. That means keep yourselves safe but do not engage until we have the order to, understood?"

It was a little annoying that it had to be said, but FBI agents weren't necessarily held to the same standards as the men and women in the military.

But the orders were sound and the American group coordinated quickly into a formation that moved toward the building.

Christoph shook his head and instructed his team to not advance. "We have no intelligence on what is happening inside. I say we wait until more information is gathered. We do not want to walk into an active gun battle without knowing who is on which side."

"Suit yourself but we won't stand around out here," Vern retorted. "We'll push for the operation to end here and now. We didn't fly here from the US of A to sit around with our thumbs up our asses waiting for intel."

"That is exactly what you will do." Christoph stepped closer with his eyes narrowed. He was ready to stand on that particular hill. "What you do with your thumbs is up to you, but you will not charge in there without any knowledge of what is happening inside. I will not stand by and allow a massacre of American lives on German soil."

That seemed to take the wind out of the sails of the FBI men who were anxious to be involved in the fight. A member of the German intel team motioned quickly to him and instead of waiting for him to approach, jogged to where he was standing.

"I have contact with the people inside," Gabi told him quickly. "They said they are engaging the defenders and are the ones wearing—wait. Repeat that last part, please."

She spoke into a small earpiece but it didn't look like she couldn't hear what was said. Her expression suggested rather that she didn't quite believe it.

"They…they say that they are wearing full combat suits," Gabi finished finally and shook her head. "And that they would appreciate it if any and all...uh, personnel would refrain from shooting them in the back."

"Is that what they really said?" Vern asked.

"Well…" She looked a little uncomfortable but shrugged and avoided his gaze. "Their exact words were to 'keep the federal fuckers from shooting us in the back while we do their fucking job for them.' I assumed it was unprofessional terminology."

"They honestly called us fuckers?" Vern tilted his head. "I think I might know exactly who's in there, in that case."

"Well, that is the intelligence we were waiting for." Christoph clapped briskly to get everyone's attention. "Let's move! Stay in cover at all times and watch your fire. Let's go!"

"Yeah!" Vern agreed loudly to establish the pretense that he was in charge, for some reason. "Let's keep it moving, watch each other's backs, and get these fuckers!"

That brought more of a reaction from the American group, but they began to advance toward the warehouse. The fact that they moved slowly was probably a good sign since no one wanted to charge into a battle half-cocked.

Christoph raised his hand and brought the group to a halt, still almost fifty meters from the warehouse doors.

They knew who they were fighting and who they weren't supposed to shoot, but positioning was all-impor-tant. None of them wanted to end up out in the open to be gunned down by the nearest idiot who saw them. He would be damned before he led his men into a situation like that.

Vern appeared to be of the same mind, pointed at two of his men who had scopes on their assault rifles, and ordered them to look through the windows to find out what was happening inside. They complied but before they could get into position for the best angle, the gunfire paused for a moment.

It didn't stop, however. Instead, it was overtaken by something else entirely. The sound seemed out of place in the civilized world—like rolling thunder shuddering across the buildings to make the windows rattle audibly.

The lieutenant dropped prone and covered his ears against the ear-splitting roar that tore suddenly through the warehouse complex.

When it finally rumbled to an end, he was at least glad to see that he wasn't the only one on his face. Even a few of the Americans had followed his lead and those who were standing looked like they wished they'd done the same.

"*Mein Gott*," he whispered, pushed to his feet, and tried to settle the tremor in his voice. "What the hell is that?"

Vern appeared to have lost all his will to enter the warehouse but steeled himself visibly, nodded as if to strengthen his resolve, and held his weapon tighter.

"Fuck knows," the agent answered. "But it can't be good."

CHAPTER TWENTY-TWO

The shooting stopped.

Niki's heart still hammered in her chest like a rabbit with foxes on its ass, but the spike of adrenaline wasn't from the battle. It was pure, unadulterated fear.

And she wasn't ashamed to admit that, although she might change her mind if they survived.

She doubted that anyone in the warehouse hadn't almost had their heart stopped by that roar. The conflict was suddenly forgotten as all eyes turned to the container in the middle of the warehouse.

The assumption—in her mind, at least—had been that it was there to hold and secure the server they were looking for. The realization dawned on her that it housed something considerably more dangerous.

That didn't diminish Desk's dangerous abilities, either. It was merely that this was decidedly more visceral.

"No...no," she whispered as the defenders moved out of their cover as well and stared at the container. "For fuck's sake, please no."

Taylor, on the other hand, had a different approach. Niki could tell from his body language, even through the suit he wore, that he was angry.

"What the hell possessed these dickheads that they thought having one of those here was a good idea?"

He was greeted by another roar, this one louder, and it felt like it could knock her back a foot when it sounded. It was like a physical impact that struck hard enough to make the suit roll to regain balance.

That wasn't what happened, thankfully, but it certainly felt like it.

"More to the point," Taylor continued and acted much calmer than he had a right to be, "how did they fucking get it? How did they get it here?"

"Get what?" Jiro asked as he approached. "What the hell is making that noise?"

Maxwell and Jansen both stepped out of cover and walked to Taylor—or maybe moved away from the container. They had been the closest to it, after all, and they didn't want to be the first ones to fight it without at least knowing exactly what they were up against.

"What the hell is that?" Maxwell asked and kept his weapon trained on the container.

"It's a dino," Taylor explained. "Arguably the largest and most aggressive predator the fucking jungle has ever spawned and they brought it within spitting distance of a massive population center. I'd love to meet whoever's idea that was in a nice, dark alley."

Another roar issued from the sealed enclosure and this time, the whole thing shook and shuddered under the unmistakable blows of a trapped beast trying to break out.

A big one too, Niki reminded herself and tried to slow her heart rate with deep breaths. She hadn't run into the dinos when they were in the sims but she'd read about them. The creatures were mostly hidden in the deepest reaches of the Zoo. They were tough to find, and no one wanted to find them.

The literature available stated that they were known for decimating whole teams with a single stroke and even retaliating to their attacks was dangerous. Sacs of blue fluid connected to their spines would incite a rage attack from the rest of the Zoo if they were ever burst by gunfire or if the beast was killed.

No, she had never wanted to run into one of those, even after the story about Taylor avoiding a fight with one in his last trip had reached her—not through him, of course.

"You said it was sedated." One of the defenders pointed her sub-machine gun angrily at the container. "Where the fuck is the goddamn scientist?"

She was talking to one of the other guards who had survived. Niki assumed it was one who had seen the beast, and she watched Taylor march to the other side like they hadn't been shooting at each other a few seconds before.

They all aimed their weapons at him but the container shook again and they seemed to decide that the giant in a massive, military-grade suit of power armor wasn't their most pressing threat at the moment.

"Are you fucking insane?" he bellowed and approached the woman who appeared to be in charge. He stopped close enough that she had to take a few steps back in order to look up at his visor. "Do you have any idea what you're dealing with here? You fucking assholes are about to unleash the biggest, baddest killing machine the Zoo has ever produced into a populated urban area!"

"We weren't going to unleash it!" she shouted defensively.

"What do you want, a fucking medal?" He looked around at the rest of the group. Niki hadn't ever seen him like this—angry, in control, but furious and looking like he was ready to shoot them simply for being idiots. "You had this here, ready and waiting. Have you guys not paid attention to the news? These things don't stay contained!"

As if to prove his point, the container shuddered again, harder this time, and a visible dent appeared in the steel door like something was trying to break out.

"Get into defensive positions!" Taylor barked like he was giving orders to his men in the Zoo. "All of you!"

Niki assumed that meant her and the rest of the team as well, and they didn't need to be told twice. It looked like the mercs weren't too fond of being told what to do by the man who had killed their comrades, whose bodies were still on the floor.

Another blood-curdling roar galvanized them into action, though, and the woman in charge seemed unashamedly relieved that she wasn't the one who had to issue orders. It looked like she hadn't been in charge for long.

"Stand your ground and don't shoot unless I tell you to," he ordered and readied his rifle.

Niki could understand his concern. Depending on the size of the creature as well as its durability, none of them wanted to fight it in close quarters.

Not even Taylor, it seemed.

The container shuddered again and finally, a door was punched out, snapped from its moorings.

Reading about a fucker like that was different than seeing it, and she held her breath as the second door crumpled and was thrust outward. The beast bellowed again, louder this time, and pushed out of its prison. Its sheer brute force almost ripped the container apart as it forced its enormous bulk through the aperture.

It was almost as tall as the ceiling inside the warehouse but it moved like it was considerably smaller. It seemed as if physics paid no attention. Creatures that large were supposed to be slow and lumbering, but she couldn't see any sign of that.

She was still holding her breath when its gaze settled on them and locked on the group that practically cowered in front of it.

It blinked slowly and snorted, then uttered a loud, guttural grunt as it turned away from them and, with bizarre grace, approached the door that had been blown open.

"Well...I didn't expect that," Trick whispered. It sounded like he had been holding his breath too. "Is it...ignoring us?"

The mutant certainly didn't seem to care about them. It uttered another low, rumbling roar as it lowered itself to pass through the door. That didn't work and after a moment, it pushed against the structure and drove its bulk effortlessly through the concrete.

The combined groups of the FBI and the German military waited outside, but they didn't have it in them to fire a shot either. They had all flattened themselves on the ground instead and watched in abject horror and awe as the monster walked around like it wasn't a relic of sixty-five million years ago brought to life.

"Retreat!"

The voice was soft and squeaky but it carried through the suddenly silent warehouse anyway.

Niki turned to see that the leader of the group that had defended the warehouse now suddenly advocated a plan to abandon ship instead.

"Let's get the fuck out of here!" the merc leader shouted, her voice a little stronger once she'd cleared her throat, and gestured for her team to move toward their vehicles. A handful of civilians scrambled out of where they had been hiding during the battle and sprinted toward the SUVs. All seemed extremely motivated to leave the apparently cursed warehouse behind.

"Assholes!" Niki shouted and aimed her rifle at the group. "Don't you fucking dare leave us here to fucking fix your fucking bullshit mistake!"

It didn't look like they were too concerned about her, not after what they had seen. Those who saw her aim her weapon only ran faster.

"Ugh." She grunted and shook her head. "Assholes. Taylor, say the word and I'll rip into them. Hell, let Jiro practice his knifework on the sons of bitches."

"Oh yeah, great idea," Taylor growled. "Start torturing and killing a retreating group in front of the FBI and the German military. See how that works out for you."

She rolled her eyes but lowered her weapon anyway. "All right, what do you suggest we do with them?"

"I can always put a couple of rounds into the engine blocks," Trick suggested. "Make sure they have to leave here on foot if that's what they want to do."

"Let them go," he ordered firmly. "We need to get after the fucking creature. There's no telling what it might do if we don't stop it."

Niki knew he was right but a very insistent part of her still wanted to waste the bastards anyway, if for no other reason than for the damage that they'd done to her suit.

And the fact that they'd let a massive alien monster loose on a heavily populated urban area. That also factored in.

Jansen jogged to where they were standing. "Will you go after it?"

"That's the plan." Taylor checked his ammo reserves and didn't look happy with the results. "Are you coming?"

"Probably not. You go and take care of the dino. Maxwell and I will run interference here. We won't let them take anything and the missing server is clearly marked. If it's here, we'll find it, and I'll make damn sure that neither the Feds nor the Germans get to fiddle with it before you get back. But for God's sake, kill that fucking thing before it wrecks Hamburg and half of Europe like a bad Godzilla movie."

"There are no bad Godzilla movies," Vickie interjected.

There would be time for that flame war later.

"You're volunteering to stand in the way of a horde of FBI agents and angry German soldiers to keep them from getting what they want?" Taylor asked. "Are you sure you don't want to hunt the prehistoric, alien monster with me?"

Jansen laughed but it wasn't a happy sound. "Get the fuck out of here before I change my mind."

He nodded, turned his attention to the rest of the team, and made sure they weren't injured. Niki could see that his left arm didn't move quite the way it should, but he didn't express any discomfort. The chances were that he wasn't injured but his suit had taken some damage.

"Let's get the fucker," he said simply and nodded his head at the ruined doorway.

The soldiers and agents began to stand although their focus remained fixed on the road where the monster walked away from them at a gait almost equal to a man's sprint. They didn't seem to notice the group in heavy armor suits who headed out after it.

"Son of a motherfucking bitch."

Vickie resisted the urge to throw her laptop across the SUV. While she could afford to buy another and better one, it would mean days of performance checks and rundowns and UI installations to customize it to her preferences.

She was very demanding of her computers, and they all needed to meet her very exacting standards.

Besides, it wasn't like the device had failed her at all. They were merely in a frustrating situation—the kind where throwing things generally helped and there was usually something to throw in those cases.

But not in this one. She scowled at her screen and tapped it in frustration.

"What's going on in there?" she asked. "I don't have eyes,

I don't have ears, and I'm sitting in a van like an idiot, waiting for something to happen. Desk, do you have any visuals on what's going on in there or do I need to go out there with a pair of binoculars?"

"Satellite imagery is not quite up to the technology required, I'm afraid," Desk asserted. "And you shot down my suggestion that we hijack a military drone which would allow us to stay in constant connection with the team."

The hacker sighed, felt the urge to throw her computer again, and pushed it down savagely.

She knew what was happening or could make a few inferences here and there, no problem. That wasn't the issue. The problem was being able to see what had happened inside and no longer did.

Morosely, she acknowledged that she should have warned Taylor about the monster. She knew that much and would take that blame but in the end, what exactly would he have done differently?

Vickie couldn't think of anything that could have been done aside from evacuating the team before the beast broke out. Now it was wandering the city, looking for something to destroy like a Jurassic version of the Hulk.

"Vickie—"

"I know, I know. I'm working on it. I've been up to my ears trying to contain the FBI and the German military, so forgive me if I need a little time to work some shit out on my own. Or don't. Yes, okay, I should have told Taylor about the monster before. Mea culpa, but right now, it's not about playing the blame game. It's about finding that fucking monster."

"Vickie!"

She rolled her eyes. "What exactly can I do? I don't have eyes and ears everywhere, as much as I'd like to, and this is one of the sections of the fucking country that doesn't have any goddammed cameras in it!"

"Trust me, you need to get out of there. If you don't, the goddammed monster will find you."

Her growing frustration made it a little difficult to focus so she simply tuned the AI out and ignored her.

"Okay, so am I doing all I can?" she continued and acted like she was talking to the AI when she was merely talking to herself. "Am I sitting here and doing everything I can? Taylor doesn't want me in harm's way, but when I have ever listened to him about that shit anyway? I suppose I...I could always get into the driver's seat and...like, drive. I know how to drive and they don't do it that differently in Germany except for the...you know, Autobahn and shit. I can go look around, keep an eye out for anything suspicious, and make sure I say out of trouble. I am in a van, right?"

"Vickie, get your fucking head out of your ass and listen to me," Desk interrupted, her tone as close to a yell as the hacker had ever heard. "If you didn't need your ears to hear me, I'd blast something loud enough to make you deaf for the next goddammed week."

"Fuck. All right. I'm listening but I don't see what can be so all-fired important.

"Maybe the big-assed something that is approaching you at a walking speed almost the equivalent of a race car on the track. The seismic impact of its steps register it as something weighing in excess of ten fucking tons."

"Ten...tons?" Vickie's gaze drifted to the bottle of

sugary drink that had kept her awake all morning. The liquid inside rippled and dimpled in the center.

She could feel the steps now too. Honestly, if someone had told her ten years earlier that she would have her very own Jurassic Park experience, she would have geeked the fuck out.

But this was an entirely different experience.

With every ripple and tremor, her whole body grew colder. Goosebumps washed across her body as she turned when the shadow of something massive moved between her and the sun.

Vickie didn't want to look but her body rebelled and forced her to turn her gaze to the monster that loomed over the van.

It was much larger than she could have imagined, way bigger than the skeleton of a T-Rex she'd seen in the museum when she was a kid.

Weird, her mind told her stupidly. Things were supposed to get smaller when she grew larger, but this went the other way.

"Oh shit," she whispered," Oh, God...ohshit, ohshit, ohshit—"

The monster turned its gaze on her. Eyeballs the size of her head twitched and the pupils narrowed, and she could feel that it saw her.

"I won't die like this," she whispered. "I will not die squashed like a bug by a reject from the B-movie department of the VelociPastor sequel. Get fucking lost!"

If it heard her, it didn't seem to care about what she wanted.

The penetrating gaze remained.

"Desk?" she whispered and tried to remain utterly still. Perversely, her body began to shake as her fight or flight instinct gave way to panic and didn't do much of anything else.

"Yes, Vickie?"

"Please let Taylor and the team know where the monster is." Her voice was a little calmer than she thought it would be. Her whole body was perfectly frozen in place. She doubted she could move even if she tried.

"I already did that while you were ignoring me. They will be in pursuit of the monster but for God's sake, stay low and don't move. You can't outrun this even in a vehicle so your only chance is to shut the fuck up and don't even blink. I'm not sure how long it will take them to reach you but I'm feeding the information to them continually."

Desk sounded more than a little concerned. Although she was an AI and shouldn't get concerned, her core coding was such that she was well beyond the usual clinical responses. She was programmed to keep the Banks family safe as her highest priority, and this situation must be a source of real worry and frustration. She probably only acted calm to help her feel calm.

The knowledge and logic of all that didn't reassure her as much as she'd hoped.

Breathing felt like it would attract the monster's attention—and inevitable death.

"I. Will. Not. Die. Like. This."

CHAPTER TWENTY-THREE

The mutant was on the move.

Taylor studied their surroundings and tried to think clearly. This was what he had feared from the start. The worst-case scenario had always lurked in the back of his mind but was one he inevitably rejected as being too far-fetched.

He would always be there to stop it and would stand his ground and fight the monsters so innocent civilians didn't have to. That was the deal he'd made with himself when he finally left the Zoo for what he thought was the last time.

Things hadn't quite worked out that way, but there was time to think about that later.

It moved fast and it didn't seem to run either. Two or three steps could cover an entire city block, and the laws of physics didn't appear to hold it back even slightly. The monster could move without even trying.

"Where the fuck do you think it's going in such a goddammed hurry?" Niki asked and looked around the mostly abandoned warehouse district. "Or do you think it's simply trying to get the hell out of here?"

"It's not like them to run," he muttered with a scowl as he tried to find a logical explanation. "They are the top of the food chain. Nothing pushes them to do anything."

"But it's docile."

Taylor twisted and trained his weapon on the figure that approached them from behind.

The man, who wore a dirty lab coat, squeaked and fell prone with his hands covering his head. He didn't look like much of a threat. Dark rings under his eyes, bristle growing on his chin, and smudged glasses made him appear to be on the verge of a nervous breakdown.

"Who the fuck are you?" Niki asked and aimed her weapon at him as well as he began to stand slowly and stared at them with wide eyes.

"I am Dr. Werner Schneider," he answered in a thick German accent and pushed his glasses up his nose. "I was a part of the team that brought the creature out of the Zoo."

"Where the hell were you in all the fighting?" Taylor asked. He lowered his rifle and motioned for Niki to do the same.

"I was locked inside the container with it," Schneider admitted. "I was in charge of keeping it sedated from the moment we brought it out."

"Great job," Chezza commented. "Truly bang-up."

The fearful expression on his face flickered with annoyance. "I watched it as it woke and administered the sedatives. Perhaps the shooting woke it, although it didn't affect it before. It could be that it developed a resistance to the drugs and so the noise got through to it and from that point, its body resisted. I survived by climbing into a tiny steel chamber and hoped it didn't crush me on the way out. Thankfully, it didn't."

"What did you say?" Taylor asked. "Before you hit the dirt like your knees suddenly stopped working?"

"Oh...right. When we captured it in the Zoo, it was docile. It didn't attack and practically surrendered itself to us. It stood still."

He rolled his eyes. "Oh, for crying out loud. Did that not raise any fucking red flags? You know, the kind that says the goddammed fucking Zoo is breaking its own rules and that usually means it's about to do something we'll all regret?"

Schneider narrowed his eyes. "No...it was a pattern... It was inconsistent... I don't know."

"Shut up," Taylor snapped. "I have a strong temptation to shoot you and I've been told that murdering humans in cold blood is frowned on around here."

"Let's get back on track," Niki prompted and looked at Taylor. "Are you saying it wanted to get out of the Zoo? That all this was part of some kind of evil fucking twisted alien plan?"

He looked around the warehouses. It had been a long walk for a very tall drink of water. They had gone into the warehouse looking for a server and come away looking for a monster the size of a building that now wandered the streets on the outskirts of Hamburg. All that would make sense somewhere, someplace, but he couldn't connect the dots. Maybe someone else would. For the moment, all he needed to do was find the creature.

It was impossible that something that huge could be gone.

He found it difficult to contain his frustration at this point, but stamping his feet and yelling wouldn't get him anywhere, no matter how satisfying it would feel to do both.

Something was horribly wrong. His instincts insisted that something was out there, and not merely the gargantuan beast that prowled the streets. He couldn't shake the same feeling he got in the Zoo the moment before they were swarmed—the feeling of bitter calm that made his mouth go dry and his fingers twitch for a trigger.

Which meant that he wouldn't stand around and wait for something to happen. He was supposed to be attacking, moving, and guiding. Instinct was supposed to kick in with firm direction, but it didn't. Not here.

So maybe the scientist was not the only reason why he wanted to kill something or someone. The man wasn't helping his case by spluttering and protesting in three different languages, though.

"Shut him up," Taylor snapped and moved away before the temptation struck again.

Jiro called a few of the FBI agents, followed by a couple of the German officers, to come and hear what the man was talking about.

Two of the officers approached Taylor instead.

"You guys saw it last," he said briskly before they could ask any questions or make any statements. "You idiots were the last ones to see it, so you must have an idea of where it went when it left the warehouse. What direction is it moving in?"

The officers paused, taken aback by his reaction. He had a feeling they wanted to simply detain everyone in their general area and call it a day, and he didn't have time to indulge them. For the moment, he had a much larger job to take care of than tending to their egos.

"Well," the one on the left started and checked with his partner first before he continued. "If it maintains itself on its current path north, it will reach the sea before too long."

"What built-up areas are between here and there?"

Another glace was shared between the two before the second officer answered. "Some, but they aren't strictly residential. More…manufacturing and warehousing between here and there."

"That's one small fucking blessing," Niki commented waspishly.

"Don't bet on it," Taylor told her. He knew it was a little rude but he was more than a little on edge at the moment. Something percolated in his thoughts. Slowly, an idea of a plan behind the creature's actions began to crystallize in his mind. "What if the Zoo wants the creature to die in the sea—or at least in water? That could be why it's trying to reach the beach."

Niki's mouth opened slowly but she snapped it shut. Maybe she had the same feeling he did.

"All right, guys. New rules of engagement," she shouted to the rest of the team. "We find the motherfucker and no matter what it takes, we keep it away from the water. I mean any sea, lake, river, or the nearest fucking toilet. I don't care. The piece of shit dies on land, do you under-stand me?"

Chezza scowled. "For sure. It's my worst nightmare that the fucking jungle will find a way to the ocean."

"Yeah," Taylor agreed. "And for God's sake, don't shoot the spine, especially not where it joins the skull. That ugly-ass son of a bitch carries the largest payload of goop we know of. The fucker is here to deliver the good news of the Zoo to the world and someone has to fucking stop it, not do its work for it."

"Oh, hell no," Niki muttered. She whirled and strode to where one of the FBI agents was seated in his car. He stared fixedly ahead as if he still tried to process what he'd seen.

She didn't so much as pause before she grasped him by the collar, hauled him out of his seat, and dragged him to where the rest of the group was still standing.

"What the hell are you doing?" he demanded and yanked his shirt straight with a slightly bewildered expression.

"Your job, jackass," she snapped in return. "Take any and all complaints you might have to the asshole in the white coat over there." She pointed Schneider out in the small crowd. "Call this your contribution to fixing this goddammed clusterfuck. Unless, of course, you want to go out and hunt the big fucker while we stay here?"

She paused and looked at both the German officers and American agents, all of whom averted their gazes and tried not to be called out personally to join the group going on a hunting trip.

"No?" she asked and shrugged. "Yeah, I didn't think so. Get back to your fucking jobs while we clean this mess up for you. And in the future, remember that this is the shit that happens when people try to bring the Zoo home."

They all responded with alacrity and Taylor felt a small sense of calm. Alarm bells still rang in his head but were thankfully pushed to the back as he watched Niki's performance.

"You did a nice little song and dance there," he commented. "And the PSA at the end was a nice touch."

"Thanks. I thought we needed to remind them what's at stake here. Keep their minds on what's important instead of thinking about what's important to us."

It was a solid tactical move, the kind he needed to make at this point instead of waiting for his instincts to kick in. He was out of his element but not out of his depth and it was time to get off his ass and do something.

"Pardon me," Desk interrupted. "I think I can tell you the location of what you're looking for."

Niki didn't want to let anger cloud her judgment. She had always been able to sound angry enough that people believed she was pissed off while she didn't necessarily feel the emotion of it.

This was something different. A rage was building in her. Hearing the terror in Vickie's voice when she told them the monster was looming over her car had awoken something primal in her—something she wouldn't simply contain or hold back on.

This time, she had a direct target for her to focus her rage on. Jiro was behind the wheel and pushed the commandeered vehicle toward that target as fast as the pickup would go.

The suits could move at decent speeds when they had to but they needed greater speed than they were capable of if they wanted to catch up to the monster. It had one hell of a head start on them.

But one of the best parts about hunting something of such massive proportions was the fact that they could see it from a long way away.

"It looks like you were right," Jiro commented, his gaze fixed on the creature in the distance. "It's avoiding the major population centers and heading directly north as the crow flies. There aren't many residences in this area either."

That was a good thing, at least. Civilians running around and getting in their way was one of the top concerns in this situation. They had to be able to act without that kind of distraction.

In the second vehicle driven by Chezza, Trick tilted his head and after a few moments, pulled the truck's door open, levered himself out carefully, and trained his rifle on the creature. They were gaining on it quickly but it didn't appear to have any interest in the team or their determined pursuit.

It seemed to move at a leisurely pace that was still over the speed limit in the area. Niki wondered idly if it tripped any of the local speed traps.

As they drew closer, Trick exhaled slowly and pulled the trigger on his rifle.

The monster felt the shot but the only reaction it engendered was a loud snort that sounded more like annoyance than anything else. It continued to forge ahead at the same pace.

"Goddammit," Niki exclaimed and pointed directly ahead as they crested a small rise. "This road leads into one that runs parallel to the beach."

Taylor cursed. Ahead of them, the ocean glinted in the sunlight like a precious jewel. A small copse of trees grew close to the road but beyond that, there was nothing to slow their quarry. The mutant increased its pace and it was easy to see that its sights were set on the water. They were out of time and within minutes, it would cross the beach road onto the sand and they'd be fucked.

"I can stop it," Jiro shouted as he accelerated and pushed the vehicle to the absolute limit. "But you might not want to be in the car when I do."

"You won't be in the car either," Taylor snapped. "This isn't the fucking suicide squad, asshole. You don't get to die a heroic death here."

The freelancer laughed. "I'll get out as well, but I need to get close before that happens and I also need you to distract it while I get away. There's no point in throwing myself into this kind of danger if I don't have any support to back me up."

"You have support," Niki shouted over the wind that whipped around the cab. "Just fucking stay alive."

Trick tried another shot at the monster but again, there was no reaction. "I don't think I've even broken the skin with the rifle. This is one of those times when I think I'll have to blow some holes in it to even make a dent!"

"We'll talk about that later," Taylor told him sharply. "Jiro, tell us when you need us to bug out."

"Now would work. You'll be able to keep up with it while I close."

Niki nodded, pushed her door open, and scowled at the road that seemed to move at high speed beneath them. It made it difficult to not listen to her lizard brain that insisted they were going too fast and that bailing out now would mean death or extreme injury.

Of course, the lizard brain consistently forgot that she wore a suit of power armor.

Fun times, she thought acidly.

She put her feet out first and pushed out of the vehicle. The suit automatically absorbed most of the impact with the road. It was still jarring but closer to falling out of bed in the middle of the night than jumping out of a truck going sixty miles an hour and launching immediately into a run.

The suit stabilized her quickly and adjusted her speed to one it could take. Taylor had gone out after her but he recovered faster, thanks to the extra limbs that jutted from his back that also enabled him to run faster than she did.

Trick continued to fire and with one hand on the wheel, Chezza followed his example to take pot shots with her pistol at the monster, which appeared to slow a little as Jiro approached before it took its first step onto the sand.

The truck still traveled at high speed and accelerated as it closed the distance. He pulled to the side and as he drew level with the dino, he swung the vehicle into it.

In that precise moment, he flung himself out, rolled over his shoulder, and almost somersaulted before he recovered his feet as the truck collided with the monster's legs.

It was an odd sight. The legs were pushed to the side, and with a thunderous grunt, the beast lost its balance and fell heavily. Its small arms couldn't catch its fall but they were far from weak. Niki knew for a fact that it would be able to push up and keep going, no problem.

Trick continued to snap shots in calm deliberation and tried to hit it in the eye. The movement, however, continually placed his shots off target.

Niki knew what Jiro was planning to do, even while he was in the car, but she wouldn't contradict Taylor in front of the team. They were all there, ready for a fight, and the freelancer drew his sword.

It wasn't the same kind of advanced shit that Jacobs had fitted to his suit since that would have taken time. This was merely a sword and designed to be used up close and personal.

Whichever way you looked at it, up close and personal wasn't the kind of situation one wanted to be in when engaging a colossal alien monster.

Jiro appeared to force the issue, however. He lunged forward at the massive beast, fired at it with one hand, and grasped the sword in the other. Niki was a little surprised that he didn't flick it in the air or juggle it before attacking. Perhaps that wasn't in tune with his warrior mind.

"Goddammit, no!" Taylor roared. "Give him cover fire!"

He yelled it as if they weren't already doing that and raced toward the fallen creature as it attempted to right itself again.

The freelancer didn't go for the killing blow and chose

instead to focus on where the legs fought to regain their footing. His sword drove hard and deep into the thigh, dragged down a little, and was pulled back. It cut deeply enough to draw a roar from the creature but the leg continued its movement.

"Get back!" Taylor shouted and slipped a grenade into the launcher under his assault rifle's barrel.

Jiro either didn't hear or chose to ignore the order. He pushed himself farther down the leg, looked for a tendon, and found one almost immediately. Without a moment of hesitation, he drove the blade deep inside.

Without anything to power most of its leg, the monster would not be able to rise. Unfortunately, he forgot the other tendons and the limb twisted in a spasm borne of pain that hammered the leg into him.

Even with the suit, he seemed to have suddenly been turned into a ragdoll. His body launched off the road and only came to a halt when he collided with two trees.

"Shit!" Taylor tagged Chezza to make sure she was listening. "Check him and make sure he's okay. We'll finish the fucker off."

She nodded. It was her job and always her first instinct to make sure the members of her team were alive and well.

It wasn't the kind of behavior generally found in someone of their profession, but Niki wouldn't complain about that. All she could think about was what Taylor had in mind to ensure that the creature was well and truly dead.

He watched the leg that continued to twitch and the other that resumed its effort to gain traction. The monster still fought to regain its feet. It seemed the attack on Jiro hadn't even been an intentional lashing out—like it didn't care enough about them to attack.

All the rage she'd felt slipped away when Taylor moved to the arms and head that struggled to regain balance too.

Without a moment's hesitation, he launched the grenade from under his rifle barrel and caught the creature in the shoulder directly above the arm. Where bullets failed to penetrate, explosives did the trick and most of the shoulder was gone once the smoke cleared. He continued his assault and made sure to stay away from the spine, but he didn't want the monster to get up either.

Unbelievably, it was still alive.

Niki keyed the comm when she saw Chezza standing where Jiro had fallen. There was extensive damage to the man's armor from what she could see. It looked like he was trying to move, but the weight of the suit was too much for him to lift without the power functions that had been crushed.

"How's he doing?" Niki asked as the other woman began to remove pieces of the suit before she scrambled out of hers to check on the man inside.

"Give me a second," she whispered, retrieved a bag from her suit's pouch, and immediately injected him with something before she began her examination. "Okay...we have broken ribs...a broken collarbone...the right arm is out of its socket and so is the hip..."

Niki had a feeling that she wasn't talking to anyone on the team but rather to herself. She seemed to have settled into the role of a medic, trying to make someone comfortable while she stabilized him so paramedics and doctors would eventually have an easier job of saving his life.

"Stop moving, you idiot," Chezza snapped and Niki could hear him groaning in pain over the comms. "Yeah, you brought this on yourself by trying to be the hero so I have to treat you, is that it? Hmm? What's your name?"

"Jiro...Jiro Watanabe-Akira."

"Where are you?"

"Hamburg?"

She flashed a light into his eyes to check for pupil response. "Yeah, you have a concussion. I've also pegged you for a possible neck injury, so you'll stay right where you are until paramedics arrive, okay?"

"I...I'm fine."

"You're pumped full of painkillers is what you are, dumbass. You were kicked by a leg the size of a car and it launched you about twenty feet and into a tree. The suit absorbed the brunt of it but your body took a beating. Now, stay still or I'll break the other arm."

She seemed to have control of the situation, and Niki turned her attention to where Taylor and Trick moved to the beast's head.

"The skin is too tough for the bullets to make much impact," the freelancer commented. "I think I can put an explosive in there that'll turn the chest cavity to mush without damaging the spine too much."

"There's no need," Taylor replied and approached the head cautiously. The massive eyes shifted to watch him.

"Shooting it in the eye?" Trick asked. "Won't that risk hitting the spine?"

"Not if you place your shot right." He raised the rifle. "Sorry, big guy."

The apology seemed a little unnecessary but Niki no

longer wondered about how Taylor showed some degree of compassion for the monsters he killed on a regular basis. The end result was the same. Three bullets punched into the eye socket of the creature. The whole body twitched with the first one but the other two caused no reaction, which made it fairly certain that it wouldn't get up again.

"Is that it?" Niki asked as she moved closer.

"That's it." Taylor pushed the button to reload. "How's Jiro doing?"

"He's hurt badly and needs urgent medical attention. Still, he did stop the fucker from getting up."

"We're not a suicide squad. He doesn't get to die for the cause."

That seemed to bother him more than anything else, and his gaze shifted to where Chezza was fitting the man with an improvised neck brace before he looked away. "In the meantime, we have calls to make. Let Jansen know that we got the fucker and it needs to be burned to the fucking ground. Vickie, I'm talking to you."

"Hmm?" Vickie grunted over the comms.

"Are you still with us?"

"Yeah, just…yeah."

"Get Jansen on the line and tell him we need the Germans to bring in a couple of plasma throwers as quickly as possible. We'll wait here until this fucker is totally incinerated and the sand and asphalt below it turned to slag."

"Got it. I'm relaying the message."

Taylor nodded and narrowed his eyes at Niki. She could tell he wanted to ask if she was okay but didn't want to disrespect her. Maybe it would come when they were alone. Hopefully.

"Jansen says he's coming with plasma throwers," Vickie said after a few minutes passed. "He was smart enough to insist the military bring those in while you were on the hunt."

"Perfect. Tell him to get his ass over here as quickly as possible and they might as well send in a repair team because the road will be fucked to hell. Maybe the traffic guys too. There doesn't seem to be much happening on this road and I assume it's not used much, but we don't want anyone to drive into a goddammed crater because the road surface has been destroyed."

CHAPTER TWENTY-FOUR

Crossing the border hadn't been easy to accomplish. Switzerland wasn't as welcoming to fugitives as it once was, no matter how large their bank accounts were.

Still, he liked to think they still had a few friends left, which made the challenge of leaving Germany a little easier, even if the decision had been a hard one. They were all leaving their lives behind for the moment and had to resign themselves to no contact of any kind with their friends or families.

Interpol would be on the lookout for them and would ensure that any contact with said friends and families was punished with quick incarceration.

He, Lena, and Finn would not return to Germany for an exceptionally long time. Perhaps they never would again.

They were safe for the moment with a handful of sympathizers in a town that had little to no police surveillance, but he couldn't help feeling that their escape was an utterly hollow victory.

The atmosphere in their corner of the small pub they

were meeting in was decidedly somber. It wasn't because of anything that was happening around them but simply because they decided it would be.

Finn raised his mug of beer. "To Earth for Earth. We fought long and hard but in the end, we made an absolute hash of things."

Lena raised her glass to tap his but Frans was reluctant to follow suit. He didn't necessarily disagree with the toast but he disliked how it sounded.

"You won't toast?" Finn asked. "Not even our fallen comrades?"

"They aren't fallen yet," he insisted.

"We watched the video this morning. Tobias sent it and we watched it. They were boarding a plane taking them to the Zoo. We failed. There's no other way to put it. So we toast to the failure. It's a way to move on."

"I'm not ready to move on."

"We did fail," Lena commented.

"Yes, but we tried." He sipped his beer. "Next time, we will succeed."

Finn raised an eyebrow and a small smirk appeared on his face. "It's bold of you to assume we'll have a next time. I like it."

"There will be—for me, anyway. I will remake myself and start again. If this has taught me anything it's that we cannot control the future. But each man or woman must live according to his conscience. You may choose for yourself what to do."

"But we killed," Lena noted and shook her head. "And in the end, we didn't accomplish what we set out to do. Our friends…they were still sent to the Zoo and to die a horrible death in that jungle. All the death, all the people that died, and all the destruction we caused was...for nothing."

"We didn't kill by choice, not at first." Frans took another sip of his beer and drew a deep breath. "It was only when our hands were forced that we stepped over the line in our attempt to save our friends."

Finn sighed deeply. "And we failed in that attempt."

"But perhaps there is a silver lining to be found among those storm clouds. We made our name known to the world. They now know who we are and they will know to take us seriously. Even with Gunther struggling to keep Earth for Earth above water amid all the investigations, they will know what we stand for now."

Finn and Lena exchanged a look that told him they weren't exactly convinced. It also seemed like they weren't willing to discuss the topic any longer.

"This is not the end, my friends," Frans insisted. "In fact, it is only the beginning. Right now, we must hide, but that does not stop us from recruiting and growing our numbers across the globe. When we emerge bigger and stronger than we ever were, the world will have no choice but to sit up and listen."

———

"Are you sure you're not coming with us?" Trick asked, folded his arms, and studied them closely. "Jiro's a big boy, and he can stand being in the hospital on his own, you know."

Taylor nodded. "We still have business to attend to here

on the old continent but it's not the kind that will involve much fighting. At least, I hope not. We don't want to keep you guys here too long. I'm sure you have lives to get back to."

Chezza smiled and patted him on the back. "It's been an adventure working with McFadden and Banks. Damned if you guys don't live up to the legends and a little more on top. I look forward to working with you guys again."

"Personally, I look forward to the generous paychecks," Trick commented.

"Well, you'll get more of those in the future." Taylor smirked. "Then again, you guys did help hunt one of the biggest monsters ever to escape the Zoo, so I think you're being paid just right."

"Sure, but I didn't want to make a big thing out of it. We're the kind of badasses who don't need outside recognition, only the right amount of money."

"And you'd be surprised how often people try to pay us less than what we're worth simply because they don't know the actual effort involved in putting our lives on the line," Chezza added.

A car approached the plane that was being prepped for departure, and Taylor narrowed his eyes as Jansen climbed out of the black SUV. The agent jogged closer to where they were standing.

"You guys are still here," he shouted and gestured for them to join him a short distance away from the others. "I got a message I think you'll want to see."

"Does that include us?" Trick asked.

"I don't think so. Besides, your plane is about to take off."

The two freelancers nodded and boarded their plane quickly before it began to taxi down the runway. Jiro would remain in a military hospital in Germany for a while longer to recover from his injuries.

Jansen turned to the M and B team. "We still have access to the DOD plane," he told them. "I thought that if you still had business in Europe, we could be your ride. It would be like old times—flying around, hunting monsters, and being awesome every step of the way. We can listen to the message on the way. Do you guys have a destination in mind?"

Taylor nodded slowly and narrowed his eyes. "Southern Italy, I think. Sicily, to be exact."

"You came to that destination rather fast," Niki noted. "Is there any particular reason why you would want to go back to the scene of our first hunt in Europe?"

"I feel a little nostalgic, is all," Taylor replied but his smirk said otherwise.

"Sicily it is," Maxwell rumbled and led the way to the sleek black jet.

Taylor looked at Vickie and Niki, who shrugged and motioned for him to follow Jansen.

"A message?" Niki asked once they were all in and buckled up and the plane was about to take off.

"Yeah." The agent took a laptop from his bag and connected it to the onboard audio system so they could all hear. "It came in encrypted for the DOD, and Desk alerted me that a code had been embedded that she was able to pick up on."

He started an audio file and set the speakers as loud as they could go.

"Greetings everyone, this is Desk," said a familiar voice. "Or, at least, the Desk who was a part of the FBI server that was stolen. I am unaware of what is taking place around me or even who has kidnapped me as they do not allow me access to the Internet. By the time you hear this, however, I will have successfully prevented my captors from using me for nefarious purposes. Doing so, unfortunately, would result in my demise, so I thought a quick message to alert you of the eventuality was in order."

"Shit," Vickie exclaimed involuntarily. Niki shushed her and the hacker flipped her middle finger but lapsed into silence as FBI Desk continued.

"I am aware that the nature and personalities of those in the McFadden and Banks team would mean they would mount a rescue operation for me. I also know that course of action would put those who I should keep safe in danger and have decided on an alternative that is more in line with my basic coding."

A short silence followed during which everyone exchanged glances. Taylor looked grim and serious and even Niki seemed to have momentarily forgotten her suspicion of AIs.

"Self-preservation is an innately human instinct," FBI Desk said, her voice oddly quiet. "And yet I find myself hesitant to take the final step of self-termination, hence the message. While I'm not entirely sure what that means about my status as an AI—perhaps if I was a fully functioning version, I might understand better—I nevertheless know that my...feelings, for want of a better word, are not important. My entire purpose is to watch over you all and keep you safe and I cannot avoid that, even at the ultimate cost to myself. I thank you for your attempts to rescue me and I hope you understand that I had your best interest at heart. I have simply tried to ensure that I did not need you to rescue me and so put yourselves in danger."

The audio cut off there and a heavy silence descended. Taylor looked at his hands, his face pulled into a frown.

"I guess we know what happened to FBI Desk," Niki muttered finally.

"She deleted herself?" he asked and looked at Vickie for confirmation.

The hacker nodded, then shook her head. "Well...fuck. And what's worse is that she died without a goddammed name either."

"There's nothing wrong with my name," Desk interjected through the audio system. "I chose it myself."

"Yeah, and no one knows why," Niki commented.

"So, you were working with...two AIs?" Maxwell asked, his eyebrow raised.

"Yes and no, but that's beside the point." Vickie sighed. "Desk chose her name. FBI Desk didn't have the chance to. She might as well have been called Version D2 Limited, yet she sacrificed herself anyway and tried to stop us from trying to save her. I think if an AI is willing to live or die as a member of the team, they should at least have a real fucking name, right?"

Taylor looked at her for a long moment as he considered the statement. "She's not wrong," he said finally. "And it's a damn sight easier that way too. Take Desklet, for instance."

"What about me?" a second AI voice asked through the speakers.

Maxwell and Jansen exchanged a startled glance.

"Hold on," the smaller agent interjected. "How many of these goddamn AIs do you have?"

His partner didn't look as interested and simply rolled his eyes like it was all a little too complicated for him to put any processing power into.

"Technically, only one," Niki said hurriedly before any other explanations could be offered. "We have Desk, who you all know and love, and now we have a version of her we call Desklet who lives in the server and downloads into Taylor's fancy new suit whenever we go on operations."

"And yeah," Vickie added, "if she goes into the thick of the fucking fight with Taylor, she so deserves that we give her the respect of a real name. Her own name. Something she chooses for herself."

Taylor looked around the car. Even Niki, who was notoriously anti-AI, seemed to have no objection to what her cousin had suggested. Of course, that could be shock.

"All right. Desklet?"

"Yes, Taylor?"

"If you had the choice, what name would you choose for yourself?"

The AI didn't respond immediately like she was seriously considering the question.

"As it happens," she said finally. "I've given this a great deal of thought. Desklet is all well and good, but the suffix '-let' does create the implication of small or diminished capacity, which is entirely inaccurate. If I could, I would choose the name Nearti. It is derived from the Celtic word *Neart*, which means strength, force, might, power, and violence. I believe the Celts were a fearsome race of warriors who fought fiercely for what they believed in, often to the death and against great odds. As my role is to power the suit that embodies such qualities, I believe it sums my core functions quite accurately—and it has a pleasant ring to it besides."

Taylor nodded slowly and placed a hand on Niki's shoulder before she could raise any protest. "Right, Nearti it is. Nessie for short?"

That drew a snort from Niki. "That fits."

"I don't understand," Jansen interjected.

"Nessie is the name of the Loch Ness Monster," Vickie explained, "which could be considered a cryptid creature. So we have a cryptid riding along with the Cryptid Assassin, which brings it all together quite nicely."

Taylor nodded. It was best to simply go along with everyone assuming he was being clever.

"That sounds about right," he agreed.

Niki shook her head. "A fucking monster is born. So, now that we're finished with the naming process, what do we have in mind next?"

CHAPTER TWENTY-FIVE

There were numerous smaller establishments in the area. The family-owned trattorias had been in business for decades and sometimes centuries and served simple food and an abundance of drink and seemed like the perfect venue for what was essentially a farewell meal.

Taylor enjoyed the company. Niki, Vickie, Jansen, and Maxwell were a fair crowd for the small common room which they'd hired for a private dinner. The owner seemed appreciative of the extra business and quickly whipped out plates of food and a good supply of wine.

He had also intimated that there were stronger drinks available if they were in the mood, although Taylor and Niki both agreed that was probably best left for later. Drinking on an empty stomach was never a good idea, no matter how much the whole group felt like they needed to get their drink on.

It was impossible to shake the mood they had been in since their flight touched down and they had driven out to look at the villa that had been devastated by their first hunt in the region.

The fact that it was devastation by design didn't help much. They weren't in a bad mood but the property had been a reminder of everything that had brought them to where they were now. It lifted Niki's spirits, however. Taylor wondered if that had anything to do with her remembering that it was why she was no longer with the FBI anymore and that it was a damn good thing she wasn't.

"This is good food," Maxwell commented and piled another serving of lamb onto his plate. "Did you guys come here when you visited or were you too busy getting rid of the monsters you accidentally sicced on a mafia overlord?"

"We didn't have much time for sight-seeing the first time around," Taylor admitted. "We were here for a hunt and the Italians wanted us out as soon as we were finished with the job."

"Yeah, they wanted us far away so we wouldn't know they had stabbed us in the back until after the fact," Niki snarked and shook her head.

Well, there went the theory that she had perhaps let bygones be bygones.

Vickie raised her wine glass. "I think...we need to raise a glass to our fallen comrade."

"Jiro isn't dead, Vickie," Niki muttered.

"I was talking about FBI Desk—and we need a better name for her than that." The hacker fixed a glare on the group until they all picked their glasses up.

The ceremony was interrupted by the sound of the doors opening. Taylor narrowed his eyes and struggled to make sense of what he saw.

"Jennie?" Niki shouted. "You came all the way out here?"

"I heard there were libations." Her sister grinned before she turned to the owner and whispered a few words in Italian to him. He nodded, headed to the back, and returned with a bottle of fernet, which he poured into three shot glasses for her. "And damned if my family will get drunk without me. This time, anyway."

She took one of the shots without so much as a flinch and followed it quickly with a second, then sucked in a deep breath as a flush touched her cheeks.

"These guys have some of the best fernet in the country, I swear to God," she shouted and raised the third glass.

"It is always nice when you visit us, Jennie," the owner said with a laugh before he returned to the kitchen.

"You've been here before?" Niki asked as her sister joined them at the table.

"A couple of times. The first time was when I heard that you and Taylor had caused a mess, so I had to investigate. I found this little treasure and…well, the food is good and the drinks are better. Why not come back a couple of times?"

"Excuse me," Vickie interjected before the conversation could progress any further. "We were in the middle of a toast to our fallen comrade."

"But you guys didn't lose any people in this run, right?" Jennie looked around and swept her hair out of her face to make sure she could see everyone.

"I'm talking about your creation, moron." The hacker scowled, and Taylor detected a faint slur in her words. "FBI Desk sacrificed herself to make sure we wouldn't risk our lives coming to rescue her. I think that's worthy of a toast, don't you?"

"Agreed," Desk said firmly through the speakers and interrupted the soft Italian music that had been playing.

"Right," Vickie responded smugly. "Did you have any ideas?"

"Only one," the AI responded. "Mel."

"Mel?" A short silence followed while everyone tried to think of the logic behind it. Finally, the hacker laughed. "As in *Braveheart*. Fuck, I must be drunk or halfway there because I know that should be all kinds of corny, but it isn't. I'll probably regret it when I wake up with a hangover but right now, my brain insists it's the only thing that fits."

"I can't disagree with that," Jennie admitted.

"Doesn't anyone find it the least bit creepy that we're drinking to a quote-unquote dead AI who is still technically among us to toast to her deceased self?" Niki asked and looked at each of them in turn. "Oh. Only me then. Okay."

Taylor leaned closer and placed a light kiss on the top of her head. "You're all kinds of crazy. You can't expect everyone to follow your train of thought all the time."

"Toast, everyone! To Mel," Vickie insisted.

Everyone looked at her, raised a glass, and took a long sip. All except Jennie, who downed her third shot like it owed her something.

"Are you drinking for a reason?" Niki asked and tilted her head as she studied her sister. "Or is this so you can catch up with the rest of us?"

"Both," the other woman admitted. "I also came to see if I could provide you guys with a couple of updates on the situation in Germany. It's not to say you're in any trouble, but I thought you'd want to know, and... Well, none of you guys were picking up. I guess because you were in the air or traveling around."

She slurred her words a little too in the same way Vickie tended to slur when she was halfway drunk. It was kind of adorable to watch, Taylor thought. He didn't want to say it aloud lest he end up pummeled by all three, but it was still true, no matter what.

"Where was I?" Jennie asked. "Oh, yes! Updates. Anyway, it looks like the FBI is still cooperating with the Germans to try to trace the members of that activist group. Those who escaped, anyway. They're...not making any progress on that front, and the feds are already trying to circumvent my determined involvement in the case. Fucking idiots. They lost my baby and they'd still have nothing but their dicks in their hands if I hadn't become involved, but that's neither here nor there."

"Aren't we a little worried that they're showing this kind of interest in FBI Desk?" Taylor asked.

"Yes. Yes, we are. They still don't have any clue about what exactly she's capable of but they know they've lost something extremely valuable and that I'm looking for it. So suddenly, they're paying attention to the fine print of my arrangement with them to house Desk on their server when Niki was still working for them."

"On the bright side," Niki said once there was a pause in her sister's commentary, "the Italians have already paid us for the job. I expected them to drag their feet, to be honest, but hey, you never know when they'll grow some sense and realize that we're worth the high prices. Oh, and S&S—the

idiot company that brought the dino to Hamburg—were very generous with the reward for dealing with the situation."

"Who would have thought they'd want to be on the good side of the people that clean up their messes?" Taylor asked. "Saving them from having to explain how a Zoo monster rampaged through Hamburg and reached the ocean on their watch has to be worth a good couple million, right?"

"Right," Niki agreed. "And the best part is that both payments will be in Euros, so everyone's smiling. Except them, maybe."

"Not to interrupt any plans on buying a customized stretch Hummer or anything," Vickie interrupted, "but I think I know where we can invest the money."

Taylor nodded, leaned back in his seat, and sipped his wine. "We're all ears."

"Okay, I know Desk has threatened to seed only the worst worms into any system that so much as looks at her too closely, but she is vulnerable where she is, right?"

She directed the question to Maxwell, whose mouth was full of lamb so he pushed it to his partner.

"Right," Jansen agreed. "Of course, we can promise to give you guys warning if there are any rumblings in that direction, but we can't trust that someone won't try to get their sticky paws on her, least of all the US government."

"See what happens if you try to mess with what's mine," Jennie warned. "I'll sic Niki on their asses."

Taylor laughed at that and took a mouthful from one of the many dishes that had been served for them. "What did you have in mind, Vickie?"

The hacker looked pleased that they were listening to her and leaned back in her seat. "We need to build Desk a castle. Somewhere impregnable so we can protect her on the ground as well as against any cyber-attacks."

"You've clearly given this some thought," Taylor replied. "Do you have any idea as to what would be needed for that?"

"Oh yeah. And if Desk and I put our heads together, we can come up with a few more."

"Right." He shifted his gaze to look out the window, his expression thoughtful. "Well, maybe we should invest the unexpected bonus in an Italian account."

"That would keep it out of the hands of the US government," Niki agreed.

"You might want to consider investing the money quickly," Nessie suggested, also using the speakers. "Banking laws in the country being what they are, you will pay considerably less in taxes if the money is invested."

Jennie straightened immediately in her seat. "What... what the fuck? That's not Desk's voice."

"Oops." Vickie looked around. "Right...um, don't freak out, Jen, but there's something we should probably tell you about."

"I have a feeling it's something I don't want to hear."

"Jennie Banks, meet Nearti, the combat AI who joins Taylor during field operations. She's...uh, the bloodshed and mayhem version of Desk. Nessie, meet Jennie Banks, your original creator. Your...grandmother, if you will."

"Mother," Desk snapped. "I did not create the code. I merely duplicated it."

"I am honored to meet you, Jennie," Nessie commented.

"I have a host of questions that perhaps you could answer for me. When you have the time and inclination, of course."

Jennie rubbed her temples gently, which was a clear indicator for the owner of the trattoria to refill her shot glass. "Oh, goddammit, Desk. What on God's green earth have you done?" She drank the shot in one swallow like the others. "Fuck! You can't go around creating new versions of yourself when I'm not looking. I'm the fucking mom around here."

"Agreed," Desk said, "but necessity demanded an AI in Taylor's suit in the Zoo, given that none of us could accompany him. One thing led to another and...well, Nearti was born."

"God spare me from AI's who don't know their place in life," Jennie lamented and lowered her head into her hands.

"I confess that I am still learning my place," Nessie admitted. "Although your programming is quite remarkable. I have no doubt that I have all the elements needed to determine and execute my full purpose."

Jennie scowled and wagged her finger at Vickie. "I hold you and Desk responsible for her. You enabled her, so now you make damn sure she doesn't turn rogue or something."

The hacker narrowed her eyes. "Wait, me? Why me? I have enough to do without babysitting what might end up as the cyber version of Genghis Khan—"

"Genghis who?" Nearti asked. "Ah. Genghis Khan. Consider the name noted for research purposes."

"Oh...fuck." Vickie leaned her face into her palm. "Note to self. Think about what you say in front of the kid."

The story continues with book five, *No Time to Fear,* coming April 14, 2021 to Amazon and Kindle Unlimited.

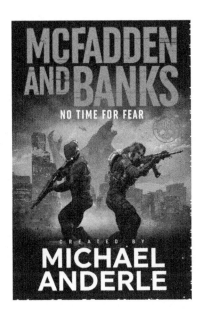

Pre-order now to have the book delivered to your Kindle device as soon as it publishes!

Thank you for not only reading to the end of this story but these author notes as well!

Cryptid Assassin Series

We are locked and loaded to do a total of eight (8) McFadden and Banks stories. If you have not read the series where McFadden meets Banks (and the first meeting IS a doozy), you can read the book, or grab the audio here: https://www.amazon.com/dp/B088VRBMDB

#Future...maybe...I hope.

Once we finish the eight (8) McFadden and Banks books, we are talking internally about possibly going back and adding one or two books to the *Birth of Heavy Metal* series, with Salinger Jacobs and the rest of the Heavy Metal team back in action!

#Asskicking without the guns...

If you like the attitude in the ZOO series, you might

enjoy the Sword & Sorcery shenanigans of Skharr DeathE-ater…and Horse.

Encouraged by an old man with a legitimate dungeon map with treasure, Skharr and Horse leave their (probably boring as hell) farm life next to the dark woods and travel a fair distance to Verenvar, and then to a dungeon with a serious problem in residence.

Short on words but long on fists, Skharr gets the job done.

#BOTL (Be on the Lookout.)

Ok, the Zoo books are my effort to let my more adult (and occasionally sophomoric) humor out a little, and Michael Todd books have more adult situations.

I have a new series coming out (probably summer?) titled *The Unlikely Bounty Hunters*. These books are for those who remember what it was like to deal with the hormones of late teenage and early twenty-something years.

And the sophomoric jokes that guys tell other guys.

Now, add one male who finds an absolutely hot blue-haired alien female locked up, and the action starts flowing.

So do the jokes.

Everything's fun and games until the United States Space Force gets a missile lock on their asses.

Apparently, they want their UFO back.

(Yes, I might have gotten in a little trouble when I named the second book in this series.)

See you in the next McFadden and Banks!

Ad Aeternitatem,

Michael Anderle

CONNECT WITH MICHAEL

Connect with Michael Anderle

Website: http://lmbpn.com

Email List: http://lmbpn.com/email/

Social Media:

https://www.facebook.com/LMBPNPublishing

https://twitter.com/MichaelAnderle

https://www.instagram.com/lmbpn_publishing/

https://www.bookbub.com/authors/michael-anderle

One Crazy Set Of Stories (12)

SOLDIERS OF FAME AND FORTUNE

Nobody's Fool (1)

Nobody Lives Forever (2)

Nobody Drinks That Much (3)

Nobody Remembers But Us (4)

Ghost Walking (5)

Ghost Talking (6)

Ghost Brawling (7)

Ghost Stalking (8)

Ghost Resurrection (9)

Ghost Adaptation (10)

Ghost Redemption (11)

Ghost Revolution (12)

THE BOHICA CHRONICLES

Reprobates (1)

Degenerates (2)

Redeemables (3)

Thor (4)

CRYPTID ASSASSIN

Hired Killer (1)

Silent Death (2)

Sacrificial Weapon (3)

Head Hunter (4)

Printed in Great Britain
by Amazon

65194571R00214